THE SHEPHERDS OF THE SUNSTONE

BOOK ONE - THE SUNSTONE SAGA

NICOLIN ODEL

This story depicts a married male/female couple in an open LGBTQ2S+ relationship.

CONTENTS

Chapter One
WATER

Simon held his breath. Darkness was closing in; he could see a sliver of light on the ripples far above, edging away. He felt himself being pulled down into the depths, as if by countless taut, grasping hands. Pressure filled his chest. *I need to breathe.* Fading, sinking, lungs burning, he sucked in a breath and felt the murky cold fill him.

"SIMON! SIMON!" Simon's wife clenched her hands and pounded her fists onto his chest. "Gods! Why are you drowning in bed?!" Another thud of her hands. He coughed, spewing up muck. A fit of wet heaves as he rolled onto his side.

"What in all the hells happened, Simon?" Saudett asked, her eyes watering.

Inhaling profoundly, Simon said, "I dreamt I was drowning." He let out a long sigh of relief. "Remind me to avoid swimming for the foreseeable future, my dear wife." He rolled onto his back and gave a wry smile.

She burst into tears and began sobbing.

He slowly sat up and put his arms around her. "It's all right. I'm all right." They held each other. After a long moment, he took her head and looked at her. Her short black hair was messy, her bangs hanging over her dark brown eyes. Her lips were deep mulberry. The double-looped golden rings on the right of her small nose matched his own. He caressed her cheek; her warm brown skin was soft. *By Hettra, the Goddess of Love, she is beautiful,* he thought. Saudett had stifled her sobs by this point, and her eyes darted down to Simon's lips, then back to his eyes. He gently moved his hand from her cheek, around her ear and neck, slowly guiding their lips together.

A distant bell rang. Saudett paused and counted the tolls. Nine. The day was getting on. Simon had left for work, overseeing the construction of some new provision cellars on the outskirts of town. She thought back to their conversation after they had made love.

"You're taking this rather lightly, are you not?" she said as she had lain next to Simon earlier that day. Her head rested in the nook of his shoulder, her leg over his as he lay on his back. His pale skin looked bright against her bronze tone.

"What's that?" He grinned.

She smacked his chest playfully. "The *dream*, by Skrull's ass! The drowning!"

"Of course, of course. I'm trying desperately not to think about it." He paused, staring off into the distance for a moment. Finally, he said, "I'm sure it will never happen again. Perhaps I vomited in the night and choked on that. I did have a bit *too* much wine last night."

She peered at him sternly.

"Ahem. *Anyway*, I need a distraction; I should head to work." Simon paused and arched a brow. "Speaking of distraction, perhaps you can invite Cad over tonight?" he asked.

It was Saudett's turn to grin; they both enjoyed the company of others in and out of their bed-chamber often. Their open relationship was pleasurable for them. She particularly enjoyed it when her husband used another man for excitement. "I will inquire if he is available this evening."

He nodded. "Well, off to work I go. 'Another sunrise, another pence in the pocket,' as they say."

"Only you say that, dear husband," she said as he began to sit up, pushing him back down. "Not yet. A little longer, please."

He lay back. Saudett felt him put his nose to her hair and breathe deep. He gave a contented sigh.

"Of course, my love."

They lay in silence for a long while, enjoying the moment together.

Saudett's mind wandered. "Please pick up a plucked chicken from the market on your way home from work."

He coughed and gave a flourish with his free hand. "Ahem, of course, my love!"

She smacked his chest again, slightly firmer this time.

"Ouch!" he yelped. He quickly stood and dressed, brushing his tawny-colored mess of hair out of his eyes. "I'll watch out for any wells or overly deep puddles to fall into!" He shot her a mischievous grin as he closed the door on his way out.

"He's in an oddly good mood," she muttered as he left.

After a sensual morning, fuelled with the emotions of potential loss, Saudett smiled as she thought of the man she had taken for her husband. Her smile quickly turned to a grimace. *How could a dream nearly drown him? What does it mean?*

The sea was weeks away from Dagad, and a vast desert lay before it. There was the river Droe, which bordered the town's western edge. In the summer months, it was little more than a creek. Simon had grown up playing in that river, and the people let their children use it with little care. *There must be something more.*

During her musings, she had slowly been dressing in her regalia. Over a light tan linen undershirt and loose leggings, she strapped on the hardened leather armor. The chest piece had bronze scales on her torso—a belt with scales draping around her hips. Bronze-plated shin guards and soft leather sandals wrapped her feet. She wore matching bronze bracers around her wrists and a bronze-plated leather cap. Scales attached to the cap protected her ears and the back of her head and neck. Similar tan-colored linen twisted into a headband around her forehead. The headband could be easily lowered around her face against the dust storms from the desert's east winds.

The dark blue braided rope tied around her upper arms indicated her rank of sergeant among the Shepherds Eye's law enforcement and soldiers. She took her spear, headed out the door, and stepped into the dusty street.

Dagad was a large town, residing on a small flatland before the foothills slowly died into desert sands. The surrounding hills were pastures for sheep, goats, and camels. Primary stables sat at the northwest and eastern edges of town, providing any transportation needs. Dagad was the last stop on the road before the forested mountainous region to the northwest descended into the desert to the east.

For a town of around seven thousand citizens, Dagad was prosperous. Each week, caravans would arrive from the western kingdom of Aurulan, making their way east to the bountiful coastal nation of Xamid, on the far side of the Burning Sea or vice versa. These kingdoms, countries, and dangerous domains made up the world of the Earste Lân.

From silks and spices to iron and copper, it all came through Dagad at some point, though it was not a straightforward journey through the vast, deadly desert. Saudett made her way to the town center, strolling past the equilateral beige sandstone dwellings. The closer she came to the center, the taller the structures became, adding new layers to existing foundations. *Simon aided in the construction of most of those,* she recollected as she passed them by. The thoroughfare widened into a market of colorful canvas sheets stretching across the tallest buildings, giving the area some much-needed shelter from the heat.

The Shepherds Eye barracks were just past the eastern edge of the market. Saudett slowly made her way through the shops, keeping an eye on the dealings and bustling activity of the inhabitants. Many people traveled through the town, and many, at some point, decided to stay, contributing to the diverse mix of Dagad's citizens. Dagad was officially in the Aurulan Kingdom, on its easternmost border. Though many Xamidians had made Dagad their home, like herself, most of the Aurulan populace was pale-skinned and fair-haired—*just like Simon's scrawny arse.* She grinned to herself.

Saudett continued to stroll through the market stalls. *No caravans yet this morning,* she observed. She was very familiar with the comings and goings of trade. She was, after all, the daughter of the heads of the esteemed caravan guard unit, Caravan House Kafilah, operating out of Xamid.

A commotion at one of the stalls to her left caught Saudett's attention. A circle had formed before her.

"Clear the way!" she ordered as she firmly moved bystanders aside with the shaft of her spear.

A large man with a bald head and dual thunderbolt tattoos arching over it was bellowing at another man, his face turning pink as he shouted. The source of his wrath seemed to be a small Xamidian merchant trying to shrink back into his own skin.

Saudett realized she could not understand what the large man was saying, as he spoke a different language. He was a Vouri, come down from the mountains in the North, known for their primary occupation of mining and skull-cracking abrasiveness and brutality in battle. He was twice her size, waving a pouch of some sort in front of the little shopkeeper's face, pointing at it, then back to the keeper. She put on her most polite smile and approached the man.

"Annoitko tämän tyttärelleni!?" His voice was deep and raspy, and his long, braided red beard shook as he shouted.

Putting her hand on his back, she said, "Sir, please explain—"

The man swung his arm around full force, trying to connect with her head. She bobbed under the arm, simultaneously slipping the butt end of her spear between the man's legs at an angle as he twisted. He lurched. She sprung up, landing her feet square in the man's chest. He landed with a heavy thud on his back. The pouch he had been carrying burst into a black cloud. She spun her spear around and aimed the tip at his throat.

"Hold!" she barked.

The man groaned and held his hands up in submission. She looked back to see two more Shepherds Eye guards coming to her relief. She looked closer at the powder sprayed over the man's clothing, then touched it and rubbed it together between her fingers and thumb. A tingling sensation shot up her hand.

"*Grit.* Where did you get this?" she asked.

The bald man turned his head toward the merchant.

She looked, and to her surprise, the little merchant was gone. She turned to one of the newly arrived guards, nodding to him. "Go have a look for the owner of this stall. Inquire with some of the witnesses to find out who he is."

"Uh, yes, right away, Sergeant!" the man said hesitantly, then jogged off.

"Help me get him to his feet," Saudett said, indicating to the other guard, and together, they grasped the man's arms and helped him stand up. "Did you buy this from that merchant?"

The large man stared at her blankly.

"Can you understand Auru?"

The same long stare.

Repeating the question in Xamidian yielded the same results. She let out a heavy sigh. "Bring him to the barracks."

"Steady!" Simon watched as his men lowered a sizeable rectangular brick into the excavated circular pit. The pit descended nearly the height of three tall men into the earth, and it had to be deep to keep provisions cool, dry, and completely enclosed to keep out the spring rains.

The thought of water brought him back to that moment of suffocation. That moment of liquid filling his lungs. *Skrull, take me.* He shook the thought out of his mind. "Good lads. Let's get another ready."

They worked on the staircase that descended into the pit; large bricks stacked on one side. The stairs were simple; building the enclosed dome roof would be more challenging. A frame of pine reinforced by iron would need to be built nearby and hoisted up and over the hole. Then, the triangular cross-sections would need additional strapping, wrapping around the circumference at different heights. Thin, flexible strips of wood would be woven between the main frame. After that, Simon and his crew would slowly apply sandstone mud, beginning at the dome's base and rounding upwards.

Simon surveyed the area around them. They were toiling just outside the town limits, at the base of two hills, where the domes would have shade most of the day. Even with the cover of the foothills, it was blistering hot today. A dust cloud was peeking over the horizon to the east, toward the desert.

"Could be a caravan or a sandstorm rolling in," drawled a deep, Tal'tulu accent behind him.

Simon turned to regard his foreman, Naurr Andiges. "Aye, I'll keep an eye on it, my good man."

The dark, stocky man always awed Simon with his physicality. He was wearing only a cloth turban on his head and loose, billowing trousers. The man's chest and arms glistened in the heat. Simon arched a brow; the view added a bonus to construction work. A few years back, Simon had offered for Naurr to accompany his wife and him for some enjoyment. Naurr had politely refused, as he was in a happy, *exclusive* relationship. *By Qav, the God of Greed and Luck! My men sure are a treat to the eyes.*

Naurr flashed a bright white smile through his gray curly stubble. "Want me to send a drudge up the hill for a look-see?"

"Give it an hour," Simon said. "If it looks to be a storm, we'll retire for the day. But I'm sure it's just a caravan."

"You're the boss."

Simon frowned. "Come now, you lot! I do not pay you to be in a state of comatose!" He shouted at his crew, who had begun idling while listening to the two men's conversation.

"What's comatose?" one of them questioned. *Ilan, of course. Another handsome Auru chap.*

"It means dead to the world. Sleeping indefinitely. It means use your thick skulls and get back to work! Especially you, Ilan!"

The men bustled back to business. Simon sighed. *We've completed four domes in under two months, but we still have five more of these damned things to build.*

"You're late."

Saudett waved the guard succeeding her forward, guiding the large detainee into the office. "My occupation begins the moment I step out my doorway, Lieutenant," she shot back.

The lanky Auru hesitated, then cleared his throat. "Ahem, well, what are you waiting for? Report on the situation, Sergeant."

"Aye, sir."

She studied her superior. Ryon Laniel dressed in the heavier accouterment of the Shepherds Eye soldiers: more plating and additional shoulder guards attached to the man's garbs. *I prefer to be able to move during combat, but to each their own,* she thought. He had a double-braided blue-and-black rope wrapped around his bicep. His sharp facial features could be handsome if he added a few extra pounds and got some sleep. He failed to keep eye contact with her as she began her report. His attention focused on the sizeable Vouri man.

"A disturbance in the market with a particular merchant I have never met before. The alleged merchant running off in the middle of the fray," she said.

Ryon nervously brushed back his shoulder-length blond hair. "And what was the source of this disturbance?"

"This man," Saudett waved a hand toward the hulking man and paused, tilting her head. "Do you have a name? *Name?*" She touched her chest and said, "I am Saudett. You are?"

"Baal," he growled.

"My friend *Baal* was either trying to purchase or sell grit to the merchant, as far as I could tell."

"Grit? Where is it?" The lieutenant stared intently at Baal. "A merchant, you say? What was his name? A description, perhaps? Can't you say anything other than your name?" Ryon rattled out questions sporadically.

Baal grunted, "Home. Go."

"Unlikely," Ryon muttered with a sigh. "Take him. Lock him up for now; charge him with possession of illegal alchemical substances." He nodded to the guard still at the man's side.

As the guard moved to restrain Baal, the large man roared, "HOME! BRENA! HATA!" He twisted out of the guard's grip, then charged.

The guard stood there stunned, only having time to put his hands up in terror. Too late. Baal's shoulder impacted the man, sending him into the wall, plaster covering him as he slowly slumped down.

Baal turned back to the door.

The lieutenant was sweating profusely behind his desk, his bloodshot blue eyes darting back and forth between Baal and Saudett. He had edged toward the corner of the room, his sword now in a trembling hand.

Saudett stood in front of the only exit. *Gods, I wish the captain were here to see this.* She shrugged. *Oh well.*

"Why did you not restrain him properly!" she heard Ryon shriek.

Dropping her spear, the cramped office would hinder her weapon use. Baal gave a toothy, bearded smile, then, like a bear, charged again.

A herd of sheep was wandering past, ushered by a couple of ragged, brown-speckled sheepdogs and a shepherd holding a long, crooked cane. Another man walked alongside the shepherd. Simon recognized his father by his slow hobble. *Come to ensure I am building these cellars correctly,* he assumed with a scowl.

"Greetings, my son!" His father waved, a broad smile on his face. Medium-length gray hair parted to reveal an old yet charming face and a short-cropped gray beard to complement.

The Meridio's were of Aurulan background. Having had Simon later in life, his mother had passed nearly a decade ago, somewhere in her late sixties. His father, Yakeb, still puttered around town, keeping busy, checking in on his son's construction projects, and giving *much* guidance.

"Father," Simon said dully.

"I was just telling Qunid, here," Yakeb said, "about how you used to draw structures, castles, and whatnot as a child. I had to slowly integrate the theoretical knowledge of engineering into that little head from the get-go. Soon enough, your sketches had measurements, material lists, and the whole lot. He caught on quick, Qunid!" Yakeb slapped the sheepherder on the back.

The sheepherder just smiled and nodded. It seemed Qunid was reasonably used to Yakeb's storytelling.

"So, what brings you to my site this...uh, what time is it?" Simon asked curiously.

"Time to eat, ya lazy bastards! Take a break!" Naurr shouted at the men.

"What a coincidence." Yakeb's bright blue-green eyes sparkled with amusement. "What are we having to lunch on, my son?" he asked enthusiastically.

"A coincidence indeed," Simon muttered. "Red lentils and goat meat curry, with some flatbread. Join us. Father. Qunid."

The men gathered around a fire pit, which had a pot simmering. They sat cross-legged on simple rugs or rested on large boulders and piles of lumber around the worksite. Naurr served each man a wooden bowl of stew and a couple of flatbread pieces. The shepherd let his sheep graze free up the side of the hill to their northwest, leaving his faithful dogs to ensure none strayed too far off.

"How is the cellar construction coming along, my son?" Yakeb asked.

"'Another moon, another mountain,' as they say. We should finish with this one in a handful of days."

Yakeb grinned. "I fear only *you* say that, my son. Iron banding for the reinforcement of the dome?"

"*Yes,* Father."

"How old is the pinewood? Don't want it to be too dry and crack."

"Arrived on yesterday's caravan from Aurulan, fresh from the sawmill. Black pine from Tobak. We've been keeping it in one of the finished cellars."

Yakeb smiled and patted Simon on the back. "Ah, that's my son." Filling his mouth with a spoonful of curry, he mumbled through a mouthful, "On another note," he swallowed, "my dear daughter-in-law had a little run-in this morning with a thug of some sort."

"Oh?" Simon raised a brow.

"Safe to say, it didn't end well for the thug."

Naurr barked a laugh. "I don't envy that criminal man; your mate is kin to a red-hooded sand viper, says I." The burly foreman could not contain his chuckling. "How she fell for the likes of you, Skrull only knows."

"Skrull had nothing to do with it, my good man!" Simon exclaimed, grinning. "My dashing looks and inquisitive brain won her over!"

"Leave it to my son to catch a beautiful fox." Yakeb joined in the laughter.

"Thank you! At least *someone* is on my side."

"I'm always on your side, my son. Speaking of which, did you mix the gravel with the sandstone mixture in two parts of water?"

"Gods take me, Father! Just let me do my Skrull-forsaken job. We've built how many of the damned things already!"

"I'm just trying to help, my—"

"Enough help; can you not just trust my judgment and go home?"

Yakeb's face fell. He stood. "I'll be on my way then." Dusting off his gray robe, he turned and began hobbling away.

"Skrull, take me," Simon exhaled.

"Boss."

"What?" Simon turned to the Tulu. He was staring at the top of the hill directly to the east. A massive cloud of dust shrouded the eastern sky.

"Hells!" Simon shouted. "A sandstorm!"

"Nay." Naurr pointed. Simon followed his line. A single rider sat at the top of the hill. A glint of bright golden light flashed off the metal back at them.

Simon squinted his eyes. *It's too far to make out any details of who the rider could be.* "Make haste! Get the men back to town! Make sure my father is safe," Simon ordered.

"What you going to do?" Naurr asked.

"The only other thing I know how to do. Try to speak with them!"

He began rushing toward the hill. As he made it to the base of it, he looked up. A glint of silver above the man's head was waving back and forth. The ground began to shake. A rumble began to build—louder and louder—accompanied by undulating shouts and war cries. Then, what seemed like thousands of riders crested the hill and descended like a tidal wave toward him.

Saudett took a few steps, then dived headfirst under Baal's grasping arms, right between his legs. The massive man had tottered far over in his effort to restrain her. He was looking back between his legs, dumbfounded.

Saudett propped her knees on her elbows for a heartbeat, then lunged, pushing her feet together as they impacted the back of Baal's knee. He buckled, falling to his knees. With the man closer to the ground, she leaped onto his shoulders, wrapping her legs around his neck, hands pulling his chin up, leaning back so his flailing arms could not connect with her body. Squeezing hard and increasing the pressure with her legs, she used her strongest muscles to her advantage.

His head began to turn bright pink as his massive fingers dug into her thighs, trying to pry her legs apart. The pain burned through her like iron spikes, slowly pushing into her.

She held on.

His grip tightened, harder and harder.

She held on. Her vision became hazy from the pain.

"Skrull, take me!" she yowled through clenched teeth. "Give in!"

Finally, his grip loosened, his hands falling to the floor, limp at his sides. They both tumbled backward, with Saudett's weight still leaning back on his shoulders. She rolled into a seated position as they hit the ground, holding her thighs tenderly. Baal lay on his back, eyes closed, snoring loudly, looking almost peaceful.

"Gods, I hope we don't have another go of this, Baal," she murmured. She looked up at Lieutenant Ryon, who was standing shakily. "Your aid was ever so welcomed."

He puffed up his chest as if to retort, then sighed heavily. "I'll go find someone to move this beast." He swiftly exited his office.

She slowly reached her feet and went to the unconscious guard against the wall. She crouched down and examined him. His chest gradually rose and fell. *Still alive, thank Hettra.* She brought her thumbnail to her lips in a thankful gesture. She tapped the man's cheek lightly. No response.

"I don't think he's waking up," she thought aloud as a shadow fell over her.

"Saudett," Baal growled.

She slowly turned, holding her breath. Baal stood over her, a giant grin on his face. "Saudett strong!" He put one fist to his chest and held the other out, palm open.

She mirrored the gesture. They clasped forearms as Baal pulled her to her feet. "No. You are strong, my friend." She smiled back, amazed at how fast he had recovered. "Though, we need to figure out the plight of this grit predicament and why you were in possession of it."

"Grit, bad. M—Merchant gives to my young girl."

Saudett's eyes widened. "How old is your girl?!"

"Old, what is word?"

"Age, years, seasons, time, sunrises, sunsets."

"Ah, she is birthed," he started counting on his fingers, "humph, near twenty summers?"

She felt a flash of rage fill her. *Gods, trying to get a young woman addicted, and then what? Grit is a highly addictive substance.* From what she had heard, someone's first use of it could knock them out cold, though frequent users began to build a tolerance to it. She frowned; she didn't know enough about the substance, as it had never really been a problem in Dagad. "I will track the merchant down and figure—"

A bell began to toll—a clamor at the door. Ryon rushed in, surprised to see Baal standing in front of Saudett.

"What is going on? Never mind. We're under attack from the desert. Rally with your squad at the Road's End!"

"Baal, go home. I'll find you once this is over." Saudett picked up her spear.

"What?!" Ryon exclaimed.

She stared at him.

"Fine. But this will be in my report to Captain Dermont."

"And mine won't leave out a single detail."

The lieutenant's face paled.

Chaos surrounded him. *Dust.* Thundering hooves made his ears ring. As the wave of attackers reached the bottom of the hill, Simon had just enough time to jump behind a large boulder in a stony outcrop near the base. The horsemen would not ride here without tripping and breaking their steed's legs, especially at full speed down the hill. *Once they had turned around, on the other hand...*

Dust. All he could see was dust and dark shadows fleeting past his vision. He could do nothing. He sat whimpering. *I hope it is a quick death.* What had led up to this moment? Meeting the love of his life, his better half. *We were going to start a family soon.* He would never get to see his children's faces. The countless hours he put into building a profitable operation. *All for what? Studying under my father. My father.* He was still in this madness with no cover and a bad leg. *The last thing I had said to him.*

Simon stood, then set out back toward the town through the chaos and the dust.

There are too many of them. Saudett looked at the massive cloud, maybe three hundred paces away. Nearly two hundred Shepherds Eye had formed a triple line across the Road's End. Yet, more guardsmen were creating columns behind, snaking back into the market. To run out into the open field on foot against such cavalry would be suicide. She had never seen a tribe of this size in the desert.

They have an army, and all we can do is watch.

The tribe seemed to circulate, the dust cloud spinning in their wake. Simon was out there, working on those cursed cellars. *Did the fool not see the dust cloud approaching?* She wanted to run out and find him, to stab and cut her way through if she had to. She knew better; she would quickly be downed and die alone—leaving Simon to his fate.

A horn sounded behind her. At the head of a few hundred cavalries, the captain of the Shepherds Eye was coming up the main road behind them—the infantry line parted in unison at the sound of a double blast of the horn. The columns moved aside to let the cavalry through. The horsemen picked up speed and surged past, forming a wedge to pierce the side of the circling nomads. As the tip of the wedge collided, another horn blast sounded. Saudett sprinted ahead. *I'm coming, Simon!* The rest of the infantry close on her heels.

The dust lessened slightly as Simon approached the building site; he could see the outline of the four domes they had constructed looming through the dust. *Praise Hettra, I haven't received a spear to the back yet.*

Approaching, he could finally make out a group of people on foot huddled beside one of the domes. *My crew!* They had picked up tools and loose reinforced boards. They were trying to fend off the horsemen.

Simon thought it strange the tribesmen did not just ride them down and trample them to death. Then he saw several horsemen coming in for a pass, bolas spinning above their heads. The stone-weighted ropes shot out from the riders just paces away from the workmen. Two of Simon's men went down from the impact of the bolas, yanked off their feet, and dragged away from the group. One man grasped at his neck as the rope constricted.

As Simon stumbled forward, another wave of riders passed, and more of his men were hauled away. He heard their muffled shouts as they disappeared into the dust. Only two figures remained. He made out Naurr's stocky silhouette and another man standing behind him.

"FATHER!" Simon screamed through the turmoil.

Three nomads had halted fifty paces away from Naurr and Yakeb. Two of the riders dismounted and approached, large curved scimitars flashing. One held back on his horse, watching. Horse and rider alike clad in golden scale and plated armor, the man wore the speckled fur of a hyena around his shoulders. A jagged gilded helm was atop his head, and his mouth and nose were covered with strips of cloth. Simon had seen the other riders dressed much more simply in plain boiled leathers and light linen robes.

Naurr carried a massive piece of iron inset lumber in both hands. As the nomads closed in, he rushed them. The first raised his scimitar, defending himself from Naurr's two-handed swing of the hardwood. Simon could hear the resounding clash of metal and watched as the scimitar flew to one side. Then, the lumber came up under the man's chin with a thud. The nomad took a precarious step back, then crumpled into a heap.

The second man had come up behind Naurr as he had finished his strike. A deadly slice of the scimitar flashed toward Naurr's neck. Naurr ducked and spun, the lumber arcing in a massive sweep, connecting with the man's legs. Bones snapped; the man screamed. Naurr stood over the man, lifting the wood high over his head in both hands. He crunched the butt end into the man's face. Blood sprayed; the screams abruptly cut off. Another sickly thud. Thrice. Naurr slowly turned toward the golden-clad rider. The pulp of the dead man's brains and skull scattered everywhere, an eyeball rolling into the mud.

"Enough," the golden-clad figure commanded, raising his hand. Three riders pounded past their leader, bolas soaring out at Naurr. He blocked one of the bolas as it wrapped around the lumber. But he could not fend off so many at once. One of the stones spun and collided with Naurr's head, and he fell to the ground.

As Saudett reached the multitude of horses and bodies, she vaulted off the corpse of a horse, using it to gain more height, and extended her spear into the nearest bandit. The spear punched into the nomad's left side, below his armpit, and into his heart. She pulled the spear free as she landed. He slumped off his horse and toppled to the ground. Blood pooled and clumped in the dirt to form a dark muck.

"FORM UP!" she shouted. Her battalion gathered about her.

Two more enemy riders went down in a flurry of reaching spear tips.

Suddenly, bolas whistled out of the dust toward the group. The volley snared a couple of Shepherds Eyes and ripped them out of the formation.

"They are trying to take captives!" Saudett hollered.

A hooded Shepherds Eye soldier reacted quickly, coming to the aid of one of the tangled men. Dropping a short bow, he swiftly unsheathed his long scimitar and sheared through the rope, connecting the catch to the rider. Saudett watched as the hooded soldier clenched his teeth through his chest-length black beard and hauled the entangled soldier to his feet. *Xamidian,* she determined, catching a glance of his tan complexion under the hood. His bushy, slightly greying eyebrows frowned with focus while he cut away the tangle of cord. He pushed the man back into formation. Unfortunately, the other snared soldier was far gone, pulled off into the turmoil.

"Yah!"

She heard a shout as another Shepherds Eye, a Tulu woman, hurled a throwing ax at a rushing nomad, her white dreadlocks tied up tight behind her yellow-scarfed head. The ax sunk into the rider's chest, and he toppled backward off the mount.

Slowly, they pushed on, step by step, the compact cube of soldiers bristling with spear points outward. *Killing* their way to her husband.

Simon's father straightened his usually hunched back, standing tall and unwavering but alone. He looked back at his son.

The man in gold reined his horse beside Yakeb. He murmured something Simon could not hear.

A few dozen paces distant, Simon was pleading, his hand outstretched. "Wait! *No.* FATHER!"

Yakeb smiled at Simon as his head fell from his shoulders.

Simon halted in his tracks.

"You can help me, Father," Simon murmured in despair. "Tell me what to—" He was yanked to the ground, face thudding hard into the dirt. A rope compressed around his legs. He tasted iron in his mouth, and his vision blurred with red. He saw his father's body fade into the dust while he was dragged away.

They were gone. The dust was settling on the landscape, settling on the *bodies.*

I'm too late! Saudett sat cross-legged, face bowed, looking down at Yakeb's head in her lap.

Chapter Two

DUST

Simon winced at the pain in his chest and stomach. *Let me die,* he thought. He was straddled over the back end of a horse, harshly bouncing as the horse galloped. He could only see the ground beneath him, changing from the patchy grasses and rocky dirt of the foothills to the hot sands of the desert. The gallop slowed to a trot, then eventually subsided into a walk. The ride continued endlessly, or so Simon felt. He slowly slipped in and out of wakefulness from the pain and exhaustion. Then suddenly, it was dark.

Simon was maltreated off the rump of the horse and dropped face down. He choked on a mouthful of sand. Someone rolled him over and sat him up. Putting warm water to his lips, which he eagerly sucked back, swallowing some of the sand already in his mouth. He did not care. He was lifted to his feet by a couple of nomads on each arm, both faces hidden by layers of wrapped linens, only their dark eyes regarding him. He was then ushered to other captives huddled in the sand. The two men joined a few other sentries and watched the group nearby.

"What are you going to do to us?" Simon asked.

A different guard strolled over, wearing baggy brown robes and hard-boiled leather. The guard paused, standing over Simon, then struck him across the jaw with the backhand of their fist. Simon reeled, tasting blood again.

"Do not speak," said a fluid, feminine voice.

"By the Gods. Ah, well, can I have more water for this newfound blood in my mouth?"

She raised her fist again. Simon covered his head in a defensive cower. Yet no blow came to him as he parted his arms slowly to see her walking away, back to her post.

Simon arched a brow. *It's hard to tell she is a woman under all those heavy robes. A warrior woman as well. Reminds me of Saudett.* He let his imagination wander to the mystery beneath the bulky clothing. He soon found his thoughts come back to his spouse. Saudett had been pressed against him this very morning. Her soft, bare skin against his. Hands clawed into his back as they—

He shook his head, then shrugged to himself. *I need to keep my spirits up in such a stressful situation.* He whispered, "Saudett, my star, will you come to chase me across the desert?"

"I wouldn't be putting it past her, boss man," a familiar voice whispered.

Simon adjusted around to see Naurr. "Thank the Primus, you made it." He put a hand on Naurr's shoulder.

Naurr gave a silent chuckle. "Be missing the wife there? Mark my words, she will come for you." He half-smiled before his face winced with pain. Naurr had a massive welt on his forehead, looking raw and bruised.

"You know what, my good man, I think you're correct. She will come. *And!* I was thinking about her in the most loving of ways possible, of course!"

"Of course, the most loving of ways." Naurr paused for a long moment before finally speaking again. "It breaks my heart. I couldn't protect your father, my friend."

Simon's mischievous antics instantly fell as the realization and horror pierced into him. *My father is dead. How could I be thinking of sex at a time like this?* He gave Naurr a weak smile. "You did better than I could have. Far better. I am the one who should be apologizing. I got us into this mess. And as you suggested, I was responsible for not checking on the dust cloud. It's my fault he's dead."

"Don't be blaming all of fate on your shoulders. Only the Primus and his gods know the paths we take. Let us rest while we have the chance. They likely to break camp before daylight."

"Aye, Naurr. And thank you, thank you for fighting for him."

"If we don't be making it out of this, I will seek you out in whatever hell you find yourself in."

Simon chuckled and curled onto his side in the sand, still thinking about his father. The regret of his last words weighed heavily on him, and a sinking feeling crept in. *I told him off, and now he is gone forever.* Simon began to focus back on a time when he was a child.

He remembered his father hovering over him as he sat at his small table in their modest home. Soon, his senses filled with the sounds and smell of his mother busily preparing a meal in the background, humming as she worked.

He heard his father as clear as day: "Walls need to be properly supported with a base lamina before the studding and reinforcement pins. Once the lamina is in place and timber forms are attached, mix and pour the wall composition, whether sandstone or the more traditional Aurulan limestone thatching."

Then, his mother's warm voice. "My dears, our meal is nearly prepared. You finish this up now, Yakeb." Her tone suggested she had not asked a question.

"Of course, my fair-haired maiden! Just after we finish up with this topic," Yakeb said.

"My hair has gone mostly grey, no thanks to you."

"And ever more beautiful as the days go by, my sweet. As gorgeous, dare I say, oh my, as the eve that our son first suckled your teat."

"You devil man. Hasten yourself, or I'll fetch my black-pine ladle."

"Yes, yes, quite right. We can alter our course after dinner, Simon. I'm in the mood for some poetry or the history of Al'Jalif, the Jewel of the East. I think I have a text around here somewhere on that particular subject. Many a romantic ballad out of Xamidian nights. Enough mathematics and practical knowledge of whatnots for one day."

"Ahem," Simon's mother cleared her throat menacingly.

"Indeed, let me just wrap up here. Where was I? Simon? *Simon?*"

He listened to his father's voice fade in his mind as exhaustion swiftly overtook him.

Simon's eyes shot open. He could not breathe, sinking again into the dark gray-green depths. Then, he saw a faint light at the furthest depth of his vision. He felt himself being pulled deeper, trying to struggle against it.

He could not hold the air in his lungs any longer. *Primus, help me!* He felt the familiar feeling of the cool liquid rushing into his lungs.

He coughed up the water, the sand turning brown with the moisture.

Choking and catching his breath, he gasped, "Damn, fu—perhaps I should start sleeping with a bucket at my side. Then, I can quench my thirst with this unholy liquid. 'Two birds with one bucket,' as they say." He smiled wryly to himself.

"I've never heard such an expression before, and, well, that was *quite* disturbing," came the sultry voice of his aggressor, the sentry from the past night.

"I couldn't agree more!" Simon piped up. "Madam?" He hopped to his feet energetically and gave his most flirtatious grin.

"All of you, up!" she shouted at the groggy prisoners.

Dawn was just arriving, a low orange glow from the distant eastern horizon. The oppressed group groaned as they stood.

The golden-clad man leisurely walked his speckled white stallion up to the prisoners.

Simon felt his blood boil, his face becoming suddenly hot with rage. *This man killed my father!* He looked around for something to use as a weapon. There was nothing but sand. *Maybe I could stuff the man's throat full in his sleep.*

"Your occupation?"

He had not realized they were questioning the prisoners and were directing the current query toward him. Standing taller, he composed himself and announced, "Chief architect and owner of Meridio Enterprises."

The golden-clad man nodded. Then, to Naurr, he asked, "And you, warrior? Some sort of bodyguard, I assume?"

"I am but a simple drudge hand," Naurr answered.

"Nonsense! Don't cut yourself short, my good man," Simon exclaimed. "This gentleman here is the leading foreman of Meridio Enterprises."

Naurr sighed.

Simon tilted his head in confusion. Then, realizing Naurr was trying to lay low, his face flushed at his stupidity. *Gods, for all my studies, I sure am an idiot.* Naurr was so much more intelligent sometimes, perhaps because he had more experience in the outside world. Simon's childhood had been relatively sheltered in his lessons. Regret panged through him as he thought of his father once more. "Skrull, take me to your hell and back," Simon murmured.

The golden-clad man laughed shortly through his mask, golden helm jingling. "A bookman, but much to learn, this one."

Simon felt his neck heating up again. *I could just run at him and die, get it over with.*

"Meridio? This is your house name?" the golden man asked.

"Aye, it is my house name. You-you cowardly fuck of a whoreson!" Simon screamed the last words. "It is the same name of the defenseless old man you murdered in cold blood yesterday!" Simon took a handful of steps toward the golden man. A sword instantly slid under his chin.

He halted. His mistress, the jail guard, stood to his side, the tip of her tulwar blade drawing a thin line of blood as she circled to his forefront.

"Do not throw your life away so readily," she whispered.

He looked into her eyes, their radiant, almost unnatural violet with gray-gold flecks gazing back at him. All he could see were her eyes, long black lashes, and dark brown skin around them; the rest of her face remained hidden behind the wraps. What an intriguing mystery, he pondered as he found himself lost in her gaze.

"We need them alive," said the golden man. "There is great labor to prepare in the valley." He waved a hand at the rest of the prisoners. "These are your workmen?" he asked, looking at Simon.

Simon recovered from those gem-like eyes and gave his head a shake. With a scowl, he tried to spit in the golden man's direction, but his mouth was barren of moisture, making only a pitiful puff.

The golden man turned to Naurr.

Naurr nodded. "Some Shepherds Eye soldiers, too, be looking the like."

The town's guard and a *literal* shepherd of sheep, Simon noted. Qunid sat discreetly among the prisoners, looking at the sky, minding his business. *At least he had survived,* Simon thought.

"Good. Let us depart." The golden-clad man shouted to the surrounding nomads, "Split the prisoners into partners. Otsoa's, take one hundred of the Pack each. Have one prisoner walk half the day while the other rides with the beasts of burden. We will throw off any pursuers by leaving in all directions. Split your force in half four days from now. Any more resilient pursuant will lose the scent in days. We'll meet at home in the Valley of Hasiera."

The golden man mounted his horse. Then, looking down at Simon, said, "Give him half rations," he paused to grin wickedly, "and make him walk the entire way."

Chapter Three

GRIT

"Skrull, take me. I should have been there! Simon, I swear on your father's grave. I will come for you," Saudett hissed angrily as she surveyed the carnage after the attack. Having been occupied with Baal and Ryon, perhaps she could have reacted faster if only she had been closer to Simon. *Yet, what could I have done against the horde of nomads?*

The bastards had taken everything: weeks' worth of grains, dried fruits and salted meats, yams, onions, garlic, and many spices packed into large hemp-woven sacks. The vaults belonged to the municipality. As such, they stipulated the food to the town's administrations—such as the Shepherds Eye, the Court of Freemen, cemetery workers, street cleaners, rat catchers, and other offices that kept the town functioning.

Saudett fumed, pacing back and forth before the half-finished excavation. *On the bright side, at least all the cellars had not been fully stocked.* Almost one hundred heads of sheep had also been taken, along with the preserved goods. The nomads could not be traveling that quickly with such livestock and cargo, not to mention a half-hundred prisoners.

By the Primus, the creator of the gods. She gripped her spear impatiently; *I need to set out! I should be thinking about my husband, not the welfare of the damned town.*

A small group of horsemen was approaching from the town, riding past a mound of bodies piled to be burned. She scowled as she noticed Lieutenant Ryon at their head. "Took the wretch long enough," she grumbled aloud. The group reined in beside her.

"Where is Captain Dermont?" she asked.

"He is in the infirmary," Ryon answered. "Took a slash to his leg, and he's unable to walk. He placed me in command."

"Fair enough." *Skrull's sack, why does it have to be him?* She held back her thoughts. "Shall we be on our way? Daylight fades, and my husband gets ever further from us."

"I will take our swiftest riders and track the bandits; you will stay here and prepare for another attack."

"Hettra's fucking tits, I will not! They took *my* husband. Does that not mean anything to you?" She gripped her spear, knuckles whitening.

"Hold your tongue, Sergeant! Or you will do something rash and become a corpse in the desert." He looked down at her from atop his horse and sneered.

She wanted to hurl the spear through the man's face. She took a deep breath and composed herself. "I have more experience in the Burning Sea than most. I've traveled across it many times. They'll throw you off their trail after the first day. You need me!"

"Nonsense. These are my orders; best you tend to your dead." He turned his horse and motioned the other riders to follow.

She stood, her face and neck hot with rage. "By Skrull's unholy torment," she cursed, "take that man swiftly to your hell." She contemplated fetching a horse and going out alone. But what would she do if she found them? She'd also be cut down or captured, *but at least I would be with Simon.* She could also find herself demoted or expelled from the Shepherds Eye—or worse, tried for desertion and sent to the labor camps of Aurulan.

Composing herself once more, she tried to rationalize the situation. That many bandits must have some sort of stronghold out there. The best option would be to track them back to their hideout and then muster a force to wipe them out. She would have to bite her tongue and wait until the lieutenant returned. She needed to busy herself in the meantime. *First things first: I will put Yakeb to rest.*

Two dozen or so dead nomads had fallen in the fray. She watched townsfolk scurrying about butchering dead horses on the spot, stripping nomads, and dragging them over to the pile of bodies. They began tossing torches on the mound. The smell of charred flesh wafted past Saudett's nose.

She covered her mouth and nose with her linen head wrap to lessen the smell, pondering the nomad's folly to sacrifice so many to obtain little supplies and a few slaves. The nomads could have lost many more had they not dispersed after the captain's charge. They had also shown restraint in direct combat. Instead, they focused on skirmishing, mainly with the bolas to apprehend and short bows to fend off any immediate pursuit by the

Shepherds' cavalry. *Why attack now, after all these years?* She would visit the captain later tonight and hear his take on the assault.

She wrapped Yakeb in a thin beige length of linen from head to toe, placing the head as if to reattach it. Then she laid him on a leather canvas attached to two aspen poles, fastened to the sides of a camel, to be towed back into town.

Others were doing the same for some of the fallen guardsmen. With the brunt of the fatalities where the two mounted forces had struck each other, not so many on Dagad's side had died. *Thank Hettra.* The families of the dead would bring the bodies to their households to observe their culture's interment customs.

Yakeb, being from Aurulan, would be laid to rest beside his wife in a cemetery for the Auru peoples of Dagad, which was a day's march west into a woodland grove. The body would first stay a day and a night in the Meridio home while dressed for burial. The embalmer would prepare the body with oils and herbs and do his best to reattach the head to the torso for observation. *I will carry this practice out in Simon's stead, and with Qav's luck, we will one day look upon your father's grave together.*

It was approaching sunset; she wanted to report to the captain before nightfall. She began the quarter-hour walk from their home to the barracks near the Road's End. The streets were dead. Everyone was shut in with their families after the assault on the town. She again found herself in the market thoroughfare, shops shut down.

What's this? She noticed activity at one of the stalls, where she had a run-in with Baal earlier. A small, timid-looking man, nervously looking about, hastily directed a couple of brawny men to haul off his containers and sacks as if to close the booth permanently.

She sauntered up behind the fidgety merchant. "Primus tell, where are you off to at this time of night?"

The man squeaked as he turned to face her. His eyes widened when he looked upon her face, and his beady black eyes darted around. "Sergeant! Thank you ever so much for dealing with that brute earlier. It is awful for business and much too dangerous to stay in this town. I am headed to Xamid on the next caravan, where my services will be better appreciated." Jewelry jingled on his green-and-gold trimmed full-length robe as he spoke animatedly.

"Grit dealing being your primary source of income? Or perhaps a more human trade? Selling your captives to be used for their genitals?"

His eyes seemed to widen even further. Finally studying the man, she could see he was Xamidian, though with a much lighter skin tone than Saudett. *Not used to the out-of-doors.*

A long, black beard hung down his chest, and an elegant bright red turban set with green gems adorned his head.

"I haven't the *faintest* idea of what you're talking about, Sergeant. I am but a simple spice trader." He turned his head around as if looking for the whereabouts of his hired hands.

One of them had ambled away a good twenty paces from where the merchant stood, hands up, indicating he did not want to fight. The other was nowhere to be seen.

Saudett began to turn and check her flank when two thick arms wrapped around her, crushingly tight; her spear fell from her grip. Pain shot through her arms. She tried to throw her head back and catch the chin of the man holding her, but the back of her head bounced harmlessly off his chest.

"Get involved in my business, and you'll become it," the merchant snickered. His bony fingers grasped a pouch off his belt. "Hold her legs, Kem."

With the other thug grabbing her lower legs, she could not move. One of the thin hands of the merchant covered her mouth while the other took a pinch of the black powder from his pouch. She tried to turn her head away, but the scrawny hands were more robust than they looked, holding her head still. He pushed the powder into her nostrils, and her vision exploded. Her nose burned, and she felt a prickling in her throat.

Grit. It caused the user to become lethargic and unresponsive—helpful in getting people to do what you wanted. It was also rumored that it could rarely increase the potency of magical energy in a being. If one believed in that sort of thing. Magic users were one in ten thousand—and Saudett had never seen anyone use magic in her life.

Unfortunately, she wasn't one of those lucky mythical beings. Her head was spinning, and she felt warm, pleasantly relaxed. Her senses dulled; she could only make out the colored canvas coverings overhead moving along. Moments later, the canvases were gone, and the group was between two buildings in a narrow alley, the stars beginning to appear through the dusk.

"Oi, let us use her before you sell her off," one of the thugs grumbled.

"Well, if you insist. But I will be the first," said the merchant. "Hold her down over those crates."

The thugs unfastened her belt, and her girdle fell to the ground. Then, she was sharply pushed over onto her stomach atop the crates. She wanted to scream and fight, but her body did not respond. *Primus, help me!* She vaguely felt the tearing of her linen trousers and under wraps. She could not defend herself; she could hardly distinguish what was happening with the fog clouding her mind.

"Simon," she murmured, overcome.

The next moment, she heard a muffled bellow as she was pushed hard off the crate, falling limply to the ground. Her head slammed against something. Blinking in confusion, she couldn't keep her eyes open any longer with the combination of the drug sapping her strength and the knock to her head, though the pain was dull and distant. There was the faint sound of a struggle, but she could not see well enough to determine what was happening. *Some soldier I turned out to be.*

She lay, unable to move at the mercy of some grit slinger. Muffled voices were shouting? An eternity of silent minutes washed away. Finally, a vast silhouetted form lurched over her, and she was being gently lifted as she slipped into a hazed slumber.

Consciousness slowly came to Saudett. Her head pounding; she could feel each heart-beat pulse through her skull. One spot on the back of her head began to burn. She closed her eyes, focusing on the sounds around her. She heard faint murmuring and realized people were whispering in a rough dialect. *It's an oddly familiar idiom. Vouri?* Slowly opening her eyes, Saudett saw a small hearth and two figures seated in front of it: one vast and bulky. Firelight glistened off his shaven head and dark black thunderbolt tattoos.

"Baal?" she murmured.

"Saudett, friend. Home." He gestured to a sturdy figure, an equally tall woman stirring a large pot over the hearth. Baal turned and gave a toothy smile and grunted, "Brena, mate."

A woman's pale face smiled, producing a slight crinkle of laugh lines around her eyes and mouth. Her bright blue eyes shone in the firelight. Black dye darkened her eyelids, and her long blond hair reached her lower back in a large braid. Two jagged lightning bolt tattoos, matching her partner's, ran down her neck and into her blouse.

"Shepherds Eye," Brena softly stated in clear Auru. "Thank you for releasing my husband." She smiled warmly. "As you may have noted, he tends to take matters into his own hands. He is also not overly sensitive to diplomacy."

Saudett lay on the bed, propping herself up on one elbow. "No need to thank me. It seems I am the one who should be thankful." *Skrull take me; I should have been more aware of the second thug! Years of training. I am better than this!* "Hettra's blessing that Baal arrived when he did. I am equally in his debt, as I was on the verge of a life of drug-induced slavery." She winced at the pain in her head. "At any rate, I would not be aware of the greater threat posed by this dealer if not for his harsh confrontation. Your daughter had a similar experience?"

"She was not so forcefully confronted. That merchant offered the grit to her at the market; he could not blatantly kidnap her in such a place. Luckily, we found her on the verge of collapse nearby. The two thugs were shadowing her but ran off at seeing us. She is still recovering." Brena pointed a finger past Saudett.

Saudett turned onto her other arm and realized there was another person in bed with her. A girl with short-cropped fiery red hair was sleeping soundly. "You have a beautiful daughter, Brena, and Baal. What is your house name?"

"Vasara."

"My pleasure, Vasara House. I am in your service." She felt exhaustion creeping back upon her. "Do tell, what happened to the merchant?"

Brena asked Baal in Vouri, and he spewed a quick reply, becoming noticeably irritated.

"The grit dealer escaped, prick in hand, while Baal was preoccupied with the two hired muscles. One of whom will meet Skrull at the gate to his hell." Baal gave a victory grunt before his wife continued. "The other will have trouble using his arms for a long time."

"My thanks to you both, Baal, Bren..." She trailed off. *I'm so weak,* she thought as she lay her head back on the bedding. A warm, damp cloth was draped over her eyes, and a gentle hand brushed her hair for a minute as sleep quickly came to her. *Just as my mother used to do.*

CHAPTER FOUR

DESERT

The glaring sun beat down upon them. Simon walked on; the heat caused an endless wave of distortion in the distance as if a massive lake was always out of reach. The dunes rose and fell like monstrous waves in the sea, slowly drifting by. It was only the second day in the desert, and Simon felt depleted. Each step took everything he had. Though he managed to stay upright for that first day, the knowledge that Simon was only getting half as much food and water as the other prisoners sapped his strength.

He stumbled and fell into the sand, content to let the camel pull him along. *This is fine,* he thought. Unfortunately, the camel stopped.

A loud *crack* and pain lanced through his back. A burning sensation and cool dampness began to soak through his shirt.

"Get up."

He stayed prone; he was ready to accept his fate. *This is as good a place as any.*

Another *crack* and more pain shot up his back. Simon lay still, clenching his teeth, dark thoughts consuming him: *The world doesn't need me. Nobody needs me.* With yet another *crack,* the pain was gone. Saudett's face flashed before his eyes, an image of her cradling a babe. Then he felt hands upon him, pulling him to his feet.

"He's had enough for now; he can ride for a half-day to recover," said a familiar female voice.

"This is against First Otsoa's command," a man's voice answered.

"The First Otsoa is not present, Mittal Gohra. I lead this Pack."

"As you say, Sixteenth." The man rode on ahead.

His mysterious vixen gave Simon a sip of water from her skin.

"My thanks," he murmured.

"You can thank me by cooperating. By using your skills and working for our people."

All he could do was nod his head. He was about to ask what she meant, but fatigue kept him from speaking further. She helped him get hoisted onto a camel's back. The saddle was surprisingly supportive, and he could sit slouched over. The relief was instantaneous. With the camels hitched together in a train, he did not need to take the reins, only keep himself upright. The solemn group continued through the rolling dunes.

Nearly a score of blistering hot days and bone-chilling nights stretched by, though it was hard to keep track, as every day seemed much the same. His abductors were well-versed in their landscape's boons. Even so, only twice on their passage had they come upon small muddy pools to refresh their water skins. In a jagged outcropping, the spots were riddled with patchy brown vegetation stuck between the rocky surface. Quite a rare occurrence in the league upon leagues of sand. Fortunately, Simon could alternate between walking and riding. He had also been given what appeared to be more significant portions of a rice-curry mixture, flatbread, and water. Soon, he found himself recovering and feeling more energetic.

He watched as the woman, this Sixteenth Otsoa, led their group. She brought the column to a stop at the crest of each dune. Then, she sat atop her mount and surveyed the landscape, sometimes for what felt like an eternity. After a while, she would raise two fingers, and the column would set out again, descending the dune.

Simon estimated nearly a hundred nomads in his group, a dozen camels laden with goods, and some ten heads of sheep. Naurr had been separated from him and taken with another group on the first day. Five days in, they found water. After the resupply, the Pack, as they called themselves, split their force in half by roughly fifty. Just as the golden-clad man had commanded them to cover their tracks.

He had but the company of his captors. The Sixteenth Otsoa became disinterested and was primarily heading off the assembly. *At any rate, I cannot cut the camel loose and ride up beside her for a chat.* He would have to wait to find out more about this woman. He was bored, so he did the next best thing. He spoke to his camel.

"So, *Marigold*, got a husband? Any children? What do you do in your downtime besides running with this unfavorable bunch? Do you get off on the slaughter of innocent old men? *No?* Please enlighten me. How did you find yourself in this group of cutthroats and bastards?" Simon paused as if to listen to the camel's response. "Indeed? From Xamid, you hail? What brings you to these parts?" He took another long pause. "You're looking for a new lover? Well, well, old Simon here can help you with that! 'The frogs and the fishes, as they say.' I just so happen to have great finesse in the art of seduction; you should ask my wife! We'll seek out and apprehend a suitable man camel just for you."

"That camel is a he," a voice said behind him.

He twisted around in his saddle. He was surprised to see the enticing lady, her violet eyes glistening with amusement at his antics behind her masked face.

"Well, maybe he, Marigold that is, fancies the man. Which I have nothing against! Quite enjoy them myself, as a matter of fact."

Her eyes flickered.

Was that curiosity? Simon pondered.

"And how would he come about having his own children this way?"

"Naturally, he takes to the slums of Al'Jalif to find a promising orphan camel to pass on his knowledge of banditry and *murder*." Simon spat the last word; sarcasm sharp like a knife.

She exhaled heavily, "Our needs surpass your thin moralistic views on killing and stealing. We do what we need to survive in this world..." the woman trailed off. "And prepare for worse."

What does she mean by that? Instead, he asked, "Sixteenth Otsoa, is it? Do you have a name? How are you on this fine day? What will I be tasked with at our odyssey's outcome? Please do tell. I'm longing for human interaction."

"I will answer one of your questions." She paused, and he could swear she was grinning behind that mask of hers. "Yes, I am Sixteenth Otsoa." She spurred her horse ahead.

"Wait!" he called after her. "Come back!" Then, he sighed with exasperation. They were the first words spoken to him since they had started on this road into Skrull's hell. He shrugged and thought, *well, that was progress, at least.* With a renewed sense of hope, he resumed his previous conversation. "Where were we, Marigold? Oh, yes, where do you see yourself a decade from now?"

Marigold groaned and spat into the sand.

Chapter Five

AWAKEN

Saudett slept fitfully on the night of her attack and, for most of the next day, waking feverishly and vomiting occasionally. Brena was always by her side with a wooden pail, food, and water. Saudett could eat a few morsels, but the solid food was hard to keep down. At least Brena's daughter, Hata, was sitting up in bed and looking much livelier, color returning to her face. During Saudett's restless sleep, she could hear the two whispering to each other quietly.

"Isä will not stop until that man is dead."

"He'd best stop, or he will end up in jail and shipped deep into Aurulan to work in a convict camp. Or, Teras forbid, he'll end up dead. This merchant is far more dangerous than your Isä warrants."

"I will help him," the daughter said resolutely.

"Skrull's hairy balls, you will not, Hata Vasara."

"Language, Mother." The two women giggled softly as Saudett drifted back into darkness.

Saudett dreamt of her past before Simon. She had fallen asleep many times after waiting hours for her parents to return home when she was young. They were rarely present, always off on the next contract, traveling the world. She impatiently awaited the day they would come home and tell her she was ready and old enough to join them. She had been working hard, participating in every morning drill since they left, under the direction of Ismael Kaur, the recruiting master and sergeant of Caravan House Kafilah. House Kafilah was an estate that resided in the beautiful city of Al'Jalif, the Jewel of the East, on the coast of the Sea of Xamid.

Saudett slightly opened her eyes when a hand gently stroked her hair. The fire-red head of the young Hata looked down on her. Saudett closed her eyes again, enjoying the feeling.

Blinking them open again, she did not see Hata, but instead, Saudett's mother's face was smiling down as she lay in bed, her hand still stroking her hair. A memory from the past returned to her.

Young Saudett sat up excitedly. "Mother! You're back!"

"I am. I missed you, my sweet Saudett."

As they embraced, she cradled her head on her mother's shoulder while her mother stroked the back of her head.

"I miss you too," Saudett said as she pulled away slightly to speak face-to-face with her mother. "I hope you aren't leaving again soon.

Her mother's face fell. "I'm sorry, my dear. We have an urgent contract lined up to depart in the morning. I have only this night with you."

Saudett saw tears welling in her mother's eyes as she asked, "Why? Why do you have to go so soon?"

"I must. I am sorry. But let's make the most of tonight. Shall we take a stroll together, just you and me?"

"I'd like that very much, Mother. Let's."

Her mother stood, wrapping a light linen sheet around Saudett before grabbing another off the bedding for herself. Then, taking her daughter's hand, she pulled her close, and they slowly crept out of the bed-chamber. Her mother looked both ways down the hall before guiding Saudett quietly to the left, toward the back of the estate grounds.

"Where are we going, Mother?"

"Shush, just for a walk to the gardens, my dear." Her mother's pace quickened. Stopping at the door, she stood silently, listening. After a handful of heartbeats slipped away, her mother slowly opened the door; it creaked and groaned loudly, and her mother froze.

"Why are we sneaking, Mother?"

"It's alright; we are just going for a walk. No more questions, please, dear. Be patient; wait until we're in the garden."

They made their way through a pantry laden with goods: crates of fruits; shelves of jars and other multitudes of vegetables and spices; barrels of wine, ale, and other liquors; and smoked meats hanging from hooks in the ceiling. Suddenly, they heard footsteps on the cobblestones in an adjacent hall. The footsteps grew louder, and they listened to a low melodic humming. They stopped once more, holding their breath. Whomever it was, they were coming right for them.

The door across from them opened; with a noticeable limp, a man holding a candle in one hand entered the cellar. He stopped abruptly upon seeing them.

"Lady Kafilah, little fox? It's a bit late to be tromping around the pantry, is it not? If I do say so myself."

"Ismael!" Saudett ran over to the man and squeezed him.

"Ahem. My pardons, lady. The girl seems somewhat attached to me since I gave her a training spear." The aged Xamidian man chuckled, his bushy gray beard shaking.

Her mother smiled, raising her brows. "You did what?"

"Pardon, my pardons, Lady Kafilah!" The man bowed repeatedly.

"I jest, Ismael. She is in good hands. I wish only to be here more often to help raise my daughter."

"Ismael is teaching me the three-point parry," Saudett chimed in.

"Is that not a fair bit advanced for a ten-summer-old?"

"The little fox catches on quick, lady," Ismael said. "Never hurts to know how to defend oneself if I do say so. At any rate, you all out for a late-night feast?"

"I plead guilty, Ismael," her mother grinned. "Do we have some cheese and smoked mackerel about this place? I have a hankering."

Ismael nodded and set about gathering a handful of provisions for them.

"Ismael." Her mother's tone of voice had changed.

"Aye, lady?"

"I beg of you, don't inform my husband of this."

He nodded again and, without a word, handed them the cheese and fish, then turned and departed. They listened as his humming quietly disappeared down the way he had come.

They found themselves in the long rectangular garden at the back of the estate. Saudett chewed on the dried salted fish, admiring the many bushes trimmed to look like different wild animals, yet they were part one animal and part another. One such sculpture was the form of a lion's head with the body of an elephant; another, a vulture and a boar, and a horse with a long neck reaching up high. Saudett enjoyed watching the gardener come to keep the bushes in shape every fortnight or so. There was a new yet-to-be-sculpted shrub, and she was excited to see what would become of it.

Saudett heard a rattle at the iron gate at the back of the grounds. She turned to see her mother fiddling with a sizeable black padlock and key.

"Where do you think you two are off to at this time of night?" a harsh voice said in the darkness.

Saudett followed the voice to see the shadowy figure of her father appearing from behind one of the shaped animals. His face was cowled with a hood.

"We're just having a moment to ourselves. I haven't seen my daughter in months. Just give us some time! Please!" her mother pleaded.

"Girl. Go back inside."

"But, Father," Saudett started.

"I WILL NOT REPEAT MYSELF!"

Saudett turned and ran back into the hallway's darkness, back through the cellar, and back to her bed. She started to cry, covering her head with her blankets; she wept until no more tears came out.

"I want my mother," she kept repeating until she closed her burning eyes and slept.

Saudett, her present self again, blinked her eyes open once more. Some hours had drifted away, and light began to brighten the room, seeping through the small square openings on one wall of the Vasara home. It seemed Brena and Baal had gone out. Saudett lay on her side, facing Hata; she slowly opened her eyes to look at the girl.

She was sitting up in bed, fiddling with something in one hand. Her hand swayed around in patterns as if to catch a firefly. Saudett vaguely realized that something was following Hata's palm, floating about. It was, she realized, a tiny sprinkle of sand, changing shape and drifting around, moving in rhythm with Hata's gestures.

By the gods, this grit sure makes you see things, Saudett thought.

Hata stopped as if she'd heard her words. The sand fell to the sheets, and the girl turned her head to look Saudett in the eyes.

"You're awake," Hata said.

"Aye, I just saw the most extraordinary thing."

"Extraordinary?" The girl's brows raised.

"Something extraordinary indeed. Can you show me again?"

"Oh, yes, please! I've longed to tell somebody other than my parents for days! Ever since I took that black powder, I've felt differently. I can feel the earth under my feet through the soles of my sandals. When my hands touch the bare rock or sand, I can ask it to move and do things, make it appear how I choose." Hata held out her hand, palm faced upwards. Slowly, the sand and dust traveled in wisps through the air to the center of her hand, floating slightly above it, forming a perfectly shaped ball. Hata plucked the ball out of the air with her other hand. "Feel it."

Saudett picked up the ball from Hata's outstretched hand. Her brows raised in surprise. "It is lightweight, yet hard as steel."

"Yes. Now, watch this," Hata urged excitedly.

The ball rose from Saudett's grasp, hovering mid-air for a few seconds. Then, with a whistle, it shot toward the hearth with such force it left a dent in the iron cauldron. A resounding clang echoed in the small chamber.

"That is spectacular, Hata. I've never seen anything like it in all the Earste Lân! You have told your parents and me, but this shouldn't get out to the townsfolk. Perhaps we should keep this secret safe. Some of the people here are averse to things that are beyond their comprehension. And there are those in the capital that would covet such power. Have you heard of the Council of the Aerie?"

Hata tilted her head, "No, what is it?"

"It is a gathering of mages, the shadow rulers of Aurulan. They have much sway with the king. It is rumored we common folk never see the likes of magi because the council hunts them all down."

"Why would they do that?"

"I'm afraid I do not know. I've been to the capital, Nidhaut, many times. The council's various towers pierce the city's skies like magnificent mountains, yet I have never met a council member. I've never witnessed magic before now."

"I'd like to see that city one day."

"Poking the hornet's nest, Hata!" Saudett squinted at the girl.

Hata grinned, dimples forming on her freckled cheeks. "I know, I know, very well." The girl nodded enthusiastically. "Our secret then, *old lady?*"

"Old lady?!" Saudett smirked. *I am perhaps a decade older than the cheeky girl, to be sure.* She sighed, "Our secret, then. Just keep practicing, try out new things, experiment—whatever comes to mind. Just don't do it in public. If you are willing, we can ride into the hills and try some things together."

"That sounds terrific!"

At that moment, Baal and Brena returned. Baal was laden with baskets of fruits, vegetables, and meats.

"Good afternoon, you two," Brena said, seeing them sitting in bed. "It appears that you're both getting on better."

"Profoundly so," Saudett said. "Your care and hospitality are—"

"I told her about the magic!" Hata blurted out, cutting her off.

"Hata. You must be careful about this. Tell no one else," Brena scolded.

"I must agree with your mother, Hata," Saudett reassured.

"I know, I know. I won't tell a soul. We're still going to go train, right? Old lady?"

Saudett looked at Brena and winked.

Brena smiled and nodded, "Very well."

"When will we go?" urged Hata.

"Perhaps tonight. I need to hasten and make a report to Captain Dermont. It's been a couple of days, and I have not checked in. Not to mention a personal matter I need to attend to. The body must be turning foul by now."

"Body?" Hata asked.

"Oh," she paused as the memory returned to her, anger building in her chest. "My husband's father died during the attack. *Gods,* I should have been there!" she cursed, slamming her fist into the bed frame.

Brena said some words to Baal in their language.

"Joo," Baal grunted.

"We will help you bury your husband's father. What came of your husband?"

"Aye. Simon, my husband, was seized by the nomads. I've truly lost my entire life in a matter of moments." The weight of that was finally bearing down upon her.

"What will you do?" Brena inquired, plowing through Saudett's growing despair.

"I'm under orders by my lieutenant. I must await our scouts, who are in pursuit, to return. I have my doubts they will find anything."

Baal gave a guttural growl, "Lewtan, what was name?"

"Ryon."

"I should crush Lewtan Ryon's head, hmm, or snap neck."

Saudett chuckled. "I may not stop you next time, Baal. Anyway, let me go home to a hot bath and redress. These clothes are in tatters." She felt at her ripped linen trousers; her mind flashed to the thought of her attackers nearly having their way with her. She grimaced, laughing misleadingly. "Once I've cleaned up, I will make my report. After that, perhaps, I will see you this evening, Hata."

"Joo, kitos," Hata smiled widely.

"Please come back to dine with us if you can," Brena added. "We are having a recovery feast."

"Thank you for your kindness, my friends." Saudett exited the small one-room home with a smile. She stopped and let her inner armor fall as she turned a corner to head toward her own. As the trauma of *everything* washed through her, she knelt in the alley and began to cry.

Chapter 6
Innocent

Hata was overjoyed. Saudett was the first person in Dagad she had connected with. *My first friend.* She was the first person to share her newfound powers with. *Other than my parents.* Full of excitement, she reflected on her encounter with the drug-dealing merchant. *I would still be a nobody if I had not fallen to his temptation.* She found herself daydreaming of that day.

***

"Young lass!" an elaborately green-dressed Xamidian man with a bright red turban and profoundly hooked nose called out to her. "Fair jewels for the lady! Brought in from Al'Jalif this very morning."

Hata strolled over to the canvas-covered sellers' stall. Examining the jewelry, spices, and trinkets strewn on cloth-covered crates, she picked up a simple, pretty, beaded necklace and asked, "How much for this one?"

"Fine taste, young lass!" the merchant grinned. "It's on the house!"

"What? I have a few coins. Please tell me the price."

"The price! You can pay me by testing these new smelling salts from the Isles of Tal'tulu. I need comprehensive reviews to sell them to the good people of Aurulan and beyond."

"Smelling salts?" Hata tilted her head curiously.

"Indeed, my red-headed colleague. I have *luscious lavender, rose rains*, and *berry wine*. So many flavors to swell your senses."

"Those sound delightful. Just one sniff; then I must return home."

"Of course, of course." The merchant guided her gently around the crates and under the stall's beige canvas ceiling. Leading her to a table at the rear, canvas curtains surrounded the back of the shop. Presented neatly on the table were different colors of powder, organized into small, colorful lines.

"They are so pretty. Do I just sniff them?"

"The key to taking in the entire magnitude of the products is inhaling the powder into one's nostrils. Otherwise, you will be left *unsatisfied*."

"This pink one is pretty. Can I try it first?"

"Aha! *Rose rains*. Excellent choice!" The merchant took a thin wooden square and scraped the product forward for easier access. "Go ahead, darling. Inhale quickly."

Hata carefully leaned in, put her nose as close as possible to the powder, and sucked in through her nostril. *Wonderful. Like soft flowers on a rainy day.* She could almost taste the rose on the back of her throat.

"Mmm, that does smell lovely, sir merchant."

"Very good, let me mark that down. Please try another."

Hata proceeded to try two more, which smelt remarkably like their namesakes. She made small compliments after each, and the merchant wrote her words in a small notebook.

"Now, the main event." The merchant produced a pouch from his person and handed it to Hata.

She gingerly opened the pouch and peered inside. The powder was pitch black. "Oh, what is this one called?"

"Lucid liquorice. Tough to procure this one. Enjoy the morsel, my compatriot."

Hata shrugged, poured some onto the table, tucked the pouch into her sash, and quickly sucked in the powder. Light blossomed before her eyes, and she stumbled back out of the covered stall. *In Teras' name*, she cursed. But pleasure and warmth washed over her, though her sight was blurred.

Suddenly, many vibrations were growing from the very soles of her feet. Sensations shot up her legs, some stronger while others were faint. As if every footstep of the people around her could be felt through her sandals. It became thunder.

"Lass, do come back!" She barely heard the merchant's voice as she stumbled through the crowd, miraculously avoiding collisions.

Hata's head began to throb, and there was a tickle in her nose and throat. She licked her lips. *That powder.* She wanted to feel that same sensation again. *No, Mother and Father are waiting.* She stumbled toward home, becoming increasingly lethargic as she did so. *I feel so weak. What is this other feeling?* An awakening. *The thundering feet! They won't stop!* She held her head in her hands.

She felt two pairs of heavy footsteps distinctly closer than the rest behind her as she turned the corner to home. Finally, she collapsed.

"Hata?" Her mother's voice.

"Hata!" Her father's roar.

She felt herself be lifted away to the safety of home.

***

That was three days ago. Hata's headache had finally ended. The beautiful woman Saudett had undergone the same unfortunate fate.

Did she have magical powers as well? No, she was not so lucky. Hata remembered Saudett would have nearly been abused if not for her father's timely intervention. *That could have been me. Why was I so trusting of that wretched man in the market?*

Still, she smiled, gently guiding the sand through the air before her. *This power is worth it. In Teras' name, I will use it for good. I can't wait to go with Saudett into the hills and practice magic!* Hata paced back and forth excitedly. *I want to spend time with Saudett,* she thought. Her parents were outside drawing water and would soon begin cooking the night's feast.

Hata brought up the memory of the woman sleeping next to her for the last few days. She remembered how Saudett's chest raised and fell gently, her soft bronze tone warm to Hata's touch as she lay beside her, as closely as she dared, taking in the woman's scent. *Saudett smells lovely.* Saudett's beautiful, peaceful face would often contort, her thick black brows furrowing, nose rings jingling, as she would cry out in her sleep, sometimes shouting her husband's name, Simon, or the name Yakeb. *Poor woman, she has lost so much.* Hata longed to comfort her and to hold her.

Hata had fancied only one girl, her best friend, growing up in Oitilla, her hometown village carved into a mountain, but she hadn't realized her love until it was too late. *Silja...* Hata ejected the thought from her mind and focused on Saudett. But there was something about Saudett that made her stomach flutter. Like she would do anything to be in her company. Every minute with Saudett felt like seconds; she wanted it to never end. *I hope she comes back quickly.*

When her mother and father clamored through the door, Hata's mind still reeled with excitement at this newfound person in her life and the earth's awakening to her will.

"Ah, tytär, good, you are awake," Brena said. "Please chop these potatoes and leaks for a stew."

"Joo." Hata busied herself working, glad for the distraction.

"Tytär," Baal grumbled.

"Yes, Isä?" Hata answered.

"Friend Saudett, she is good strong woman," he fumbled over the Aurulan dialect. "But how you say?"

"Just be careful with her," Brena added warmly. "We don't want you to get hurt. The woman has a raging flame within her."

"That's what I like about her," Hata grinned.

"Hata."

"I know, Mother, I will be. But she is going to help me practice the magic. She is a trained soldier. She will know what to do."

Baal grunted.

"You have two reasonably seasoned warriors at your disposal here, Hata."

Hata groaned, "But you're my parents! Training with Saudett will be more *enjoyable*."

Baal chuckled and said in Vouri, "Let the girl be. She never took to our training back home. Why start now? It's about time she made some friends in the Aurulan flatland."

True. Hata had not enjoyed learning the way of the sword, ax, mace, or shield. Both Baal and Brena were renowned among the Vouri for their skill in combat, but Hata had much preferred to coast through life, focusing on household chores.

Cooking, cleaning, and sewing, she relished. Even hunting and sleeping on the mountainside for days tracking a beast had been more up her alley. *My father taught me how to survive in the cold. He taught me how to hunt.* Skills that would help her live. *However, I don't doubt a little combat experience would significantly increase my survival chances.*

As she chopped the vegetables and added them to the cauldron, she let her senses focus on the vibrations brought on through her feet. The sensation was always there, but she had started to tune it out when needed. She let her mind picture the people behind the footsteps walking by their door. After some time, the vitals were ready and on the table. She realized one set of footsteps had stopped in front of their door. *Saudett!*

CHAPTER SEVEN

DEMON

The night had come, and the nomads were restless.

Simon's captors had found a craggy outcropping to set up camp, offering shelter. Setting up makeshift stakes, most nomads stood guard at the pickets. Simon was corralled with the animals, as close to the rocks as possible, next to a huge bonfire. The nomads were usually never this uptight at night's watch. Typically, they were lax in their nightly routine.

Why was tonight different? He could not get any answers either, as he and his camel were tied together, with a small rope length between them and the other animals. He would have to lead the entire train to the nomads to ask some questions—most likely only to be beaten or lose the next day's rations.

"Well, Marigold? What do you think is going on? Perhaps a rival band in the area?"

The camel chewed his cud, staring unfazed at the question.

"Perhaps it is the myths you hear from travelers about the desert beasts that slaughter everything in sight." He laughed aloud. "What nonsense."

The animals became agitated almost as the words left his mouth. Then, an eerie screech pierced through the night air.

In unison, Simon heard dozens of swords unsheathing. Then silence. It stretched by. Simon held his breath.

The screech sliced through the night once again, closer. *Louder.* The nomads answered with a battle cry. He then heard shouting and fighting. Simon could not make out what was happening. He was too close to the fire and could only see darkness. Occasionally, the glint of a nomad's weapon reflected the firelight. He thought he could make out the silhouettes of massive hunched figures doubling the size of a man. Curved blades flashed around the profiles.

"Skrull, take me. By the fucks...perhaps I'll die for sure this time," Simon stammered.

A horse screamed behind him. He turned as the scream abruptly changed to a fluid, gurgling noise. The horse's neck had been ripped open, and a massive figure held the corpse by the head. The horse's blood gushed down into a black maw. Six long spiked teeth, three on both the upper and lower jaws, protruding in unnatural directions, cutting through flesh while a long, thick white tongue whipped back and forth, lapping the froth.

The creature's skin was cracked and boiled through slick black hair that covered it. From its feet and hands protruded massive claws over two feet long. Its right arm, much thicker and muscled than the other, pierced the horse's neck while holding the body high above its head. Gore poured down its arm and exceedingly large shoulder.

As Marigold tried to flee from the creature, Simon was pulled from his feet. It did not make it far, as all the animals were tied together, struggling in different directions, screaming, and bleating in terror. After the beast had gorged on blood, it let the carcass fall with a thud. A red-stained tongue lolled out, and it turned its head toward Simon. *Oh, gods.*

Bright yellow pupils shone in the firelight. *Oh, gods!* Blood covered the patchy, oily, slick black hair of its arms and legs and parts of its bare, gnarled body. Simon tried to push himself away, but with his hands tethered to the camel's saddle, all he could do was kick and pull. *Oh, gods! Oh, fucking gods!* The creature took a few steps toward him and extended its hand in a wanting grasp, its long claws inches from Simon's face. He pissed himself.

"PRIMUS! HELP ME!"

A flash of silver and a spray of black blood covered Simon's face. With a guttural cry, the beast reeled back.

The Sixteenth Otsoa stood before him, the sword in her right hand pointing toward the monster, its curve angled down. She held her left hand straight before her, two fingers pointed at her adversary.

The beast shrieked; bloodied saliva sprayed from the gaping jaws. Then it was upon her, taking a broad, low arching sweep of its unwounded left arm at the woman's legs.

She seemed to float as she spun, legs kicking up behind her as the blade blurred in a whirl around her. She sailed over the attack. Another shower of black blood from the creature's forearm.

Another gruesome screech.

The Otsoa was locked in combat with the hulking entity, yet she was unscathed, dancing around its attacks lethally. Black wounds began dotting the creature's hide: a vertical slash across its leg, another across its abdomen. Other nomads joined the fray from behind. Simon lay on his back, watching the struggle. The other nomads began darting between the Otsoa's attacks like giant wasps until, finally, the creature was on its knees, both arms dismembered and dripping.

The Otsoa spoke. "Back to your hell, demon."

With a choking warble, it said, "She-wolf. You will know slaughter in the wake of the arrogant." It began to laugh eerily.

Simon stared in horror at the abomination. *What in all Skrull's hell is this thing? How can it speak?*

Grasping the pommel of her sword with both hands, the Otsoa thrust deep, piercing the blade through the creature's open maw, then pushing down, splitting the jaw and neck until bone halted the blade's path. She put a foot to the creature's chest and kicked, pulling the sword free. The demon crumpled backward, then began to bubble and dissipate into a pool of black muck.

"Mittal Gohra, how many did we lose?" she called out, wiping the blade clean with a rag from her waist.

"Four of ours to the three of them. Fortunately, all this one did was kill a horse. A shame it didn't put this slave out of his misery, ha," Mittal replied, looking down at Simon, still splayed out on the ground, shaking.

"We need this slave. He is to aid us in the defense against the Daanav."

Simon coughed in surprise. His Xamidian was lacking, but he thought that was the word for 'demon'...or was it 'devil'? "What?!" he exclaimed. "What can I possibly do against these things, these demons? These Daanav? What are they? I am nothing but a simple builder."

She turned to look at him, her luminous violet eyes meeting his own. "We know very little of the Daanav. What they are, and where they come from. They are not ones for conversation. Only that they wish death upon us and do not seem to leave the desert. So that, simple builder, is exactly what you will do. You will build for Hasiera."

Simon stared in disbelief. "Build what, if I might ask?"

She strode over to him, crouching down, her face inches away. "You will help us build a haven, whatever that entails. That will be up to you and the First Otsoa to decide," she whispered.

"Me? And that *bastard?*"

Still crouched in front of him, she replied in a low and sweet voice, "I will tell you more on tomorrow's road. Get some rest now, Builder." She helped him to his feet, pulled a dagger from her belt, and cut the ropes from around his hands. "I do not recommend running away during the night." Again, he could swear she was smiling under the linen face wraps, her eyes twinkling in the firelight as she turned and walked back to Mittal. "Mittal Gohra, keep a rotating watch. Tabbi, join me in my tent." Mittal headed off, and a woman fell in behind the Sixteenth.

Simon sat down, settling his back to Marigold, who was now calm and chewing aimlessly. He heard some muffled moaning coming from the Sixteenth Otsoa's tent.

"Well, that sounds utterly delightful, especially after this Primus-be-damned nightmare. I see why anyone would want to distract themselves from such a situation." He sighed heavily. "They could have at least invited us, eh, Marigold?"

A groan in response from the camel.

"I know, I know. Think of my dear wife back home."

That is if I ever see her again. Simon pictured Saudett in his mind. Her beauty, her fortitude, her warmth. *Her buttocks!* The sudden image of the Daanav reaching out for him flashed, overtaking the portrait of his wife. *Skrull's hell, those creatures.* The mood now deflated, Simon lay down, tossing and turning, trying to shake the gruesome beast from his mind.

CHAPTER EIGHT

PAST

"Where in all the hells have you been, Sergeant? It's been five days since the attack on the town!"

Captain Cad Dermont eyed her questioningly. He sat on the edge of his bed, clothed in light silk sleeping robes, exposing a stout gray-haired chest. His right thigh was wrapped in a large bandage; a small red stain soaked through the cloth.

"Captain, please lie down; you have opened your wound," Saudett urged.

"I'm fine," Cad said. "Where have you been? I thought you had deserted to chase off after your husband."

"I admit, it did cross my mind."

"I would have been forced to send you to the labor camps. The King and his council of *vultures* do not take desertion lightly." The man scowled at her. His hair was cut in a short military crop above a salt-and-pepper beard.

"I am well aware. Therefore, I am formally resigning my station to go after Simon," she answered flatly.

He stood up. He was a head taller than Saudett and brawny. He was an Aurulan-Xamid mix, his skin a light beige tinge. He was a handsome man in the latter years of his forties. Throughout the years, Saudett and Simon had enjoyed his company as a third party to their bed-chamber activity.

"Saudett, I will not permit it," Cad said, frowning.

"You cannot order me to stay. I will not leave Simon out there alone. I must go!"

"First, I can order you to do anything I deem necessary. I am your captain!" he replied, his voice rising. "Just because we fuck here and there doesn't give you special privileges."

"Then we need not *fuck* anymore," she spat back.

He sighed, putting a hand on his forehead. "I apologize; that was out of line."

That shifted his tune quickly.

"Alas, I know. I understand that I can't stop you. There is nothing that could get between you and Simon, especially not me. You are both my dear friends. *More* than friends. So," he paused, a half-smile on his lips, "I am reassigning you to the scout division."

She stared at him skeptically. "Sir, we don't have a scout division."

"We do now." He grinned. Then, he limped over to a desk beside his bed and opened a drawer, pulling out a braid of blue and black. "I give you the freedom to do as you like, Lieutenant."

Saudett's eyes widened. "Sir! Thank you, sir!" she said, putting her thumb to her lips.

"*But* you will wait until Lieutenant Ryon returns with his findings."

"He will return with nothing, Captain. The man is not worthy of his weekly stipend."

"I know you have your differences, but this is my only condition. Then you are free to pursue on your own."

"Sir." She straightened.

"I also grant you leave to take two other Shepherds of your choice on the journey. You should not go out there alone. If you find your husband, don't do anything senseless. You should record the location, return here, and we can muster a force to deal with these brigands once and for all."

"I would prefer to infiltrate and make a rescue attempt."

"Only if you deem it safe to do so. You still haven't told me where you have been these last few days."

"Of course." She quickly recounted the events leading up to and proceeding the attack to Captain Dermont.

"Grit dealers in Dagad. I suppose it had to happen eventually. I will put someone on it. Leave it in our hands, Saudett. Try to focus on your husband."

"I don't know if that merchant has left town yet. I haven't had time to do anything since I awoke. Like you said, it's been five days, so I imagine he has flown like a winged rat."

"True, a few caravans have left since the day of the attack. He may be out of our grasp by now."

"Hells, I'll find that son of a whore as well," she muttered.

"Keep the task of your husband first and foremost. He is a good man and lucky to have you by his side." His gaze danced up and down her body.

"I will. My thanks again, Captain."

He smiled and nodded, then sat back down on his bed. "Forgive me if this is uncouth or too soon, but perhaps you could pleasure me with your company before you depart?"

"I'm afraid it *is* too soon, Cad. I'm drained and exhausted and have yet to bury Yakeb's body. My husband is gone. How can I even consider doing that at a time like this?"

"Forgive me. I thought it might help take your mind off things."

That isn't a half-bad idea...No. Simon is alone out there. I do not have time for this. She shook her head. With that, she turned and left the captain's sleeping quarters. She needed to lay Simon's father to rest soon; it weighed all other tasks down. After exiting the barracks, she returned to the Vasara household. She would need their help to bring the body and create a grave in the woodland cemetery. Hopefully, they could set out at first light on the morrow.

Then what? How was she going to deal with the hunt for Simon? Trek aimlessly across the desert and pray to Qav for luck? *I tried that before.* She did have experience in the desert from her time as a caravan guard. She took up the role once she was old enough after her parents had gone on a routine trip from Xamid to Aurulan but had never returned.

The image of her father confronting her mother in the garden returned to her. Anger simmering within her, she quickened her pace. Upon hearing the news of her parent's initial disappearance, Saudett, still too young to do anything about it, had dragged Ismael and a company of recruits across the desert in search of them. She had never once left Al'Jalif at that point in her life. *Such a fool I had been*—the cost of that irrational endeavor had been too great. After that, she had spent years training before she finally joined the caravan, hoping, *longing* that she would find a clue to their disappearance, but nothing ever surfaced. Throughout her time with Caravan House Kafilah, she had come to Dagad countless times. A persistent young man constantly vied for her attention on one such occasion. At first, she had pointedly ignored him. Yet he was always waiting for her when she came through town, even after many months of being away.

Saudett recalled one memory. She had just returned to Dagad when he had found her in the market and said, "Beauty of the Burning Sea! Welcome back! Care to partake in a drink of wine, perhaps some roast fowl, and meaningful conversation?" Simon's blue-green eyes had sparkled as he approached her in the middle of the thoroughfare.

"Sir, have we met?" she mocked, remembering him from the last time he had accosted her at the northwestern entrance of Dagad.

"You wound me, my lady. Simon Meridio, semi-chief engineer of Meridio Enterprises, at your service."

"Simon Meridio, what precisely does a semi-chief engineer's work entail?"

"Oh, my, don't get me started. If you do, you will most definitely require some wine. Shall we, *Lady?* I don't think I got your name on your last visit. I was too enamored by the beacon of your beauty through the crowded streets. I spied you from a league away as you approached the city, your glow—"

She put a finger to his lips. "Shush for now; let us partake in the wine. It seems I will need it." *Hettra's tits, this man has a devil's tongue,* she had thought. "I am Saudett Kafilah, a simple caravan guardsman. Come, I'm thirsty." She put her arm through his.

His smile widened. "Saudett Meridio has a pleasant ring to it, no?"

She felt her face flush. "What?!"

"Wine! We need wine!" He pulled her along toward the nearest tavern.

At that time, it was not very busy in Grohl's Savory Inn and Brewing. The homely interior was simple; wooden tables dotted the main hall, and there was an expansive bar along one wall. It was mid-afternoon, and a few patrons were finishing late lunches while a few sat and drank alone at the bar.

"Sir Grohl, the handsome, is it? A carafe of wine here, please," Simon called the burly bartender, a slight dark mustache covering the man's upper lip.

"Wine? *Handsome?* Ye daft, man? 'Tis a brewery. Nor 'tis a brothel. We sell ale, ale, and ye guessed it, *more* ale."

"Is ale all right with you, my dear?" Simon asked, turning back to her.

She raised her eyebrows at him. "*Dear?* You sound like you've already married me."

He smiled wryly. "Well, that is the plan, madam."

She coughed in surprise once more. "Simon Meridio, you can't marry someone you have not yet come to know."

"That is precisely why we are here now in this tavern. I mean to get to know you."

She sighed. "Ale is fine by my standards, actually preferred."

He turned back toward the barkeep. "Handsome sir, what spices of ale do you present-ly—"

The barkeep interjected, "Get off your pompous arse and come to the bar if ye wish to be served."

"Ahem. Excuse me, madam." Simon stood, bowed gently, and walked over to the man. She watched as they whispered back and forth, Simon gesturing madly for a moment and squeezing the man's large bicep. Which caused a blush from the barkeep. Saudett wasn't sure whether he was flirting or bargaining with the barkeeper.

After what seemed like an eternity, Simon returned with a wooden tray of six small wooden mugs, each with different-colored liquid sloshing about inside: an amber red, a pale ale, and a dark stout, one of each flavor for them both.

Simon picked up the pale ale; Saudett opted for the amber.

"To Hettra's love," Simon toasted, holding his mug across the small round wooden table they were seated at.

"Hettra's love," she answered, tapping his mug with her own. She took a deep draft of the bitter ale; it was cool and refreshing. With a contented sigh, she said, "Simon, you were fairly *coy* with that man just now."

"Was I? Indeed, I find all people attractive, regardless of gender, *Saudett*. It's an elegant name. I remember the first time I spied on you in the market. You were studying one of the jewelry stalls—particularly something like this." He nonchalantly pulled some golden loops from his pocket—bracelets to wear on the wrist or ankle.

"Firstly, good on you for your position towards others. I am in the same boat, as they say. Primus, forgive us for going astray from your dogma."

He looked at her curiously. "I've never heard such an expression."

She changed the subject. "Secondly! You *spied* on me in the market? Surely, not the market." She shifted her head, somewhat confused. "Our first meeting was near the bridge over Droe, not in the market. And thirdly, a gift on our first tryst? You are bold, Simon Meridio."

"Ahem, I may have been watching you for the better part of the year, at least when you were in town. I just had to work up the courage to do something about it, but now, I'm all in."

"Indeed, it seems you are." She took the gift from his outstretched hand. She noted they were bright, polished, and solid gold, not waxed brass. "These must have cost a pretty penny. Is the life of a semi-chief engineer so lucrative?"

"It is never short on work. We are the only organized construction company in Dagad, besides a few craftsmen and tradesmen here and there. The municipality pays well for our services."

He appears to be charming, handsome, and well-off. This Simon is beginning to grow on me.

"What of yourself? Caravan guard? That sounds exciting!" Simon leaned closer intently, propping his elbow on the tabletop while putting a hand on his chin expectantly.

"Not nearly. It involves mostly riding or walking. I've been in an occasional skirmish with bandits, but nothing horrific. Keeps one fit, though." She casually flexed her toned bare arms.

"Those look dangerous," he poked at her with a grin.

"By the look of it, I'd have more trouble wrestling a goat than your scrawny arse," she countered.

"Without a doubt, my lady," he chuckled. "Alas, I am all brains and no brawn."

This is enjoyable, Saudett thought. She was fond of his merriment and humor.

"I'm afraid I somehow accidentally twisted the subject matter back unto myself. Where were we? Ah, yes, caravan guard, correct? Have you ever *killed* a man?"

She paused for a time. "I have."

They both sat in awkward silence for a long moment.

"I can see it brings you no joy. Let us change the subject."

She nodded in agreement. "Tell me more about your work; how did you come to Dagad?"

"If you insist, please feel free to stop me if I droll on for far too long. I don't know when to quit sometimes."

She quickly finished her ales and ordered another round, just the amber. Simon was still working on his second drink, as his talking took up most of the time. She listened intently to Simon speak of his parents immigrating from Nidhaut, the capital city of Aurulan when he was very young. She was content to listen, to learn about him, though she questioned here and there or commented on something amusing he said. A platter of roast duck legs and brown rice pilaf was brought to them, from which they shared.

"My father taught me everything I know. He is a great man. I truly look up to him and ever seek him out for his knowledge daily. He will be ready to retire soon, leaving the company in my hands. I find comfort knowing he will still be just around the corner for a quick query of his knowledgeable mind."

"I'm glad you have such a caring father."

"Your father was not such a one?"

She paused again. "No. Father was not. I am not ready to discuss these things with you yet, Simon Meridio. Nevertheless, I am savoring your company and your words. I wish to meet you again when I return to Dagad next."

Simon's smile shone through her. "And I, you, Saudett Kafilah…"

So, it went. Eventually, Saudett could not wait to return to Dagad and see him. She retired from the traveling guard, joined the Shepherds Eye, and married the man.

She suddenly found herself standing in front of the Vasara residence. *How long have I been here?* Before lifting her hand to knock on the door, she looked down at the golden rings on her left wrist. The door opened, and an excited Hata rushed out and embraced her.

"You're back! Can we go practice now?!" Hata exclaimed.

"Hold on," came Brena's voice from the threshold. "Let us sup first, Hata."

Hata's shoulders slumped. "Joo, but let's eat quickly now, old lady!"

Saudett chuckled playfully, "Call me *old lady* again, you eager, lanky, little welp! We will go after we have partaken in your parents' hospitality."

They entered the home together. The table was laden with food. There were small loaves of bread at each place, a roast of lamb, slices of cheese, and fruit. A large pot of leek, potato, and fish soup sat steaming in the center, giving off an alluring aroma.

"You shouldn't have done all this!" Saudett blurted. "This must be a week's worth of food here."

Baal gave a wide smile. "Eat! We celebrate!" He poured her a tankard of a dark, almost black ale. "Drink!"

She took a sip of the dark liquid. It was cold and creamy and went down smoothly. "To my new companions!"

The four of them lifted their mugs as one.

"Voitoon!" the three Vouri cheered in unison.

They ate and conferred. Saudett told them about meeting Simon and coming to be in Dagad. Brena, in turn, told the story of why their family was in Dagad.

"We hail from the village of Oitilla, high up in the North Iron Belt, a mining town carved onto the side of a mountain. Half of it partially protrudes from the cliff on a large plateau; the other half of the village is part of a large cavern." Brena took a deep breath as if to take in the mountain air from her homeland. "In winter, the rooftops are covered in ice;

though it is cold, the cave is always warm, bristling with the forge's heat and smithy. The ice melts during the day and freezes solid at night when the forges are cool. A massive waterfall is in the center of the village; the waterfall turns to ice in the winter, becoming a crystalline pillar and splitting the entrance into the mountain. It is a grand sight to behold."

"Ice Pillar Falls, as we call it," Hata added.

"It sounds beautiful indeed. Why did you all end up leaving such a home?" Saudett asked.

Brena glanced at her husband. "There is a bit of a story behind it. Baal oversaw the mine; only the village chieftain could overrule his direction. He found something in one of the deepest mining shafts. An archway or some such? My husband wanted to close the earth on the thing. Ota Vastaan disagreed."

Baal grunted in disgust.

"The archway was surrounded by many precious gems, and the chieftain, Ota Vastaan, coveted these. There are plenty of minerals closer to the surface. Baal wanted to start a new shaft higher up."

"Myymme rautaa, ei jalokiviä," Baal growled.

"That is true, Baal. Oitilla's main economic source was exporting iron and other common ores to Aurulan in the South. I'm sure we could have sold the gemstones eventually. This *door* under the earth gave us an unwelcoming feeling, and Baal deemed it an unnecessary risk. We recalled the elders' stories of a four-armed being skulking around the caves. Ota laughed in Baal's face at this, cast his concern off as superstition."

"That's when my Isä challenged Ota for leadership of the village. I can tell this part, Mother," Hata said excitedly.

"Have at it."

"It was not a fair fight," Hata said. "Our chief wields the clan's heirloom war hammer, believed to be blessed by our god of the mountain, Teras. Runic scripts twist around the hammer's head, made from blue volframi ore and encrusted with gems like those the chieftain sought after. Still, it was an extended fight. Isä held his own; they fought for nearly two hours, trading blows. *Back and forth.* The chief was weakening; it looked like Isä would soon strike the finishing blow. Then the chieftain's eyes rolled back in his head, and the runic holy war hammer began to glow blue-white. His next attack shattered Isä's shield and cracked his arm."

Baal was grinding his teeth; he downed another tankard of the dark ale with a grunt, froth dripping down his red beard.

Hata's face became sullen. "We were banished, and my friend was…"

Brena touched her daughter's shoulder measuredly and continued, "And so, we left the Vouri. We followed the North Iron Belt trailing south and east, skirting the Aurulan mainland. We are not fond of the larger settlements; even Dagad is overpopulated for us." She took a long draught of her ale and sighed. "It was a long journey, and we found ourselves here, on the edge of the massive sea of sand. We could not go back, so we stayed on here."

"Baal will go back one day. Baal will defeat Ota," the large man said, a grimace on his face.

Brena rubbed Baal's back reassuringly.

"I do not doubt that you can do that, Baal Vasara. You have a strong family at your side. I envy you," Saudett said appreciatively. "My praise to your storytelling, Brena and Hata."

"Voitoon! Friend Saudett, to victory on our paths!" the Vasara's exclaimed in unison. They simultaneously raised their mugs in celebration.

"Enough about us, friend Saudett. Have you thought about what you plan to do once we start after the brigands?" Brena asked.

"Truly? It's still worrisome. Once I descend into the desert, how will I possibly find their trail? They could be halfway across the Burning Sea while I run in circles, looking for a hint of their whereabouts." *It will be the same as when I chased after my parents,* Saudett thought.

"I think I can do something about that," Hata spoke up, her voice rising in excitement. "I can feel where people have walked the earth before. I can even feel people walking outside at this very moment, to the far end of the street."

Saudett, slightly inebriated from the ale, laughed and declared, "Ah yes, of course! Hata the mystic; I shall rely on her. You may be my right-hand man in this endeavor!"

Baal growled. "I will be right-hand man. *Only* man." A flat, serious expression crossed his face. "When leave?"

"Hold on. *We? Leave?* You cannot be serious? You have all done enough for me already."

Brena smiled warmly, "We have already discussed it and decided. Although, we have one condition. Baal, no, *we* are out for vengeance upon this grit-dealing merchant. After we find your husband, we ask that we head to Xamid and try to look up the swindler." She paused. "Of course, all three of us will be accompanying you."

Pressing a thumb to her lips in thanks, Saudett replied, "I am unworthy." She paused to compose herself. "Well, with your help and the aid of two skilled fighters among the Shepherds Eye, my heart is lightened. My confidence is lifted." Saudett could not help but smile, holding back tears at these near strangers' compassion. "I can use all the help I can muster, and I will forever be in your debt."

"No debt. Vouri and Vasara stand by word," Baal said. "Our word, our honor. Voitoon, friend Saudett."

"Voitoon," she whispered in response.

Hata was beaming and fidgeting impatiently. "Yes, Voitoon. Victory to our companions, our new friend, the old lady! Shall we go now? It's getting quite late."

"Hata!" Saudett got up and walked behind Hata; the girl was a head taller than herself. She wrapped her arms around Hata's neck and chest as she was still seated and squeezed tightly. "Fine! Let us head to the hills, just north of town. First, let me thank your family for the meal."

Brena waved a hand in dismissal. "We thank you, Saudett. But enough thanks at this table tonight. We will aid you with your father-in-law; we have a cart we can use to carry him to the woods on the morrow. Then, we will return and prepare to set out after your husband."

"Go, take offspring away." Baal was pulling his shirt off, looking hungrily at his mate.

"At least wait till we're out the door, Isä!" Hata exclaimed.

Brena's laugh lines crinkled at her daughter's embarrassment.

Saudett repeated the sign of thanks to her lips, head bowing gently, then took Hata's hand in hers. "Shall we, Hata?"

Nearly half an hour later, they found themselves in the foothills just north of town. Saudett broke off a long branch from a few stumpy trees nearby. Hata watched intently from some thirty paces away.

"All right, Hata, what would you do if someone charged you with a spear?" Without warning, Saudett shouted and rushed toward Hata; the branch extended out in front of her.

Like a startled frill-necked lizard, Hata gawked at the last moment, covering her face with her hands. She yelped.

Saudett tapped the branch gently on Hata's head. "Dead," she said.

"I thought we were just going to have some fun?" Hata's shoulders slumped.

"If you want to join us on our little voyage, you must know how to defend yourself. Not to mention others."

"Right," Hata straightened. "Let's try again."

With a smile, Saudett turned and walked back to her starting position. "This time, you know I'm coming!" She surged forward.

The dust began to swirl in front of Hata. Hundreds of the tiny marbles started to form at once. Saudett's eyes widened; she remembered the dent in the iron pot. Taking that many at once would be fatal, especially without heavier armor.

"HATA! WAIT!"

Saudett dropped hard, skidding sideways onto her left arm and leg, beads whistling overhead. The missiles zipped toward her. A few caught her on the upper arm and shoulder. Most pelted off because of the low angle, harsh stinging welts left in their place. A few had pierced the skin, the projectile visible just below the surface. Not very deep, she thought. Still, she would not be in good shape if she had been running full force into the maelstrom.

"Ahem," Saudett sat up, plucking the marbles from the wound in her arm, wincing. "Well, I suppose that is one way to do it."

Hata rushed over. "Oh, Saudett! I didn't mean to hurt you! Teras's stones, I could have killed you; that was foolish."

"No, Hata. That is precisely what you should do if your life is in danger. Very suitable for that situation. However, shall we ponder some less fatal deterrents for training purposes?"

A smile lit up Hata's face like a star, and she enthusiastically nodded.

She has a beautiful smile, Saudett thought. But asked, "What else can you do with the earth?"

"Hmm, perhaps I can do the same thing with those boulders there? It might be too slow to be of any use."

"It doesn't hurt to try out the theory. Can you toss one at the hill there?"

Hata nodded, then approached one of the boulders protruding from the earth. She began moving her arms in the same manner as when she formed the marbles. The boulder inched upwards; a surprising amount buried deep in the ground. After a few more moments of the boulder hovering slightly, still half in the underground, Hata gasped, and the boulder thudded back into position.

"It is too heavy," Hata gasped, panting.

"You feel the weight of it?"

"To some extent—it feels like pressure surrounding my head when I try to move it."

"Your powers could very likely be like physical exertion: the more you do it, the easier it gets. At any rate, let's try a few other things, then head back. We must leave bright and early tomorrow morning, at first light."

"Joo. Thank you for doing this. I would never have considered stopping someone from charging me until it happened. Now, I'm at least a little bit prepared."

She put a hand on Hata's shoulder. "Pray, you never have to. And for my new friend, I am with you. I firmly believe that everyone, from the remote Isles of Tal'tulu to the most distant corners of the Earste Lân, should know how to defend themselves, magic or not."

Hata's eyes began to water, and she wrapped her arms around Saudett. "Saudett, I think you are the first friend I've made in this town."

Saudett held her for a moment quietly, then put a hand on her cheek, looking into her light-green eyes. Saudett took the girl in, enjoying her beauty. "I am yours to confide in, Hata. I will be here for you."

Hata sniffled and nodded.

"Now, shall we try our luck with something smaller than a boulder this time?"

Hata visibly cheered up. "Joo!"

CHAPTER NINE

GAIN

"Good morning, Marigold! Bright and burning as ever, I see. Watch your step; those puddles of black muck do *not* look inviting." Simon was feeling jolly. "At least now we know why they keep us alive, eh, Marigold?" He patted the camel's furry neck. "Build a fortress, she says. They're surely mad."

"Rrraaarr," Marigold said in agreement.

"Truly mad indeed. Have you ever seen anything like those creatures of the night? I don't know if I even believe it for myself yet. Skrull-damned things out of nightmares! Fairy tales come to life! Bully cocks!" *I am starting to go hysterical from the shock of realizing these things exist and that I'm supposed to somehow stop them.* "However, it does make a little more sense now why they needed a builder. The poor people must be defenseless, waiting for the monsters to come for them each night, living in fear." He sighed with empathy.

Simon smiled in relief to see the Sixteenth Otsoa trotting back from the front of the column to accompany him. He grinned as she approached.

"I was just telling Marigold, here, what a fine morning it is and how we look forward to aiding you and your people in this gargantuan task of erecting a fort in the middle of the desert." Simon continued his spiel. "Where in Skrull's hell will I get the materials for such a task? Oh, and a good morning to you too, Sixteenth Otsoa!"

"Kiana."

He coughed in surprise. "Pardon?"

"Simpler to say than Sixteenth Otsoa."

"Well, *Kiana,* I would like to thank you for saving my life last night. I am at your service." He paused to ponder and grinned. "My life would not have been in any inherent danger had I not been kidnapped in the first place."

"You speak the truth," she answered flatly.

Simon regretted the jab. He decided to hold back any more remarks for the moment. The silence held for a few minutes as they slowly plodded on together.

Finally, she spoke once more. "I am truly sorry you have been pulled away from your life and that the old man was slain out of spite. I do not support the First's decision to cut down a defenseless person."

"You witnessed that?"

"I did."

"My father taught me everything I know, and I am sure I could have learned even more from him. He would have been more valuable to you all than I."

She looked at him for a long moment, those violet eyes piercing him.

He turned his gaze away.

"I will bring this up at the next meeting of Otsoa," Kiana said with a scowl. "Such a waste of life."

"What is an Otsoa?"

"Otsoa are the governors of sections of the valley camp we call home. The leaders of these sections are named Otsoa, and the peoples under them are referred to as their Otsoak." Then, her brows softened in an arch. "The First is taking on the heavy burden of defending our people. The Daanav that you witnessed; we have been fighting them for the better part of a year in this desert. So far, they only attack in small groups, but we fear they will soon gather in force to attack our home. Qav's luck to us; they haven't yet discovered its location. Thank the Burning Sea for its vastness." She brought one thumb to her lips in thanks. "We only wish to protect our own. The children and the elderly. To do so, we need skilled laborers who have experience in construction. Also, someone with the power to engineer, plan, and oversee the project."

"Yet you may have provoked an attack from the Aurulan Kingdom. They could muster an army ten times the size and march over your encampment."

"Ha!" she barked. "The Auru King would not be such a fool. He would not waste the resources on such a venture, especially not for some fringe town on the border of his kingdom. *And!* Over a small raid where he lost a few peasants. However, he may send a new engineer out to replace you, but even that is a stretch, I think. Not to mention, they'd have to find us. He would lose men to the desert, and he would lose men to the Wolves of Hasiera. To the Otsoa. Scores of lives. All for you?"

She was completely and utterly correct. Simon could not retort. He sighed, "Your logic makes sense. I stand corrected. But tell me more about these beasts. Did they just show up out of the blue lagoon, as they say? How many of them are there? From whence do they hail?"

"I'm sure you've heard the stories. They've told the same tales since I was a child. The ones of caravans disappearing on routine trips through the Burning Sea. Well, the stories were true. It began to happen with our people's raiding parties. Occasionally, a group would go out into the desert and never return. We thought perhaps they had had enough of the nomadic life and decided to move on; one could not tell.

"The First Otsoa has but one rule that he enforces: Once you come to Hasiera, you stay. *Forever.* This rule ensures that Hasiera is always kept secret. People who managed to leave were hunted down and executed on the spot, ridden down, left to rot, and devoured by Kahytul. Though a trail would go dead occasionally, they would come to a place where the tracks just stopped, with no one in sight, not even a body." She paused. "My pardons." She rode a score of paces ahead, barked a few orders to the other nomads, then turned and rejoined him.

"Just disappeared, did they?" Simon prodded curiously.

"On one such occasion, the tracks didn't stop. We encountered a single man who was part of one of our missing patrols. He was wandering the desert aimlessly. His hands and ears were gone, torn off. How he was still among the living, we knew not. We came upon him at dusk. We tried questioning him, but he was delirious and soon passed out after being given some water. Just as the sun set—that is when they first attacked.

"*He was bait.* We were unprepared; it was the first time we had encountered them. In hindsight, we believe they can use some method to follow their prey during the day, yet they only reveal themselves at night. They were trying to follow him back to Hasiera. We lost many in that attack, though only two hulking beasts were there. We put them down after a dozen of our own fell. I don't know where they come from; I imagine some other Lân. I believe they have numbers in the thousands, and it's just a matter of time before they find our home."

"That is a grave tale indeed. I wonder why these things have never attacked Dagad or one of the other towns on the outskirts of Xamid."

"As far as can be told, they don't seem to leave the Burning Sea. However, they also get more numerous in certain parts of the wasteland, which we now try to avoid like the plague."

"Very strange," he scratched his chin and pondered. "This just opens my mind to more questions. What is holding them here? Are they looking for something? Why are they here? Skrull's sweaty balls on it! I must know!"

"Please, no more questions for now. I have not spoken aloud this much in a long, long time. I must do the rounds of the column."

"What? We just started talking! Don't leave so soon! What about you? How long have you been a nomad? Were you born into it? If not, how did you find yourself here? Tell me your story!" She was already out of earshot. "Oh, Marigold. I do not understand women."

Marigold groaned as if to say, "And you never will."

Saudett was awakened by a knock on her door. Groggily, she went to the entrance wearing only one of Simon's loose linen shirts. She was sore from her little training session with Hata. She was glad she was learning how to deal with a magic user in combat, a new avenue of opportunity to grow. She opened the door to see the Vasara family waiting patiently outside. Baal pulled a sizable cart with shovels and a few sacks of goods.

Brena spoke, "Hyvää huomenta, good morning." Then gesturing to Baal, she said, "Baal, laita vartalo kärryyn. We will help load the body."

"The Primus's favor to you all; this would have been difficult to handle alone." She looked at Hata and gave a playful smile. "Good morning, Hata. How are you this day?"

Hata smiled shyly and blushed, then stammered, "Good, looking forward to spending more time training with you."

"And I, you." Did Hata have a fancy for her? "Come, I could use a hug! I am in need on this day of days."

Hata's eyes danced down Saudett's body, then back up as she quickly rushed for the embrace. Saudett realized she was essentially naked, yet it did not seem to faze the other two members of the Vasara family. She squeezed Hata tight, then ushered her inside. "Come, I'd best get dressed if we are to make good time."

As they found themselves indoors, Baal wordlessly approached the wrapped body of Yakeb, then looked to Saudett for permission to act. She nodded to him and watched as he gently put his arms under the body and lifted. He solemnly made his way back outside, Brena holding the door open, then joining him in the street.

"You have a wonderful family, Hata. You are very blessed to have such guardians," Saudett said as she removed her sleeping shirt and picked out some clean linen strips to wrap her breasts and lower region.

"I-I am," Hata sputtered, cheeks red, staring at Saudett's bronze body.

"Come here, help me with this."

Hata made her way behind Saudett. Holding the end of the linen strip against the center of Saudett's back, she used her other hand to pull the material in front of Saudett's breasts. Her hand brushed against Saudett's nipple, and she quickly pulled away.

"Ah-ah, so sorry," Hata apologized.

"It's fine, Hata. That's the most excitement I've had in days!" She laughed, but her mind flashed to the tearing of her undergarments at the hands of the criminal grit dealer, those gaunt hands touching her body. She shivered. "Please keep helping. We can't keep your parents waiting."

Hata smiled and eagerly finished the wrapping. She leaned in close and whispered in Saudett's ear as she finished, "You are beautiful."

It was Saudett's turn to blush; she turned to look at the young woman. "Thank you," she murmured back, lost in Hata's green eyes for a moment too long. She wondered if the bastard had hurt Hata as well. "Hata, did that man who gave you grit do anything to you?"

"No, he did not get a chance. He tricked me into taking the grit, but many people surrounded me in the market. Thank Teras, nothing more happened." She paused, looking back at Saudett with empathy. "He did something to you?"

Saudett shivered slightly once more. "He did. He nearly raped me. At the time, I did not feel much because of the grit, and I can see why addicts are so easily abused. But now, I feel defiled. It was against my will; I feel disgusted and angry at myself that I couldn't fight it."

"I'm sorry, Saudett. I'm so sorry that happened to you." Hata's green eyes glistened. "What can I do?'

"Another embrace wouldn't harm me." Saudett smiled weakly.

Hata nodded and held Saudett. She squeezed her tightly for a long moment. Saudett basked in the warmth that Hata offered. The touch was pleasurable. Hata smelled pleasant; she closed her eyes and focused on each part of their connected bodies. Releasing Hata, she cleared her throat and returned to the wardrobe. She picked up some black leggings and an armless black coat, then strapped on her sandals before returning to Hata.

"Let's go." She paused, giving the tall red-haired girl—*No*, the tall red-haired *woman*—a once-over. "I find you quite pleasing as well, Hata. I'm glad you're here with me."

Hata eyed her longingly, nodding in agreement while biting her lower lip.

Gods. Does she know she's doing that?

They met the two awaiting them and wordlessly departed. The slight mist of the day broke as they made their way down the dust-trodden streets of Dagad.

The land west of Dagad was mainly low-rolling brown grasslands, while the mountain range crept along the horizon to the north and west. Patches of trees spotted the landscape as they walked. As the sun approached its zenith, the woods began to thicken. They saw flashes of white squirrels bounding into the canopies as gentle bird sounds warmed their ears. The party decided to halt their journey and find shade for a meal. Brena spread a blanket under a tall oak tree and laid out some leftovers from the previous evening's dinner. *The Earste Lân is so vast and beautiful; there is such a difference in the tone of the land less than a day's walk from our dusty town of Dagad. It is truly fascinating.*

"We should make it to the cemetery in but a couple more hours from here," said Saudett. "Again, I couldn't have done it without you all."

"Thank not, friend Saudett," Baal said. "My daughter, train magic with you. Baal fights with you next."

"With fist or weapon?" Saudett asked.

"Both." He laughed heartily.

"I fear I would not last long fist to fist, but we can spar with weapons. What is your weapon of choice, if I may ask?"

He strode to the wagon, lifted a ragged sheet, and pulled out a massive pickaxe. "For smashing stone. Work too on heads." His teeth gleamed with a grin.

Saudett laughed nervously. "I'm sure it does. I will acquire some training weapons from the barrack before we depart into the desert. Your pickaxe would shatter my spear on the first blow," she paused, "of course, that is, if you managed to land a hit."

His eyes narrowed on her. "Baal hit!"

She laughed and punched him hard on the arm. Not so much as a flinch. *I am but a buzzing fly to an ox.* He laughed as well, and they continued their meal, chatting idly under the canopy of the large oak. *It is peaceful.* A moment of calm after the last few days of madness. The loss of Yakeb and the stress of getting Simon back lifted for a moment. *We will not have such tranquil days on the journey ahead.*

"I have also been thinking I will endeavor the Shepherds Eye to pay you as mercenaries for the coming excursion. That way, at least, you are not doing this for no gain."

Brena lifted her head at that and spoke up, "That would be greatly appreciated. We are lacking in the way of coin. Depending on this pursuit, we were thinking about finding a new place for settlement, somewhere near a mine. Put Baal to some good, honest work."

"Knocking heads, honest," Baal answered.

"Joo, my mountain, of course," she rolled her eyes. "We have been living off odd jobs, manual labor, and such."

"I could entertain my husband to hire him if manual labor is to your liking. Once we get him back, of course. Or the Shepherds Eye is always in need of more manpower."

"Hmm, we honestly hadn't thought of those opportunities. We shall consider it," Brena answered for them both.

Baal mumbled something under his breath.

"Anteeksi?" Brena's eyes glared into Baal.

He flinched away from his mate, trying and *failing* to make himself smaller.

"Someone is coming up the road on horseback!" Hata exclaimed suddenly.

"Are you sure?" Saudett asked. "You can determine that? Just a single rider?"

"Joo, I can tell; they are riding fast."

A rider broke their vision, rounding a bend in the road. The group sat silently, watching as the horse and rider rushed by, not seeming to notice them under the shade of the big tree. He appeared intent on his forward direction, wearing simple leather and a surcoat in the King's colors: white and yellow. Saudett assumed it was a messenger of some sort. She wondered what could be so urgent but decided she would not stop him. She had to focus on Simon, or she would never leave the damned village. She stood up once the rider had passed and was out of sight.

"Let's keep moving."

The rest gathered their things and returned to the road, heading deeper into the woods.

Simon eyed Kiana curiously when he found himself in her company again. "Sixteenth Otsoa, Kiana!" he greeted. "I implore you. Were you born into this nomadic tribe, or did you immigrate to this lovely environment?" He waved a hand at the surrounding sands.

Her violet eyes danced over him in reply. "I was born into it; the desert is all I have ever known. Though once you see the Valley of Hasiera, you will see it is not such a barren waste."

"Then it must have a water source and natural fauna, I presume. It would be greatly challenging for generations to exist in this place without water." He shifted on Marigold's back to angle himself toward Kiana as he spoke.

"Aye, you are correct. The water comes deep underground and out the side of the canyon. From there, it is said, a depthless pool feeds our outlet stream, which, in turn, is used for irrigation and other purposes."

Simon scratched his head. *A depthless pool, like the one in my nightmare.* "I would like to see this wondrous pool at some point."

"Can you swim up a waterfall? Can you swim in the pitch darkness, not knowing if there's air to breathe? Alternatively, you could take a day-long journey around the canyon and traverse the tops of the cliffs, risk falling to your death to look for a hole in the ground, among countless other holes, and barely the size of a man." Her eyes now squint at him challengingly.

"Perhaps another time then," he said, chuckling nervously; *why in Skrull's hell had I just considered going to a place where I could drown.* "Anyways, more about you. Have any family here? I hesitate to ask if your parents died in some horrific attack or incident."

"The Third and Thirteenth Otsoa are both alive and well." Her violet eyes returned to a playful smile.

"Your parents are leaders as well? And a higher rank than you? They must be skilled warriors."

"The Otsoa are not solely rated by prowess in combat alone, but in leadership and management of our camp sections. We are responsible for the security and prosperity of our Otsoak, the people under us."

"That is a very intriguing setup. I would like to see how it all works." He could not keep his enthusiasm in check, ever curious. "Still, I imagine both your father and mother are formidable."

"I am a match to my father's skill with a blade but have yet to defeat my mother."

"Better not get on her bad side." He smirked. "Reminds me of my wife."

She eyed him. "Your spouse is also a warrior?"

"She is a whirlwind, I swear it. As fierce as an ashen wolverine: one minute, a calm, soothing breeze; the next, a raging maelstrom. I have seen her put men that tower over her to the dirt. She is stubborn and lithe; the boys and I compare her to the desert viper. It is an apt metaphor."

"She will come for you?" Those violet eyes never broke contact.

"Yes," he answered, without a doubt in his heart. Saudett was stubbornly strong-willed; he remembered her tale about chasing after her mother and father in the desert for months. She would do the same for him.

The eyes looked away. "Then I look forward to meeting this *viper*."

"Oh, you two would get along," he said with a chuckle.

"I fear our meeting would not be so pleasant…" she trailed off. "I must do the rounds." Her eyes smiled behind her covered mouth and nose, or so he thought. "I look forward to speaking with you again soon, Simon Meridio."

"As do I." He bowed graciously in his saddle. But he feared she was right. If Saudett comes for him, these two women might fight to the death. At least this woman had kept him company; she had made it a routine to stop in and speak with him at least once a day since the night attack of the Daanav. *How many days ago was that?* He could not be sure. *Perhaps a week?* They had yet to be engaged again by the strange creatures.

"Marigold, when will we reach our destination? I would rather be helping Kiana, and her people, build infrastructure and defenses rather than walk another day through this Skrull- damned desert."

He paused as if to listen to the camel answer. "Oh yes, I agree. Perhaps, if I cooperate, they will allow me a bath. You could use one yourself, Marigold." He waved his hand in front of his nose. Then he remembered the pool Kiana spoke of. "Gods! It must be the one from the dream. It feels like fate is pulling me toward it. And what am I supposed to do when I get there?"

A grunt from Marigold.

"Truly, Marigold. Go for a swim?! You are mad, sir!"

CHAPTER TEN

FURY

The sun was setting by the time they had laid Yakeb's body to rest. The modest cemetery was within a clearing a few hundred paces off the main road. Black crows sat perched upon a hovel that stood upon the grounds. A little old man with wiry gray hair and beard, clad in dark gray robes, hobbled out of a small cabin to meet them.

"My condolences to you and your family," the grave keeper said in a shaky, nasal voice. "Who, Hettra's blessing to them, is departed from our midst?"

"Yakeb Meridio," Saudett said flatly.

"Mr. Meridio?! Poor soul. Did he get sick? How did it happen?"

"There was an attack on the town; some bandits cut him down."

"By the gods, it pains me to hear this news. Yakeb regularly visited to talk to his dear wife, Teresa, in the Dagad cemetery. He would always bring some food, and we would chat about the comings and goings in town and what project his son was working on." The man looked around. "Where is that son of his? Simon, was it?"

"Taken," Saudett said through clenched teeth.

"The bandits? Oh, Skrull, take us, lass. These are dreadful days for you."

"I will get Simon back, but I must put Yakeb to rest beside Teresa." She was getting impatient and irritated. She did not come here to talk but to honor her dead father-in-law and then go after her husband.

"Of course, I'll show you where she lay."

"Sooner rather than later," she muttered. She took a few deep breaths to try and compose herself.

With that, the man ushered them to a corner of the clearing where they found Teresa's gravestone, a modest slab of rock protruding from the earth with her name crudely etched into the stone. They all silently dug a spot next to Simon's mother's grave, then gently placed Yakeb's body, still wrapped in the scented linen strips, into the pit.

Crouched near Yakeb's head, Saudett whispered, "I'm sorry I was not there to protect you both. I will find your son. I swear it."

"I will get my chisel from the shack to add his name to the stone," the old man said as he walked away.

Saudett stood and stepped out of the shallow pit. Then, she grabbed the shovel and began filling the grave back in. Rage was boiling within her. *I must find Simon and kill the bastard who took Yakeb's life!* Her eyes blurred as she heaved the soil, her lips trembled, and tears caressed her cheeks. Then, suddenly, the dirt was moving. The remaining ground slowly flowed over Yakeb's body like a wave until it was a low mound of earth.

In a surge of fury, Saudett cried, "Hata! What did I say about using your powers in front of a stranger—?" She cut herself off as she turned to see Brena and Baal standing behind Hata, each of their hands on her shoulders.

They had given her permission, and Saudett realized the grave keeper was nowhere in sight. She saw tears running down Hata's face; the sight of it made her break down. She sat and began to sob. "I-I'm sorry, Hata. I am just so *frustrated*; I feel pathetic. *Useless.*"

Hata wrapped her arms around Saudett's head. As Hata held her, Saudett continued to weep.

She recalled her first meeting with Yakeb before her relationship with Simon had become set in stone. One of her many stays in Dagad while she was with the caravan. Simon was trying to impress her by showing her his building site, constructing another level on a homestead. He was shouting orders and directing his crew. Yet what impressed her most was that he became so immersed in his work that he had completely forgotten she was present.

The other men had shouted back, something like one's use of Simon's mother in bed. She recalled Simon's prompt reply: "That would be quite a *dead* bed!" Followed by an eruption of laughter from the group.

A crisp memory of that day came to Saudett. She had been sitting on a bench, watching the men busying themselves on the job site, when she heard a flat, monotone voice say,

"You know, that's my deceased wife they are joking about." An older man sat beside her, and she turned to look at him.

"That is very inconsiderate of them, sir," Saudett said agitatedly, standing up. She was about to make her way over to give Simon a scolding.

The man tried to hold a straight face, then a broad smile broke through. "It's fine, lass," he chuckled. "Humor keeps their spirits up. It is well for long days on the job."

Putting two and two together, she stopped and turned back to face him, then tilted her head to one side and said, "Your deceased wife? You're Simon's father?"

"Ah! You know him, that scrawny, adorable lad over there? You should get married!"

That mischievous grin on his face is so similar to Simon's. And like father, like son, he too brought *marriage* up on their first meeting. She nearly choked. "Sir, we've only known each other in short visits for less than a year."

"Short, enthusiastic visits, one would hope?" He arched a brow questioningly, smiling wryly.

She felt her face flush, then countered, "Oh, yes!" She moaned. "I cannot stop thinking about your son in my bedsheets—"

"Halt! I surrender." His face now flushed bright pink. "I don't need to know the details!"

It was her turn to laugh. "You started it, sir."

"Aye, I did. Please, I am Yakeb Meridio, at your service. Besides that—so, almost a year now? He has never mentioned you, though I have sighted you together before. He never speaks with me about romance, about his personal life. I could teach him a thing or two. You know, his mother was a beauty." He exhaled heavily, "We only ever talk about our work. Technically, I'm still in charge of the company, you see. But I let Simon handle everything these days for the most part. I only try to be helpful, but I see him gradually becoming irritated with me. I wish he would come to ask me for assistance like he used to."

"Your love for your son is immeasurable. I can see that after five minutes of speaking with you. I will gently encourage him to improve," she said, cracking her knuckles.

"Whoa now, careful with him. He is fragile." He laughed again. "You are like a burning fire, a powerful soul. I like you. My wife would have liked you."

"I wish I could have met her. She seems like a lucky woman."

"I was sincerely the lucky one. Anyhow," Yakeb paused dramatically. "When is the wedding?"

Saudett flushed once again.

A crow perched on two bony fingers within the little cabin on the cemetery grounds. "Well, well, well, I have seen something most interesting, *most* interesting indeed. *Did you?* We must inform the Alpha." The old grave keeper cackled to himself before calling, "Jezebel!"

Another crow fluttered down from the rafters onto his other hand, and the grave keeper whispered something in its ear.

Then, out through the window of the little shack, the crow flew and headed west above the woods, unnoticed by the grieving group of travelers.

It was still dark. A faint graying light began to creep in the early morning hours, yet the nomads had already finished breaking camp, readying to depart. Simon was about to mount Marigold. As he rubbed his buttocks in anticipation of the ride, a slap on his rear startled him.

"Tender, Simon Meridio?"

How do people always sneak up on me? I haven't the slightest idea. He turned to face Kiana, and to his surprise, the face looking back at him was uncovered. He stood, staring with his mouth open as if about to say something. *She is stunning.*

The skin around her eyes turned dark from the sun, while the skin was a lighter shade of brown just below that. It seemed she rarely removed the coverings. Her nose had a gentle curve; her dark lips were moving. But Simon had not registered what she was saying. He was bewitched by her violet eyes sparkling with hints of gold.

"...you a tender ass if you spend a night in my tent."

Finally catching some of her words, he shook himself out of shock. "What say you?"

"Need I repeat myself, Simon Meridio?"

"Madam, I was lost in your beauty—"

"Save the pandering," she interjected. "Tonight, when we reach the valley, we will bathe, have one another, and rest after these weeks of riding. Though, I will be doing some more *riding* this night." She smiled and laughed.

Have one another!? He felt himself go red. *So forward.* This woman astonished him. Her bulky clothing left everything underneath up to his imagination, but her face, the smile, *the eyes.* She was oddly *comforting.* Like he'd known her for many, *many* years.

"Ahem, well, that does sound like the perfect conclusion to a long road had. Who would I be to turn down an offer such as that?"

"Not an offer. You will be under my care once we reach Hasiera, and I will do what pleases me."

He shrugged. He made love to his wife; otherwise, the fun Saudett and he both had outside of that was just that. *Fun. It's most definitely always pleasurable, to be sure.* But nothing more than that. "At your service." He bowed.

A horn sounded, followed by shouting around the camp. Simon looked around and saw some nomads pointing to the top of one of the massive dunes. About fifteen or more massive hunched forms were silhouetted in low light on the dune's ridge. Running on all four legs, many smaller dark shapes quickly descended the sand toward them, moving fast. Trails of dust in their wakes.

"Ride!" he heard Kiana shout. "Follow Mittal." She bound onto her horse and raised her sword, twirling it above her head and giving a shrill-tongued rolling cry, "Ai-ayah!"

Before he knew what was happening, she had a score of nomads around her riding to face off with the coming threat. He could not stay and watch as he kicked his camel and gave the reins a whip. "Hyah! Marigold! By all the good gods, onward, damn it! Hyah! Hyah! Come on!"

He saw a handful of nomads herding the beasts of burden and sheep away from the enemy. He aimed his steed in their direction and quickly caught up, as they were not moving nearly as fast with the number of animals in tow. He looked back to try and discern what was happening with the attack. Dust flew everywhere in the thick of the fight. The nomads had met the smaller-sized hound-like Daanav at the base of the dune. They were leaner than their hulking counterparts, who were still lumbering down the dune to join the fray. Simon could only catch moments through the dust and turmoil.

The enormous abominations collided hard with the nomads. He saw many of the horsemen felled immediately. At that moment, a few smaller creatures broke off and began bounding in Simon's direction.

Turning about, Simon muttered, "Oh gods, that's not good." He quickly gave the camel a few more kicks. "Marigold. Marigold! Move your Skrull-fucking arse, for Hettra's sake!"

The camel gave a panicked groan and began trotting at a quicker pace.

Simon saw Mittal leading the animals and a few nomads on each flank. "Mittal Gohra!" He shouted. "They broke through! All the gods' fat tits! Mittal! They broke through!"

Mittal turned his desert brown-speckled horse quickly. He lifted a fist in the air, and three men joined him. They headed toward Simon, who was approaching the rear of the train. The Daanav were some fifty paces away and closing, one leading much further from the other two. Simon turned his head to look back again and got a better view of them. They had similar features to the hulking hunched forms: long canine-like faces and bone structure. The same long protruding teeth and matted black hair. He was caught up staring at the closest one, those yellow eyes holding his gaze. Then it leaped just feet away from him with a gaping open maw.

Ah, he thought, *this time, I am dead.*

An arrow whistled past his head straight into one of those glowing yellow eyes. The hound screeched and crashed to the ground at his side. Then, it quickly disappeared in the dust left in his wake as Marigold continued to run on.

The nomads galloped past Simon so near and fast that he felt the wind as they rode by. Mittal and one other hurtled by the crumpled beast as it tried to stand, an arrow protruding from its face. A significant slash across its chest and another splitting the side of its skull toppled it backward. Two more nomads split off, flanking in opposite circular directions, short bows firing arrows. One of the two remaining smaller beasts was zig-zagging and avoiding many projectiles. The other had taken a few missiles in the torso and back leg.

"Focus on the runner!" Mittal shouted to his archers. "We'll take the wounded one!"

Simon saw the first nomad engage in melee with the arrowed creature, topple off his horse, and roll. With a clean cut from a razor-sharp bone protruding from the knee joint of the Daanav hound's foreleg, the nomad's horse lost its front legs. Blood was spraying into the sand as the horse screamed. The monster's scythe-like blade fanned out to its sides as it bound toward the man. Just as the man was standing to face the enemy, the creature landed on him, its teeth closed on his throat, ripping clean through his spine, bone, and tissue. His head tumbled off after a sickening pop.

Mittal met the creature next. Rope and stone twirling around his head, he shot the bola out, and it tangled around the creature's legs. The monster awkwardly fell forward onto its face. Seeing this, Mittal stood on his saddle, with one hand on the reins, the other clutching his sword and tipping it downwards. He leaped from the horse, his total weight behind the downward thrust. With a thud, he landed, the blade piercing into the skull of the struggling demonic hound. Simon watched the Daanav's limbs spasmed while Mittal pulled his tulwar sword free, gore spraying out of the chasm. Mittal flicked the blade casually, leaving a streak of black blood in the sand.

Simon heard a scream and turned to see the last demon mutilating a horse and rider. It had caught one of the archers. With arrows protruding from its back and chest, it was taken by rage. So focused on the quarry before it, it kept tearing into the dead man's flesh. At the same time, the other archer kept adding to the pincushion until its fury finally slowed, and the beast lay on the mound of flesh. It began to melt away, red and black blood mixing in the sand.

Mittal rode up beside Simon. "Join the rest of the sheep, slave."

"Hettra, bless you!" Simon exhaled in relief. "I thank you immensely from the bottom of my heart for saving this helpless goat," he said with a grateful grin.

Mittal grunted, "We must make haste. The Sixteenth Otsoa keeps them at bay, but she is outnumbered, and their sacrifice must not be in vain. I will get you to the valley."

"Qav's luck be with her," Simon whispered to himself as Mittal rode off to the head of the train. They were rounding a dune as he looked back again, only to see the looming cloud of dust in the low light of the gray morning dusk.

CHAPTER ELEVEN

BLOSSOM

After spending a night camped out near the graveyard, Saudett and company arrived in Dagad by mid-afternoon the following day. Hata cuddled with her throughout the night, making for a comforting sleep after the hike and the stress of Yakeb's burial. Saudett had felt more relaxed on their way back, and they had an uneventful trip home for the most part.

But now, Saudett was anxious to head into the desert and begin searching for Simon. *I need to get out there. I need to select two others for the journey.* She departed from the Vasara's and went to the Shepherds Eye barracks to check in with Captain Dermont. She knocked on the door to his office.

A voice answered promptly, "Enter."

She opened the door to see Lieutenant Ryon sitting across from the captain, arms crossed. As she entered, Ryon scowled at her.

"Lieutenant," Ryon said smugly.

"I take it you never found my husband? Lieutenant?"

"As I told the captain, the brigands split their forces into at least ten groups and made off in many directions. We decided it was too risky to pick a single trail or split our forces to pursue."

"Too much risk or too much effort?" Saudett growled.

Ryon stood, his sweaty face pink with rage. "I should have you flogged for disrespecting an officer!"

"Enough," Captain Dermont interrupted. "Ryon did all he judged was necessary; he was in command of the operation, and we accept his verdict, like it or not."

"Sir," both officers answered in unison.

"On another note: A rider arrived from Nidhaut yesterday. Vouri refugees have arrived in mass to the northern villages of the Aurulan mainland. They have been driven out of their homes in the mountains. They're apparently having trouble getting further information from the refugees."

"They found something in the mountain," Saudett muttered.

"How in the gods would you know that?" Ryon sneered.

"Our friend Baal from the other day left his people after a dispute about mining operations in the mountains. He had concerns about where they were digging. Unfortunately, it seems he was correct."

"That is good information, Saudett. I will send a messenger. Though by the time one returns to the capital, I am certain events will have long unfolded. The King is mustering a counterforce to deploy to the north. He has asked all garrisons to send an officer and as many men as can be spared." He turned his attention to Ryon. "You will lead this detachment, Lieutenant."

"Sir?!" Ryon exclaimed. "But I—"

"That's an order. Thank you for your report. You may leave us now, Lieutenant Ryon." Dermont nodded to Ryon in dismissal.

"Sir." Ryon promptly made his way out. As he passed her, he pushed in close to Saudett and whispered, "Lucky for you, the captain only wants your cunt. Fucking *whore*."

The image of her fist in his face flashed through her mind. She felt her head heat with anger and clenched her hands. But held fast at attention, her teeth grinding. Once he had left the room, she visibly deflated.

"Don't worry about him. I thought we could construct a watchtower on the border of the desert after this recent attack. If he should return from the west, I believe he would make a fitting commander for such a station, would he not?" Cad said with a wink.

She smiled and nodded but said nothing, still irate at Ryon's comments.

"You will set out tomorrow at dawn?" Cad asked. "Have you thought about who else you will take with you?"

"Kaplan Mir and Taryn Drel."

"Excellent choices, skilled individuals. I will notify them and have them ready at the Road's End tomorrow morning."

"I am also drafting three mercenaries to be paid by the Shepherds Eye for their services."

The captain studied her, raising an eyebrow.

"They are *insurance*. In case things should get, well...*bloody*. A little extra muscle, if you will."

"Aye, aye, leave it at that."

"Sir, I will take my leave."

"Wait." He stood and limped around his desk. He took one of her hands in his. "Good luck, Saudett, be safe. Your husband is a fortunate man." His eyes did a quick once-over of her.

She pulled her hand from his. "Sir, Ryon's words just now. You did not promote me only to use me in your bed-chambers? It doesn't make sense. You've already had me with and without my husband present."

He coughed and stretched. Saudett knew him well enough that it was suspicious; he was not being entirely candid.

"Of course not. We have had our fun, and I pray that the three of us can partake in that bliss once more on Simon's healthy return."

She studied him. "Aye, *pray* for his healthy return." Ryon's words clung to her. Quickly, she turned about and exited the chamber. She felt his eyes follow her out. Nausea growing within her. Was he hoping Simon did not return so he could have her for himself?

I need to train! Sweat out these negative emotions, she thought. Also, they needed to prepare supplies for the morrow's journey. There never seemed to be enough time in the day. She stopped by the armory on her way out, grabbed some wooden practice swords, and then returned to the Vasara household.

About an hour later, Saudett's hands were ringing with pain. Each blow she deflected from Baal brought a struggle to retain her grip on the wooden weapon, her arms vibrating from the impact. She was fast, but her strikes on the colossal man only seemed to invigorate his swings. He laughed and grinned like an overgrown child having far too much fun.

She much preferred a spear over the sword for the reach and speed of her thrusts. If this man used his pickaxe, she could not deflect the weapon's point with a sword or spear. Also, the sheer strength of the blow behind it would crush through her, and the sharp pick would impact her body or skull. It was a brutal weapon, yet not many people fought with one.

She raised a hand to signal a rest. "Baal, you are truly a bear in a man's skin. If this were a true fight, I would have to finish you after avoiding your first strike and aim for a killing blow. I would be done for if it came to a prolonged battle such as this. The pickaxe is a favorable yet uncanny weapon."

"Sometimes gets stuck in heads." His shoulders heaved as he flexed. "Have time to step on dead man and pull free."

"Ah." She nodded. "Precise for finishing the job quickly, but can be a hassle in a larger engagement with many foes." She took a long swig of her waterskin.

Hata was sitting outside the front door of the homestead, watching them. "Sometimes, their heads just explode." She had a large, *toothy* grin pasted on her face, much like her father's.

Saudett coughed and spit out some of the water. "Gods," she muttered, recovering as Baal and Hata laughed maniacally.

"Alright, your turn, Hata. Let us go for a walk." She took Hata by the hand and strolled away with her. Saudett remembered the news about the Vouri people as they walked through town. Word traveled fast in Dagad; *they may already know it by now*. She thought if she told Baal and his family, they may change their minds and return to their people to try and help. *I am selfish but do not want to lose them, especially Hata*. She decided she would tell them in the morning before they departed.

As they walked to the hills outside of town, hand in hand, Hata huddled into her. Saudett flushed with pleasure. Hata was soothing and caring. She needed it in these challenging times, and Saudett felt that Hata also needed to be loved, physically and emotionally. She let go of Hata's hand and wrapped it around her waist, pulling her closer for an embrace.

Half a foot taller than Saudett, Hata looked down slightly into her eyes. "What was the cause of that?" she said, smiling.

"Need I cause?" Saudett shrugged.

Hata blushed. "I want to kiss you."

"You are so forthright; it is enjoyable." She reached a hand up and brushed her thumb along Hata's lips.

"What about your husband?" Hata asked.

"We have an agreement: we can engage others, enjoying them separately, or bring them in to have fun with us. It is mainly in favor of pleasure and fornication. The excitement we enjoy by bringing others into bed. But there is still an emotional connection between all parties involved, which is most satisfying. This is nothing new for us, Hata."

"What about love?"

Saudett smiled. "That is what binds all of us together. I've known you for a few days; can I not say I love and care about you?"

Tears welled up in Hata's eyes, and she whispered. "I love you too."

Saudett paused for a moment. *Am I taking advantage of a young woman with little experience? Am I only using this poor, lonely girl for my own satisfaction? To distract me from Simon.* She pushed the thought aside, taken by Hata's persona, longing for her.

Saudett stood on the tips of her toes and pushed her lips tenderly to Hata's. They were soft. She breathed Hata's scent in deeply. They continued to kiss as they slowly made their way to the ground. One hand caressed her cheek, the other under Hata's blouse, gently touching each part of Hata's skin. Her abdomen, first, then sliding up to the center of her breasts. Then she cupped and moved her hands over the top of Hata's breast and back down her ribs, lightly scoring her skin with her nails.

Saudett heard Hata suck in a breath with a small gasp. She then kissed her ear, then her neck. When her lips reached clothing, she untied Hata's shirt and pulled it over her head. As she put the garment gently to the side, she heard Hata whisper, "You too."

Hata clumsily unbuttoned Saudett's black vest and pulled it apart, then wrapped her arms around the back to remove the linen wraps from Saudett's breasts. Hata's cool, pale, and freckled skin sent shivers through Saudett as they pressed together.

Saudett kissed her way down Hata's naked body. Tenderly. *Intimately...*

... "Gods," Hata said after some time.

Smiling, Saudett crawled back up Hata's body slowly, then kissed her affectionately. "Mmmm," she moaned. "You taste wonderful. Shall we try it again?"

Hata bit her lower lip and nodded.

Slowly, carefully, and taking her time, Saudett kissed her way back downward.

Chapter Twelve

HUNTSMAN

Jude Nelon trudged up the winding staircase. *Fucks to this; it must be thousands of steps,* he thought. *Why do magi make their abode at the top of towers?* "Stereotypical," he muttered, then sighed as he continued. Small rectangular lanterns along the wall glowed with an unnatural violet light. No opening to the outside air offered a reprieve from the dingy interior, ever winding upward. Jude had been summoned here by the Alpha Passeriform, Ebras Corb, the leader of the Aerie of Passeriformes in Nidhaut, the capital city of Aurulan.

There was but one reason he would be summoned: it was time to hunt down another newly discovered mage-sensitive. As he finally reached the top of the spiraling staircase, Jude found himself at an extravagant golden door. An eagle made of solid gold, with its wings spread across the door's width, grasped a loop in its talons. Jude clutched the knocker and gave a sharp rap. Not waiting for an answer, he pushed his way through the door.

The reek of bird shit wafted over him. *Fucks.* The chamber within burst with the sound of cawing. He looked to see nests and branches crisscrossing about in the dome-shaped ceiling. Hundreds of crows were flapping and screaming at him. *Fucks to this shit. How can he live with the stench? Fucking disgusting.*

"Silence, fowls!" a stern voice called out. The birds fell immediately silent. "Welcome, Jude Nelon."

Jude looked at the figure behind a massive gold-inlaid, blackened wood desk. He wore elegant black robes with the same glinting golden trim. A golden pin, with a single feather signifying his place in the council, adorned his chest.

Jude gave the room a quick once over. Piles of trinkets, coins, and jewels littered the room, from jewelry to silver utensils and other bright objects. Bookshelves and the books themselves were covered in jars of strange liquids and other bits. A single massive glass door opened to a balcony, which looked upon the sprawling city below and a few other elevated, different-shaped towers stretching into the sky.

"The birds bring many gifts." The man gestured to the trinkets and the ceiling before casually brushing back his jet-black hair. "The people of Nidhaut are very generous indeed." The man's black goatee framed a wicked grin.

"Unknowingly generous, Alpha. Let us cut to the chase. Whom, Primus tell, am I going after this time?"

"A young Vouri girl with short fire-red hair. She can manipulate the earth, or so says the report. If so, she will be an excellent addition to my collection."

Jude's stomach turned. *By the fucks.* He tried not to think about what this man did with the girls *and* boys after he had caught them. "Where?" he answered shortly.

"Dagad."

"The trade town? That is a fortnight away on horseback. About a week, as your crow flies." He glanced up. "Hopefully, she is still in Dagad. Do you have a pylon there?"

"I doubt this girl will move or give you much fight. She comes from a peasant family; they live and die where they are born."

"You forget they are Vouri, who, as we know, have been pushed out of their homeland. They could still be on the move. Not to mention, the Vouri don't take kindly to being told what to do."

The Alpha shrugged. "That's why I pay you to do the dirty work. Still, the news of the Vouri situation is too current; they must have been in Dagad prior to the ordeal. I can get you to a graveyard about a day from Dagad, where she was sighted about a week ago."

"That is acceptable," Jude said, then paused. "Furthermore, my price has gone up."

"Why? You have been two hundred gold pieces per capture for years now."

"Precisely. The daily cost of living has increased, yet my income has not. My house gathers dust, and the plants run wild while I am not in and about it. The gardener needs to be paid; he keeps my vegetables and herbs alive while I'm away. I like to come home to a clean house and a tidy yard. It's two hundred and fifty now."

"Sometimes, it slips the mind that you are a ruthless reprobate with your homey lifestyle. It matters not to me; your compensation comes from the council's resources. It is a paltry sum."

"Make it three hundred."

Ebras glared at him and sighed, "Fine. Are you ready to depart?"

"Can I bring my horse?"

"I'm afraid the pylon's position is somewhat *confined*. You'll have to make do."

Jude grunted. "Why did I even ask? Didn't want to go back down those damn stairs anyways." Jude took a small metal box from his pouch, then removed the pendant hanging from his neck and gently placed it in the box before clasping it shut.

"Are you prepared, Huntsman?" Ebras asked.

Fucks to this part. Jude nodded.

Jude watched air split in front of him, light breaking through nothingness as if a crack in the wall had formed in mid-air. It was blinding; he took a few steps into the light. Then suddenly, Jude fell, slamming into something stiff and wooden, busting it underneath his weight. Rolling onto his back, groaning in pain, he waited for his vision to return. After a few blinks, he stared at the ceiling of a rickety shack. A small table had broken his fall and was in pieces around him.

"By the fucks," he muttered to himself. "Why can he not place these things so one can simply walk between them? None of this falling business."

"Master usually sends his familiar when he deems it necessary to visit me, times being few and far between. Though, see that shelf there. Occasionally, I wake up, and a white crow sits perched there, watching me. He sees through the eyes of the white crow, you see," the old grave keeper said, standing in the doorway.

"Skrull's balls, that's eerie."

"He should have been doing that the day the girl was in my graveyard; this sending of bird messages is archaic. He should provide a different form of communication, something we could hold in our hands and just speak into."

"Fucks you on about? That's the daftest thing I've ever heard," Jude said, standing up and brushing himself off.

"Mark my words; some magician will come up with it and make a fortune. He can send a body through a portal, but not a voice?"

"Perhaps he can. Did you ever think perhaps you need to be able to use magic as well in order to send the words back?"

The grave keeper looked quizzically at Jude. Then it dawned on him. "Ah-ha, I just need to learn magic!"

"Qav's luck with that. Then perhaps *I* will have to come to find you one of these days."

The grave keeper was cackling to himself, ignoring Jude now. "Oh yes, I will become all-powerful." He began waving his hands as if to cast a spell. "The greatest magi in history will be I, Petre Laith Feasog, the third of his name. I will be known far and wide!"

Jude pushed past him and out the door, the crooked man's words fading away as he rattled on. A quick look at the shadows determined the sun's direction, and he picked the path down the road toward Dagad, setting his pace at a brisk jog.

CHAPTER THIRTEEN

HAVEN

Simon heard a shout from one of the nomads at the front of the animal train: "We've made it! We're here! Hasiera!"

He urged Marigold forward and soon summited the dune where the shout had come from. Behind them, the sun was low; it was late. He saw before him a massive valley. Rocky cliffs jabbed vertically along the horizon to the left, creating a long, snaking wall. He saw the glint of a small waterfall coming out through a hole in the cliff face, forming a winding river that branched off into smaller streams.

He saw green. *Such a vibrant environment.* He was in awe. Palm trees and giant ferns. Patches of what looked like organized plantations of some sort. Opposite the cliffs on the south side of the valley, the hills slowly rolled up, jade grasses waving, then abruptly changing into the dust of the desert. He saw thousands of tents and many street-widened paths. He could see some twenty various-shaped sections of tents divided by more extensive trails from this height and distance. *This must be what Kiana was talking about: each Otsoa has an area and people to govern.*

By the Primus. How could so many people live here in the middle of the desert? It was beyond him. They began their descent from the dune. The earth quickly changed from sand to rich, dark red soil, green grasses, and ferns as they reached the bottom. The vegetation he was accustomed to in Dagad was mainly brown grasses and pitiful dwarfed bushes. This felt stronger and healthier. As they approached the line of tents, Simon noted a crude line of stakes jutting outwards in their direction. A handful of nomads were posted at multiple spots along the line. Riders immediately sallied forth to meet them.

The first rider to approach them called out, "Mittal Gohra, how fares your Pack?"

"The Sixteenth is lost; we were attacked at dawn a few days past. The enemy is close. I have brought the master builder." He pointed at Simon.

"This is grave and yet remarkable news, Mittal Gohra. You will be recommended as a replacement for the Sixteenth, as you have delivered our salvation."

Salvation? These people are mad. The Pack was ushered into the camp. People gathered near the path, watching as they rode in. Children excitedly zipped around the tents to better view the riders. Elders murmured to each other while watching the train, sitting in half-circles. Puffs of smoke rose from long pipes. They came to what seemed to be the center of the encampment. A large multi-peaked tent with a path carved out wide around it took up Simon's vision. A nomad motioned for him to get down from Marigold. He watched as the sheep and other animals were herded away.

Marigold was steered along with them. "I'll find you, my man. Primus's blessing to you. We've been through life and death together," he said quietly, putting a thumb to lips in thanks.

"Who are you talking about?" a voice said. "The camel?" A laugh he had not heard since the day of his capture filled his ears. *The man dressed in gold.*

Simon turned to face him. The man who murdered his father wore plain linen shirt and trousers, carrying a hoe over one shoulder. Simon must have looked shocked as the man spoke up. Surprised that the man looked of Aurulan heritage but was darkened from years in the sun.

"Harvesting and replanting the yams this time of year, we all aid where it is needed most," the golden man said. His face was plain and stubbly, and his light brown eyes were unremarkable.

Simon stood silently, staring daggers at the man in front of him.

"Come, sit in my home. The insects will be out as soon as the sun begins to set. Mare flies leave quite a nasty bite." He waved Simon over.

Simon did not move.

The not-so-golden man nodded, and two men grabbed Simon by the arms and pushed him forward. He stumbled into the large opening of the canvas tent. It had an extensive interior but was relatively empty. Simon noted another flap at the back of the tent, leading to another chamber, *perhaps the man's sleeping quarters.* Simon entertained the thought of sneaking in at night and strangling the golden man.

"Come now, sit."

Quickly looking over the rest of the room, Simon saw some simple rugs surrounding a small hearth at the tent's center. There was a table and a few stools off to one side, which looked to have some parchments rolled out, including a map, or so Simon thought.

The First Otsoa sat by the hearth. Simon didn't move to join him. But was unceremoniously ushered to sit across from him.

"Bring some food for my guest."

Simon snorted. "*Guest?* Truly, that is too strong a word."

"Did the Sixteenth inform you of your role here during the voyage?"

"She did. On that note, you could have approached this entire situation in a civilized manner. You could have come in person, explained the circumstances about the demons, and offered me payment for my services. You could have avoided killing anyone." Simon clenched his teeth.

"Would you truly have believed that demons were killing a nomadic tribe in the desert?"

Simon shrugged in response. "Probably not."

"You had a good life back in Dagad? A wife? Any children? No reason to leave it." The First paused momentarily. "Parents?"

Simon's fingers twitched. "I will see you dead one day by the Primus, I swear."

The two guards behind him made as if to pull their swords. A hand went up from the First to calm them.

"His rage is understandable. I tried to inquire with your father to join us. He just stood there smiling. It irked me. Extremely so. Accordingly, I decided to wipe that smile off his *foolish fucking face.*"

Simon lunged toward him, only to be met with a fist to his nose. He sprawled onto his back, warm blood running out his nose and down his mouth and chin.

"You will understand. We had no choice. People rarely come to live amongst us willingly, believing the desert is merely a wasteland. Everyone here is a person on the run from the past. We had to take you by force." He signaled for the guards to pick Simon up. "You will help us with our defense against the Daanav. Now go rest. Tomorrow, I would like to hear your plans for how we are to achieve this."

With that, Simon was dragged from the tent, where he was dropped at the waiting feet of Mittal Gohra. Simon groaned and held his nose.

Mittal gave a soft kick to Simon's foot. "Stand up. Don't nurse it like a child after a bee sting."

Simon whined, "I truly do not enjoy violence."

"Ha, get used to it, slave." Mittal put Simon's arm over his shoulder and helped him hobble away. "This is merely the beginning."

Still holding his nose with his free hand, Simon said, "Thank you, Mittal. Can you have them bring Marigold to wherever I find myself sleeping tonight? He must miss me already."

Mittal let out a hearty laugh.

Chapter Fourteen

SUNSTONE

Saudett was met by Kaplan Mir and Taryn Drel at the Roads End, the east exit of town. They had gathered six horses and three camels laden with supplies. Taryn paced back and forth restlessly. She was the tall, dark-skinned Tulu woman who had shown her value during the attack on the town. She wore the same boiled leather and scale uniform as Saudett, minus any shirt or trousers underneath, with her primarily bare legs, arms, and some areas around her torso peeking through. All Shepherds Eye wore the uniform a bit differently. Taryn sported two hand axes at her belt and carried a more extended version of Saudett's spear.

Saudett watched Taryn shade her eyes to the morning sun, putting a hand on the yellow scarf wrapped in a band around the top of her head. Three white dots were painted in a line just above the brows. She called to Saudett as she approached.

"We could be halfway along to that stick man of yours by now had we left at a decent time, eh?" Her words were almost hard to follow with the speed of her quick Tulu accent.

"That scrawny man has an enormous…" Saudett paused dramatically. "Brain." Her lips curled into a smirk.

"Of course, he does," Taryn chuckled, shaking her spear as she did so. "It must be a great oaken lumber to be having your loins in such a bunch.'"

"We'd best make way. Where are these so-called mercenaries?" Kaplan Mir said flatly, unamused by the playful banter.

Saudett looked at the other group member, another she had noted during the battle. He was a severe man. A long scar ran up his left cheek, leaving a hairless strip as it cut into his hairline and beard. His face was shadowed mainly by his tan cloak's hood. He wore plain brown robes, leather bracers, and knee-high leather boots, the toes slightly curved upwards to a point. His trousers billowed out over the tops of the boots. He carried a short bow and a scimitar.

"They will be along shortly," Saudett answered.

He grunted and turned back to fiddling with his saddlebags.

"So, what do you plan to be doing down there? How are we going to find him in that colossal sea of sand? Shall we walk an aimless trek, crossing our fingers until we up and all die of a great thirst?" Taryn asked sarcastically.

"One of the people joining us will aid us with that," Saudett answered amusedly. "Also, between Kaplan and myself, we know a few places to find water and shelter in the desert."

"Friend, Saudett!"

She turned to look and saw Baal and his family coming up the street. Baal led a donkey pulling the same cart they had used to carry Yakeb, only now with four large barrels strapped to it instead, while Hata and Brena strolled alongside.

"Well, he will be useful in a fight," Kaplan muttered in observance of the massive man. "The woman, too."

Saudett realized Brena was adorned in armor and had a large round shield on her back and a longsword at her side. She wore a silver-capped helm with white feathers cresting the top. Her nose and cheeks were hidden by guards. Her steel pauldrons matched her helm, and she wore a chain mail coat with a blue-gray topcoat and knee-high boots. Steel plates covered her shins.

Saudett waved to the approaching trio. Hata ran ahead to embrace Saudett. She wrapped her arms around her and took a moment to hold her.

"Good morning, sweet thing," she whispered into Hata's ear, then gave her a light peck on the cheek.

Hata blushed slightly and gave a shy "Hello."

Saudett laughed merrily. "Ready to set out, everyone?"

"And what boon does this girl offer to our journey?" Kaplan asked bluntly.

Baal and Brena had now reached the group. At the comment from Kaplan, Brena answered, "She is our daughter, and we cannot simply leave her behind."

"She is a liability. We will likely be killed trying to protect her if things go wrong."

"I can protect myself!" Hata cried.

Baal was growling, trying to piece together the conversation.

"Kaplan Mir." Saudett paused, gesturing for everyone to calm down. "Your fears are rightly stated; it is one of the reasons I picked you for this journey. You do not hold back your thoughts and are frank. Hata will prove a valuable part of our group, and I will explain why once we are underway."

"Isn't it obvious?" Kaplan replied. "Perhaps something to do with tracking the bandits. I'm sure these two fine warriors can hold their own, but I don't expect them to be able to pick up a week-old trail in the desert."

He is an observant one. Saudett nodded to him.

"We can be talking and riding, eh!" Taryn said as she hopped up on her horse and kicked it forward, leading one of the camels.

Saudett touched Hata's back and led her to one of the waiting horses. Kaplan followed suit and mounted, taking the other camel behind him. He was perceptive, catching on that Hata would provide direction after Saudett's off-handed comment. Hata was scowling angrily.

"You'll get used to him," Saudett reassured her. "Unfortunately, we will have to tell these two about your powers, especially considering we will be spending a lot of time together and if we wish to practice every night." She paused and nudged Hata. "Among other things."

Hata flushed again.

"They are trustworthy?" Brena interjected.

"Aye, I trust both with my life."

Baal grunted his approval and strode over to the largest horse. He heaved himself into the saddle, and the horse whined a bit. He patted the neck gently and muttered something in Vouri.

Brena and Hata giggled at the comment.

Saudett tipped her head inquisitively, then helped Hata up onto her horse. Once they were all situated, they slowly made off in the wake of the two soldiers.

They slowed their pace after crossing the foothills and entering the desert sands. Saudett caught up to Kaplan and Taryn.

"The girl has a gift."

Kaplan eyed her suspiciously. "She is not simply here to only be your warmth on cold desert nights?"

"Eh, you be having some manners there, Kap." Taryn swatted him on the boot with the butt of her spear.

He didn't react to the friendly attack.

"I care for the girl. She has been alone in Dagad for a while and had a run-in with a grit dealer." She went on to retell the story of how they met.

"Poor girl," Kaplan followed up the tale with a hint of regret.

"Eh!" Taryn exclaimed. "Now she be using the magic? A sorcerer! A witch even! 'Tis unbelievable!" She turned her horse about and rode back to meet the trio. "Girl! Be showing me some of that magic now, then!"

At this point, the train had stopped. Saudett and Kaplan turned their horses about to observe the entertainment. Surprised and still frowning from the early conflict, Hata's eyes sought Saudett's approval. Saudett nodded her the go-ahead.

Hata dismounted and took a few steps away from the group.

She pulled her hands back toward her, palms up. The sand moved and gathered into a small mound in front of her. She clenched her fists as if to perform a double-fisted punch and slowly pushed them forward and upwards.

The little dune she had created moved and grew higher and more extensive, like a tidal wave in the ocean, yet made of sand. It cruised and grew for twenty paces before she abruptly let her arms drop, and the wave dissipated weakly into dust. Hata fell to one knee.

Saudett and Baal met her simultaneously, helping her to her feet.

"Tytär, tarvitsetko apua?" Baal asked, a look of concern on his face.

"Olen kunnossa, Isä." Hata answered wearily.

"Pace yourself, Hata," Saudett said. "You haven't done that before. We need to practice more before working to greater notions."

Panting heavily, Hata replied, "I'm sorry. I was angry. I wanted to show them I could do it and be useful. I'm not just a little girl."

"Don't apologize. I understand how effortless it can be to let anger consume you." Saudett brushed Hata's hair gently with her fingertips. "I have trouble keeping my own in check."

"That 'tis damned glorious!" Taryn shouted. "You are incredible. Haha, girl!"

"Hata." Hata smiled meekly.

"Haha girl, you be needing a mage name, says I. Hmm, how about, 'Haha, the Red Mage of the Hot Burning Sands.'"

Hata laughed aloud. "That is quite ridiculous!"

"Haha girl," Taryn said seriously. "You have the red hair, and you can move the sand. You think of something better, then?"

"*Sunstone.* A reflection of the heat in this girl's heart and the earth she utilizes."

They all simultaneously looked at Kaplan, stunned.

"What?" His head tilted. "Is it not plain common sense?"

Everyone else broke out in laughter.

Baal joined in the laughter but had a slightly puzzled expression on his face.

"Truly a lovely name for a mage!" Hata exclaimed as her father effortlessly lifted her back onto her horse. He just smiled and nodded his agreement.

"Sunstone," Hata whispered to herself as they started out again.

CHAPTER FIFTEEN

PLAN

Simon strolled along the bottom of the cliffside, inspecting the stone. He brushed his hand along the hard gray-red surface. Surveying the cliffside, he saw veins of different minerals, layers upon layers atop each other. They needed materials to build the wall. The sand was abundant, but he would need limestone, shale, or another mineral to mix with water to create the blocks.

"I should have paid more attention to how my suppliers acquired such minerals," he pondered aloud. "Hadn't overly cared to ask." Typically, he ordered materials from multiple vendors from Aurulan and Xamid. "Oh, where to start? Where to start? I haven't the slightest idea. I suppose I will just have to experiment, then."

He went to the waterfall's base, which pierced the cliffside. It reminded him of a hole in a barrel. Watching the water settle out into a large pool where he stood. A slight mist rose to meet his face. It was refreshing in the midday sun. Countless stalks of a tall plant grew in abundance around the pool and along the riverbed. Pointed green leaves dangled from numerous joints every foot or so along the plant's stem.

"What a peculiar plant." He rubbed the leaves between his thumb and two fingers for a moment. Then, he meandered along the stream's path. The central strait of water ran crookedly across the valley until it disappeared into the hills on the opposite side. The stream was quite sizable, roughly twenty paces across. Simon thought it was a large amount of water for an underground river source. Given time, he thought of adding a water wheel along the side of the main flow to begin milling grains and whatnot. Smaller avenues of water broke away from the mainline; some seemingly natural, others crudely manmade. A few snaked into cultivated sections of low-growing, leafy green plants. He thought they must be the yams; among other vegetables he could not identify.

Continuing along the stream, he could feel people's eyes upon him. He ignored it and enjoyed his slow jaunt. He assumed a nomad was charged with watching him, but whoever they were, they were keeping their distance. *At least I have some privacy, and they are not hovering over my shoulder like a worrisome nanny.* Simon decided to act as if nobody was following him, and he liked it that way. Just people off to the sides being curious.

Simon reached the end of the water, where it buried itself into the hillside. The grass on the surrounding hills was astonishing. Herds of horses were kept grazing there, running free for the most part. Sheep and pigs were penned along the hillside base and led out into the rolling fields at intervals. He recognized one of the shepherds as Qunid. Simon was about to wave and shout at him when a hard hand smacked him square in the back. He jumped out of his skin with a yelp.

"Bossman! I am surprised you made it here alive," Naurr said, chuckling at his antics.

"Naurr! By Qav's tanned ass! You're the one who never ceases to surprise me. Gods, take us! How have you been? How was the trek?"

"Been eventful." He paused. "They had to be giving me my timber back so I could beat some Skrull holy abomination to the death with it."

"So, you met them too? Skrull's balls, those things were truly horrid."

"Aye, yet it does make me slightly sympathetic for these people here. Most are outcasts, orphans, or exiles. They be making a peaceful home and just want to live their simple lives. Much akin to me."

"I mean, I'm sure they raid the odd caravan now and then."

"If they need to, aye. We also met a caravan in the desert. The nomads took only provisions and building materials. Some weapons and armor from the guardsmen. They left enough for the caravan to make it home with some valuables intact. The caravan didn't put up a tussle. It was lightly guarded. Thirteenth Otsoa is an honorable sir."

"Thirteenth Otsoa?" Simon paused, pondering. "Thirteenth Otsoa...Ah! Kiana's father!"

"Kiana?" Naurr raised a brow.

"She is, or *was* rather, the Sixteenth Otsoa and leader of my company. She was a sight to behold! Truly gorgeous, witty, *deadly*. She reminded me so much of Saudett." He sighed sorrowfully. "Hard to believe Kiana is dead now."

"I don't think these Otsoa rush to the heavens so easily, boss."

"Perhaps you're right, my friend. I trust to hope." Simon straightened. "Nevertheless, any thoughts regarding this little enterprise of ours?"

"Thinking be your job, boss. Just tell me what you want to be done, eh?"

Simon slouched again. "Damn it, man, you must have some concepts of your own. I mean, I suppose we should start by mining the cliffside. See if we can't make some sandstone blocks for the walls. Perhaps, if time permits, a guard tower on each end of the valley on the hilltops?"

"Might be giving away the position of the valley to any passersby. As it is now, you can't see the place until you come up along it, eh? Alas, I will do what you say." Naurr gleamed with a smile. "I'll go round up the lot of boys. They've had enough of idling time to be sure now."

Good. Everything is getting back to normal, Simon thought. He watched as the Tulu foreman sauntered down the hill and disappeared among the pavilions. Simon turned along the base of the hillside and began to walk the perimeter of the encampment.

A few hours later, Simon had inquired with Mittal about a makeshift lean-to, stool, table, and some parchment and ink. He set up across from his crew, working the cliffside base near the waterfall. Luckily, they were forced to bring most of their tools when captured. Though mining was not something they needed to do at any time, they regularly needed to excavate, so shovels and pickaxes were a part of their regular collection of instruments. He sat in the shade of his lean-to, drawing out his plans for the fortifications.

"Thank Hettra for the natural barricade of the cliff on the valley's north end." Simon put a thumb to his lip. Sitting on the small stool and thinking aloud, he said, "We need a barrier on each side of the valley. The true problem is that another angle of attack would come from the hills on the south side." He rubbed his temples. "This is ridiculous; we'll need a miracle to pull this off."

If he built a wall on the south side of the valley, it would be better to build it somewhat away from the hills. They would have to relocate some animal pens and tents in that area. He thought of making a quick wooden watchtower on the hilltop on that side, with a warning bell in case of attack, but then thought better after Naurr's comments. "It may be a downfall rather than a blessing," he pondered aloud. "Now, on to my next problem."

There was a lack of lumber materials at their disposal. Odds and ends of what they had taken from the job sight in Dagad and others acquired here and there. He needed a ready resource that could be used as structural wood. He needed to make forms for the sandstone blocks. His eyes wandered back to the waterfall and the green plants growing at its base. *Perhaps...*he stood.

"Naurr! Grab an ax or something, and come with me!" He watched as Naurr shouted at the crew to keep working, then wandered over to Simon.

"Aye, boss."

"Those plants there. Do you know what they are?"

"Never seen the like in my own life."

"Let's cut one down."

Naurr nodded and trotted off toward the plants. Simon followed closely. Naurr carved a chunk out of the tree's base with a few swift, hard cracks from a hatchet. Then, using both hands, he bent it and broke it off at the bottom. "'Tis a tough timber, be it stringy, strong fiber. But we can be making use of it."

"Careful now. We don't want to overuse it, or we will be out of options quickly."

"I'll ensure the boys won't waste any of it. We can reuse much of it."

"All of our pavilions use this for framing; the little shelter you had set up has these bamboo poles for support," said a man's voice.

Simon turned and scowled as the eavesdropping First Otsoa stood behind the two of them. Simon had not heard him approach, and he was not wearing his golden armor again. He was middle-aged, in his forties, perhaps. His light brown eyes studied Simon. *They look almost sorrowful.*

"First Otsoa." Naurr nodded a greeting.

"Bamboo? Strange name," Simon retorted. "Well, someone could have told me before I had to go and figure it out for myself."

"It didn't take you long. Come, have some wine. Let us go back to the shade of your shelter." The First handed Simon a skin, sloshing and wet with perspiration.

He shrugged to himself and took a large gulp. It was warm but smooth and not too sweet. He let out a satisfied "T-aah." Then handed the skin to Naurr.

Naurr shouted at the crewmen, mockingly shaking the wineskin, then took several large swigs. The men threw their arms up angrily, stomped, and shouted insults at him. Laughing, he joined Simon and the First in the shade.

"You have a good crew. I am pleased," the First stated.

"They be all barks and no bite," Naurr said, still chuckling.

"Now tell me, Builder, what are your plans for the valley?"

"I am only doing this because I don't want to see any more innocent people dead at the hands of these *Daanav*, and if I can help with that, then so be it." Simon spread a rolled-up sheet out with both his hands. "So far, it's straightforward. Build a wall, a *very long wall*. It will be approximately thirty-five hundred paces long on each side of the valley and more than double that for the span across the base of the south hills."

"How long will it take?"

"With just my crew, years. One year, by Qav's luck—"

"That is too long," the First cut him off. "You were attacked a few days' ride from here; they will find us soon."

"I am no god; I cannot perform the impossible. I don't have enough manpower. Perhaps you should have prayed for salvation rather than capturing a lowly human engineer."

The First Otsoa calmed somewhat. "I apologize, but we need to make haste. Is there nothing we can do?"

"Perhaps then you will have to set forth a distraction. Lead the monsters on a wild desert wolf hunt, as they say."

The First tilted his head. "I've never heard such a saying. At any rate, that would cost us dearly; too many able-bodied people gone who could be here to defend if the Daanav were to attack Hasiera. I also fear it would not buy us much time."

"Then, as I said, you seek the impossible. Either way, we will focus on the side I arrived from, where we were attacked. We will start with a wall; it must be tall enough to stop the hulking demons from climbing over it. Perhaps, the height of two men." He paused to ponder for a moment. "Timing permit, to make the wall yet higher, a trench can be dug in front of it, and we can add to it from there. We will create a single choke point where a gate can be added if materials allow it. We need to mine and mix the resources to make the sandstone blocks for the wall." *I still need to figure out how to do that myself.* "It will take my men an extensive amount of time just to haul sand to the building site."

"Very well, Builder. I will assign four of my Otsoa and their people to your needs. They will meet you here at first light on the morrow, beginning with the Sixteenth, Mittal Gohra."

Simon's brows rose. He had not expected the people of the valley to help. *Perhaps we could pull this off.*

"What of Kiana?" Simon asked. "Should we dispatch a party in search of her?"

"The former Sixteenth Otsoa fought to keep our secret safe from the enemy," the First replied. "We honor her sacrifice and death in turn."

Simon frowned but said nothing. The First Otsoa, wineskin in hand, departed the two men's company.

Chapter Sixteen

STALK

Jude found himself in a small tavern off the main strip in Dagad. *Quite a busy little place.* It was a brewery of some sort. He forgot the name. Off-duty guards, townspeople, mercenaries, and a menagerie of people rolled dice and drank together. Jude found a spot near the end of the long bar and nodded to the barkeep to acknowledge his presence. Then he patiently waited until the barkeep made his way over after serving a few other patrons first.

"What'll it be?" asked the rotund, handlebar-mustachioed barkeep once he made his way to Jude.

"Ale," Jude answered.

"Yes!" the barkeep grunted enthusiastically. "We've got a select variety of ales here, good sir. We've got a smooth cream ale with a hint of chestnuts. Or try the light Xamidian spice lager. If that doesn't tickle your fancy, dare I say, try our strong goat milk stout of Vouri infamy."

Jude tilted his head quizzically. "I will endeavor to taste that spiced Xamidian brew. My thanks to you, sir."

With another grunt, the rotund man filled a foaming tankard and placed it at Jude's disposal. Then he went on to the next patron awaiting a beverage.

Jude would not ask the busy barkeep outright that he was looking for someone. Barkeeps rarely had time to talk at such a busy hour; they had a job, and Jude would not get in his way. He would find someone of more questionable caste, organized criminals who kept tabs on the town's happenings and inquire with them.

He scanned the room for a few heartbeats, nobody notably catching his eye. Most seemed to be average workers or thugs with nothing better to do for the rest of the day. A couple of uniformed town guards sat at a table in the corner, neither of which had a drink. *That is entirely fucking odd, quite odd indeed.*

After another tankard of aromatic ale and half an hour of minding his business, Jude noticed a man with long shoulder-length blond hair, also dressed in the guard's uniform but wearing heavier aspects of it, come hurriedly into the tavern. He ushered the two guardsmen out of their seats and mumbled something to one of them, who promptly took a flight of stairs up to a second level, where Jude assumed the tavern must have rooms for rent. Minutes later, the guard returned, followed by a well-dressed man in green robes and a bright red turban.

The bright headdress was like a beacon to all eyes in the room. Jude watched for a few minutes as the two men spoke. The man in green tried to inconspicuously hand the blonde guardsman a small pouch of something. *I need to talk to these men, the fucking scum of the Earste Lân.* The two did not appear to be criminals outwardly, yet they were the town's unsuspecting filth. Jude stood up, drained the last of his tankard, and strode to the table the men sat at. The town guards that were previously seated there stood awkwardly nearby, a look of confusion slowly crossing their faces. Confused that someone would approach them, they finally reacted and moved to block his way.

"Uh. Oi, stop," one of the guards said, red splotchy patches spreading across the skin on his face.

"I'm looking to make a purchase." Jude nodded past the guard toward the man in green.

"Oh, uh." The guard turned back around to look at the two seated individuals. "He's looking to make a purchase, he says."

"Shut it, you damned idiot," the armored man said. "Come over then." He waved Jude through.

Jude pulled a stool out from under the table and sat down, one man on each side of him.

"Who, fine sir, might we have the honor of dealing with?" the green-robed man said with a wheezy voice. His beady black eyes darted back and forth.

"My name is irrelevant; I am Magnus Huntsman of the Aerie." He pulled a black iron feather from his cloak and placed it on the table.

The two men's eyes widened as they reared back in surprise.

"We've done nothing wrong! Just a bit of grit dealing here and there," the man in green blurted in a panic.

Yes, fucking panic, you sleazy bastards.

"Huntsman, it's recorded. There are no magic users in Dagad. What brings you out here?" the guardsman asked, much more calmly than his counterpart.

"You're on the right track there," he looked the guardsmen up and down, trying to indicate rank. "Sergeant, is it?"

"Lieutenant. Lieutenant Ryon, sir."

"Lieutenant then. No magi may be recorded, but grit has magical properties, my new friend. It, therefore, is considered an illegal substance in the Aurulan kingdom, as I'm sure a member of the town constabulary is aware."

The two men tensed up again, eyes nervously darting between themselves and Jude.

"Alas, that is not my task this day," Jude reassured. *By Hettra's tits, I wish it were sometimes.*

They visibly relaxed again, both sighing heavily. Both men took a long, soothing drink from their cups.

"I'm looking for a Vouri girl, young, fire-red hair," Jude said.

The green man choked on his drink at hearing Jude's words. Red wine dripped from his chin as he spat, "That girl! A mage?"

"Well, this is fair news." Jude grinned at his good fortune. "And on my first try, too."

"The scamp departed town almost a week ago, perhaps five days hence. She is in the company of three hardened soldiers and, perhaps even more dangerous, her father. He is such a beast of a man. He left two of my largest, nastiest thugs ..." the grit merchant paused regretfully. "Let us just say, unable to partake in thuggery any time soon, one of them forevermore."

Ryon added to his friend's sentiment. "Aye, the man is terrifying, yet even worse, a woman who has bested him twice is with them. Curse that fucking cunt."

Fucks. I'm beginning to feel this may not be as simple as I thought. "Primus tell, where might they have departed to? Northwest? Back to the Vouri homeland?" He scowled. *Could they have made their way past the cemetery to the west? Did I just waste a day and a half coming here? Skrull's scrotum,* he swore inwardly. He felt his neck beginning to heat with frustration; he took a second to breathe deeply and calm himself, imagining steeping a cup of tea in his garden, sipping it gently, the faint aroma of orange rind and passionflower wafting up.

The men laughed. The man in green answered, "No, no, the fools have run off into the Burning Sea, most likely to their deaths."

"Good riddance, says I," Ryon said spitefully. "I pray to Skrull that the bitch dies slowly and thirsty for her lover's pox-ridden phallus."

"Come now," Jude said with a grin. "Show some compassion to your fellow men and women, else I report your dealings to the Aerie. Then you may have a different visitor in store."

Their faces paled at that.

"Come to think of it, how did you know about the red-haired girl in the first place?" Jude inquired, gradually moving his hands toward his daggers.

"Oh, you know," Ryon sputtered, "just seen her around town; not many red-haired individuals in Dagad, I'm afraid. Or Vouri, for that matter." He laughed nervously.

Jude narrowed his eyes at the two men.

"No signs of magic from this girl before a week or so ago?"

"We've never seen her use magic!" Ryon blurted. "Before or after."

"Before or after what?!" Jude demanded.

"Nothing!" the green man shouted and tried to jump to his feet. The two guards behind Jude made a clamor. Ryon followed suit, beginning to pull his blade from his sheath. They were halfway up when the tips of Jude's daggers flicked to their necks. They stopped in an awkward half-stand. The din of the tavern went silent.

"Touch me, and they both die," Jude said severely. "Get out of here, or you'll both soon follow them to Skrull's gate."

The two soldiers behind him slowly backed away, then turned and stumbled out of the tavern. He pushed the two men back into their seats, applying a little pressure with the blades. The familiar sounds of the tavern slowly returned to normal.

"You gave the girl *grit*, didn't you?" He pushed the tip slightly deeper into *Green's* neck, drawing a trickle of blood. The smell of piss soon came to Jude's nostrils. *Fucks.* He grimaced.

The man just nodded his head, eyes wide with fear.

"I should kill you now and spare more innocent children from becoming addicts. Not to mention whatever else you do to them."

"Sells them as slaves for those who can't purchase a simple good whore. Brings them back to Xamid and trades them off to the richest lords or ladies of the high estates," Ryon said. "Though, I doubt all they do is fuck them. Has nothing to do with me, though." Ryon put his hands up in a yielding fashion.

"Fucking bastard!" Green shouted at the lieutenant. "Gods take whoever paid for that fat cow of a whore that spawned you. You won't get another pinch of grit out of me!"

Jude smirked, "Well, well. I do believe both of you will be coming with me."

They looked back at him, once again in complete shock. He feared they would pass out at the seemingly endless surprises in store for them.

"I need provisions if I'm going to follow them out into this desert, so you will enlist me with the aid of a caravan."

They just stared at him. Then the man in green's eyes rolled back in his head, his face landing on the table, knocking his tankard, red wine pooling out around his face.

"Ha, he looks like a sleeping babe, eh, Ryon?" Jude chuckled. "Come now, Lieutenant, we must report to your superior about my commandeering your services."

Chapter Seventeen

COMPANION

"The dunes are telling me that many people have traveled this way. It feels like a flowing river, with many streams branching away from it. The one we are on now is vast and direct," Hata said, down on all fours, hands in the sand.

"This must be the most common path that caravans use to cross the Burning Sea. Truly, an invisible road," Saudett said, crouching beside her. "At some point, we will have to decide which of the lesser paths to follow, or we will find ourselves at Al'Jalif." The sun was beginning to set, and the party needed to stop and make camp soon.

Hata closed her eyes, breathing slowly. "It feels as if most of the paths that turn off are headed in that direction." She pushed herself up on her knees, still sunk into the sand, and pointed. Hata's finger aimed in a southerly direction. The sun was dipping to their right.

"Those are valuable tidings, Hata. Any routine convoy would not break off from the east or westward way; this must be the bandit's trail." She took Hata's hand, squeezed it, and looked her in the eyes. "You are exceptionally skilled at this, Hata."

Saudett pulled Hata to her feet. Hata nonchalantly pushed up against her, Saudett enjoying quite a face full of bosom along with it.

Hata grinned mischievously down at her, eyes twinkling with desire. "I'd like to try *you* this time."

Saudett flushed but smiled playfully in response. "Perhaps we can have some enjoyment of one another later, alone in our tent." She continued to smile as she watched

Hata's face light up. *I'll leave it at that.* The tension rippled through her. Turning away, she went to help the others begin making camp.

They set up tents, started a small fire, and ate dried meats and bread. Three of the casks Baal had brought were full of water; one contained the solid dark ale she had tasted in their home. Baal passed a mug of the dark liquid to each person.

"We change directions in the morning," Saudett said after a long drink. "Our gifted Sunstone has shown us the way." She gestured to Hata.

"Voitoon!" Brena and Baal cheered as one.

"This is great tidings, eh! So much so, says I, it be deserving another ale! Baal!" Taryn lifted her empty mug.

Baal smiled widely and pushed himself up with a grunt to pour the woman another drink.

Brena said something in Vouri, and Baal stopped in his tracks, then dejectedly, sat back down next to his wife with a huff.

"Eh, what did you say to the man?" Taryn interjected.

"Simply, we won't have any ale left for the morrow if you all keep drinking this night." Brena smiled coldly across at Taryn.

"Indeed, you do not want to get dehydrated either from overdrinking, especially with the day's heat coming on," Kaplan added.

Taryn eyed Kaplan. "How be it you can get dry from drinking? 'Tis the impossible, can't be true, eh?"

"Ever ponder why your mouth is so dry after a day of drinking too much, Taryn?" Saudett asked.

"From hurling up all the drink, of course. Nothing left to hydrate!"

"Even when you do not vomit? Unless, of course, you cannot handle your drink?" Kaplan returned to sipping his mug.

Taryn shot him a glare.

"Baal drink three casks before drunk," the big man added.

"Joo, my love, we know you can drink," Brena said.

"Brena mate, drink more than the great man Baal." He laughed sharply and loudly, echoing into the dimming evening air.

Brena smacked his arm as his deep, rumbling chuckles moved his shoulders up and down like a bear rubbing its back to a tree.

"It's true. In our village, I've seen my mother drink the longhouse full of Vouri warriors into a pile of snoring pigs. Isä included," Hata said, smiling.

"Hata!" Brena exclaimed earnestly, and then a smile finally broke through. "Oh my, it's true; men can't handle how a real woman can drink." She smacked both hands on her belly, grabbing some of the chubbiness that settled there from her seated position.

A chorus of laughter echoed through the small group of companions.

We are all getting along well, Saudett thought. Relief washed through her, brought forth by the comforting merriment. They had been in the desert now for perhaps a handful of days. They would need to find a water source within the next few days, though Baal's casks had bought them some time.

Saudett found herself smiling again. "Companions! I propose a toast! We have our course, all thanks to the fateful meeting of this family of Vouri. It was an unfortunate event, the grit, yet a blessing in disguise. Qav's luck awakened something latent in Hata's soul. I pray his luck holds on for the rest of this journey." She paused and studied the group for a moment. "To Hata!"

"To Hata!" they joined in.

"To Baal! For providing us with a mighty good beverage!" Taryn added.

"To Baal!"

"To Baal." Baal laughed, repeating the words cheerfully. "To Baal. Baal likes this."

Saudett returned to her thoughts; she felt self-centered using the Vasara family. They would gain a fair bit of gold from this venture, as she would enforce the Shepherds Eye to pay for time spent. At least they would not go home empty-handed, provided they managed to survive the whole business. *If we reach our destination.*

She had not thought that far ahead. Once they found where the nomads were hiding, what would she do? Perhaps wait until the dead of night and try to sneak in, seize Simon, and run like hell. That depended on where and how the nomads were living. Perhaps they could ambush a nomad patrol, take their garbs, and disguise themselves. Her head was reeling from both her thoughts and the ale. There were just too many unknowns at this time; *I've got to take my mind off it.*

Saudett stood. "Come, Hata, let's try out your new sand groundswell attack."

Hata leaped up energetically, grabbing Saudett's arm and huddling in close.

"Wouldn't hurt to be stretching the bones a bit, eh?" Taryn added as she stood and then bent over to touch her toes. She straightened up again and twisted back and forth before running in place for a few breaths, knees reaching up high to her chest. Once satisfied, she spoke, "Brena ma'ams, you training with me now."

"Alcohol before exertion? This ought to be pleasant," Brena answered sarcastically, cracking her neck back and forth. "Next time, we train first, then drink afterward, eh?"

Taryn's eyes danced with amusement at Brena's use of her slang.

The two women strode into the fading dusk, away from the camp. Soon, the clash of weapons and the grunts of exertion reached the ears of those left behind.

"Kaplan, fight Baal?" Baal asked longingly.

Kaplan shook his head. "I apologize, no. I can't read and ride at the same time. It gives me nausea. This is my only opportunity to do so." He pulled a weathered leather-clad book from the pack at his side. He then turned away from the fire and lay on his back to make use of its light.

Baal's head lowered akin to a sad puppy. "Bookman, no fun."

Saudett could not let the big oaf be left out.

Before she could say anything, though, Hata spoke up. "Isä, think you can brave my new-found wave of devastation?"

His head shot up; he bared his teeth menacingly. "Joo!" He trotted over to join them. Saudett almost thought the massive man was skipping with delight.

Some fifty paces from camp, they halted.

"Do you think you can replicate that act you performed that first day we set out into the wastes?" Saudett asked.

"I'll try," Hata answered.

"Alright, friend Baal." She gave him a hearty slap on the back. "See if you can take the wave head-on."

He trotted some ways away from the two, still baring his teeth in a half-grin, half-snarl.

"Isä, please close your lips, or you'll get a mouth full of sand," Hata shouted.

He stood, unchanging after the comment to close his mouth, waiting intently.

Saudett moved to get a view from the side to watch the two battle from a better angle. "Proceed, please, Hata," she called.

Hata planted her feet, then pulled her hands in slowly while closing them. A mound of sand began to form in front of her. It grew and grew until it was about waist-high to Hata. She shot her arms forward, her hands still clenched as if grasping hard onto a rope. The wave raced and grew taller, the sand curling inwards and crashing down at the wave's crest.

Baal roared and charged headlong at the coming wave. The two forces rushed toward each other. At the last second, Baal jumped headfirst, hands held down to his sides, bald head gleaming like a stone from a catapult. Saudett noticed Hata's hands open slightly as the wave was about to impact her father.

The bald head pierced through the wave of sand, and with a thud, Baal landed and skidded face-first into the ground. He had hit the tide near the top of the wave at its thinnest point.

Rather brilliant, Saudett thought.

Baal jumped to his feet; his face burned from the friction with the ground. Spitting filth from his mouth, he gave a sandy-toothed grin. "Voitoon!" he shouted, pounding a fist into his chest.

Saudett walked back over to the two. "I blame it on his sparkling waxed skull." She gave a wry smile. "So, what do you think you could do to try and make your wave less penetrable, Hata?"

"I could make it larger, higher, so he can't leap through the weak spot," Hata growled and clenched her fists, a determined scowl on her pleasant face. "Next time, I won't hold back," she mumbled.

Baal did not seem to notice; he was thumping one side of his head, trying to get sand out of his ears.

"I thought you might have gone easy on him," Saudett whispered. "It is alright to not want to hurt your loved ones, Hata. Come real danger, though; you must be unwavering and never hesitate. If you do, people will die."

Hata took a deep breath in through her nose, then nodded.

"Instead of making the wave bigger, you could try and change its shape. A wider wave may be good for multiple enemies, but you could make it deeper if it's just one, especially a big one like your father. An adversary must work much harder to get through, if at all. Or you could try multiple smaller ones, wave after wave. Even just enough to muddle with people's footing. That would allow one of us to follow up on your attack and catch them struggling."

Hata's eyes widen. "I never thought of that!" She grinned. "You are such a wise woman! Makes sense since you're so old and all."

Saudett snorted.

"I will try something else this time." Hata got to her knees and placed her palms together momentarily before she parted them and slapped them to the ground.

Baal began to sink before her eyes. A single pace. Two paces deep. Grunting and growling, he struggled to escape, clawing at the ground around him, but could not find purchase. A moment later, he was waist-deep in the sand. He let out a roar.

"That went well, Hata, very well indeed! You can stop," Saudett reassured.

Hata lifted her hands from the earth.

Baal grumbled while trying to free himself. Only his torso was visible, twisting from side to side. After a minute, he finally pulled himself out of the sand.

"Baal has sand in his arse," he grunted as he huffed his way back to camp, pulling his belt free from his trousers.

Saudett and Hata looked at each other for a second, then laughed. Hata ran to her. They embraced one another with relief and excitement. Spending all day riding and in the company of others led to anticipation of being alone together. It added to their excitement, building throughout the day.

Saudett kissed Hata tenderly, her head arching back, pushing herself onto her tiptoes to reach. Many minutes disappeared into affectionate touching and osculation, the enjoyment of being in one another's company washing over them.

"I want to return the favor. I want you to feel the same pleasure I did the other day," Hata said warmly.

"Well, perhaps it is time we take after your father and acquire some sand in our own fine arses," Saudett answered, a mischievous grin creeping across her face. Then, they both broke into giggles.

"Yes, please," Hata answered.

Saudett took her hand and led Hata further away, out of sight from the camp. "Tonight, let us relax and enjoy one another's company. It's been a long ride."

"Hmm, that does sound wonderful as well."

"The next time we encounter a bath, we can be more *energetic*."

Nodding enthusiastically, Hata began helping undress her. Saudett, in turn, removed Hata's long, simple beige linen skirt and dark green cotton blouse. They used their clothing as a makeshift pillow and blanket to try and remove themselves from contact with the sand. They settled beside one another, lying on their backs, huddled together, looking up at the stars and a bright crescent moon.

"A beautiful night," Saudett murmured.

"With a beautiful woman," Hata answered.

They turned to stare into each other's eyes...

...Saudett breathed heavily. Gasping, release washed through her.

Hata smiled warmly and kissed her tenderly, whispering in her ear. "Did you enjoy that?"

"Very much so, Hata."

"Stay with me."

"Mmm." Saudett turned, feeling weak. *Drained.* She snuggled into Hata's side. Saudett gently caressed her body and felt lust simmer inside her once more.

"By all the gods, Hata, you are marvelous," Saudett mumbled. "I cannot get enough of you!"

Hata laughed. "Likewise, *old lady.*" Then she paused. "Hmm, it is strange to call you that these days."

"Are you uncomfortable being with me, for I am older than you?"

"No."

Hata is two decades old; she is old enough to make decisions for herself, Saudett thought. Senior men married girls much younger than Hata in both Xamid and Aurulan.

"Just call me Saudett. It is better that way."

"Alright, *Saudett.* It is such an enchanting name."

"Thank you," Saudett exhaled in relief. "We best head back. We have another long day ahead of us; we should try to seek some rest."

They dressed, shaking the sand from their clothing and slowly pulling their garments on. Then, arm in arm, they strolled through the dark, back toward the warm glow of the firelight.

"Captain Dermont, was it?"

"It is." The poised soldier leaned forward on his desk, studying Jude readily. "What do you mean you must commandeer the services of my lieutenant here for an escort to Xamid?"

"Precisely that." Jude pulled the black iron feather from inside his jacket pocket. "Confidential Aerie business."

"What was your name and title again, sir?" Dermont asked.

"Magnus Huntsman is all you need to know."

"A mage hunter? In Dagad? Chasing after fairy tales, are we?"

"Indeed. Chasing fairy tales, Captain."

"This is completely mad, Captain!" Ryon shouted. "I'm needed here! Tell him!" Ryon wiped his brow with a greasy-looking handkerchief.

"Now, Ryon, this is far better than heading north to face this unknown threat in the mountains. You should be grateful!" Dermont's eyes seemed to sparkle with amusement.

"C-Captain, please," Ryon stuttered.

"Sergeant Proximo will replace you in leading our detachment to the Vouri lands."

Lieutenant Ryon slumped in his chair.

"Fucks, Ryon, you act as if still in adolescence, suckling your mother's tit," Jude mocked. Ryon shot him an icy glare. "Worry not; I will see that a bonus stipend is paid to you upon contract completion. Henceforth, you are under my command."

Ryon sat up at those words. "Stipend?"

"Indeed."

"It's settled then." Dermont nodded in conclusion.

Jude stood. "My thanks and Primus's favor to you, Captain Dermont. Come, Ryon, let us make haste. We have much to prepare."

Perhaps this corrupt fuck of a lieutenant will have an unfortunate accident in the desert.

Chapter Eighteen

SIXTEENTH

Kiana's blade scored a gash through the neck of the hound-like Daanav as it leaped for her atop her mount. Her horse whined and steered away as the limp body of the hound collided with their side, black blood spilling over Kiana's leg. She struggled to keep her horse under control as more Daanav circled.

Arrows whistled by, puncturing one such hound. It stumbled and slumped into the sand. Kiana's Pack was gaining the upper hand.

Then, the hulks joined the fray, crashing into their ranks at the base of the dune. The massive creatures hurtling down the slope crushed man and horse alike, clouds of blood and dust bursting from the impact. Men and women were torn to pieces, with no time to get out of the way of the assault.

Kiana jumped from her horse as its chest skewered on the long claws of a hulk as it crashed down the hill. She managed to stay on her feet, ducking under an incoming swipe of a clawing, blistered arm. Kiana followed through with a vertical slice at the beast's right leg, rolling to one side as the hulk fell to one knee, propping itself up with its thicker of the two arms. She heard a scream and glanced to her left as three hounds swarmed a warrior woman. *Tabbi.* Their jaws digging into the woman, they began a tug-of-war with her limbs. An arm was ripped from its socket. Tabbi's renewed shrieks pierced the air. She was very much alive while the Daanav tore her apart.

Kiana felt an impact on her shoulder and back. Pain shot through her. She was hurled forward but managed to catch herself and tumble into a roll. As she swung about, the kneeling hulk had lunged at her, and its head connected with her back. It was now crawling along on all fours toward her, giving a ghastly groan as it did. She stood tall. Spinning on her feet in one fluid motion, she twirled her sword around and above her head. With a flash, the blade came down on the creature's neck. Black blood gushed as the head rolled into the muck of the sand.

She took a breath to get her bearings. Her Pack was dwindling. They were being forced back into a defensive circle, surrounded. *Outnumbered.*

A man was crushed to death as two hulking Daanav collided with him.

Another man ducked under a leaping hound, deftly slicing open its belly at the exact moment, only to be impaled from behind on the spiked hand of one of the hulks.

Death screams surrounded Kiana, and gore sprayed upon her from all sides. One by one, her warriors were slaughtered.

She sidestepped a vertical swipe from another larger Daanav, her sword darting into its throat. Black liquid poured down her arm. The hulking mass collapsed forward toward her. She barely had time to pull her sword free and twist out of the path of the toppling corpse. At that exact moment, out of her peripheral, she glimpsed one of the hounds lunging at her, already in mid-air, claws out, maw open.

Not enough time. I can't get out of the way. She continued her twist, twirling enough to avoid taking the impact head-on. One of the long blades protruding from the creature's knee joint cut deep along her left arm as it soared past her. She responded by stabbing her sword into the creature's side, through ribs, and into vital organs. She kicked and twisted her blade free, and the demon crashed limply into the dirt, lying still.

Kiana was alone. Holding her wounded, dripping arm, exhausted. She gazed about her. A score or more of the abominations had encircled her. She fell to her knees to await the killing blow. Ready to accept her fate, knowing her people, the Hasieran were safe for now.

But the death blow never came. They stood there like grotesque phantoms, watching her, their glowing yellow eyes never blinking. Why had they not finished her? *Get it over with! What are you waiting for?* She fell to her side, defeated. "Kill me now!" she screamed aloud.

"Wolf," she heard a guttural voice hiss. "Show us the way—"

Light pierced her eyes as the sun crested the top of the dune at that very moment, cutting off the Daanav's words. Then, a chorus of screeches. They scattered, shrinking away from the daylight, fleeing back into the shadow of the dune. Some, too injured to retreat, struggled to crawl away, their skin steaming and bubbling. Eventually, the wounded creatures lay still, dissipating into puddles of black.

Even with the dust clouding her eyes, she saw the surviving fiend's barrel straight into the side of the dune and vanish. A few moments went by as the sun warmed her skin. She slowly gave in to the exhaustion, struggling to keep her eyes open. *I will just rest for a moment. Yes, just a moment.* As her eyes were about to close, she thought she saw two luminous yellow spots at the base of the dune, *watching her. Waiting for her.* Then, the darkness finally took her.

Kiana awoke at midday, the sun high in the sky. Her skin felt hot. Vultures had pecked her into wakefulness, pulling her out of her slumber. Praise to Hettra; it was not the vulture's larger counterpart, a Kahytul. Pushing herself to her feet, pain rippling through her body, she waved the birds away. They scattered and flapped onto other, not-so-lively corpses. She looked upon the devastation around her. The bodies were everywhere; severed limbs and innards were strewn about. The scavengers were ripping away flesh, filling their gullets.

Large gashes raked the corpses. Some of the bodies were left as mounds of gore, which had been crushed to a pulp. Mixed with viscera fluids, the sand had become a putrid mud. The black ooze pooled here and there among the fallen. Kiana felt a tingle up her spine. She turned to look at the base of the dune where the fiends had retreated. She thought she just caught a glimmer of yellow—or was it green? —peering back at her before it vanished again.

The Daanav want me to go home. To lead them back to the valley. To a massacre. She leaned over and picked up her sword, groaning in pain. Looking up, she surveyed the sky, determining her bearings. She then chose the opposite direction of the Valley of Hasiera and began to walk.

Hours passed as Kiana stumbled through the desert, clasping her left arm where the hound had maimed her. The blood had slowed but still dripped from the wound. She had fashioned a makeshift bandage out of some cloth from her robes, tying it around the gash, but it was soaked red. She needed water to clean the wound and fresh bandages and stitches. *I have nothing.* She must get as far away from Hasiera before night fell, and the creatures returned.

Her breathing became short and shallow as she panicked. She stopped in her tracks and sucked in a deep breath, and held it. Closing her eyes once more, she began to focus her mind's eye on the steps, the turns, the dance of the blade her mother had pressed into her from a young age. The countless hours of her mother hurtling small stones at her. Evade, deflect, or be struck. Those were her only options. Kiana suffered many bruises and cracked bones from those early days.

"Again!" She heard her mother's voice as if she were right before her. And then she was there in the memory.

"Again." A stone whistled past her head, inches from her ear.

To her great delight, Kiana had managed not to be struck that day.

"Acceptable." Her mother's words echoed in her mind.

Then, her mother pulled out a short bow and began the same exercise with rounded stone-tipped arrows. They moved twice as fast as the throwing stones. Kiana's delight turned quickly to despair.

Time stood still as the arrow was nocked and aimed steadily at her. The arrow flew. Kiana tried to swat it out of the air with her wooden training sword, but the blade caught the feather end of the shaft, causing the blunted arrowhead to deflect into her chin. She fell to her knees, hands clenched over her face, blood dripping faintly between her fingers, and pain burning.

"Stand up! Again!"

Kiana immediately felt a shiver crawl up her spine, coming out of her memory. The sensation of being watched swept over her. The fiends had left her alive. *I must lead them away.* She tried to gulp some saliva, but there was nothing; her mouth was dry. An image of Hasiera burning in blue flame flashed before her eyes. Kiana Ahmadi heard the screams of her people.

Hettra's mercy. Fear struck her, dread that her Pack's sacrifice had been in vain. As she trudged along, she thought about the encounter with the Daanav. *My entire Pack is dead.* There had been too many of the demons, and they had been overwhelmed and outmatched. It comforted her that Mittal had managed to whisk Simon away from the immediate danger.

That was our purpose, in the end, for the safety of Hasiera. With Qav's luck, they will have time to construct some sort of defense in the valley. She wished she could see Simon again, speak with him again. She had just started to grow fond of the handsome man and his charming way with words.

Her mind was in disarray: thoughts of her mother, the Daanav, and Simon. She felt pulled in every direction. *Am I hallucinating? Was it all a dream?* She prayed it was.

Both of her hands were limp and weak. As she walked on, she left in her wake a trail of blood droplets on her left side and a small trench from dragging her sword on her right. She struggled to pull her feet through the sand. If someone happened upon her trail, they would think some strange wounded beast was heaving itself along. Her clothing was all but gone, in tatters, and she had lost her scabbard in the fight. *I need to sleep, find some shade, and rest my eyes. Just need to stop thinking for a moment.*

They left me alive once; why not again? She headed for the base of the closest dune, out of the sun. She could see the shimmer of heat waves on the horizon, even though the sun was a quarter-way earthward on its descent into dusk. She stumbled and tripped on her feet as she reached the shade, falling face-first into the sand. Thirst and hunger scraped at her, but exhaustion crept over her like a woolen blanket. She tried to push herself up in vain but fell back into the sand. She rolled onto the wounded arm with little strength to apply pressure and hope to slow the blood loss. Then, too weak to feel anymore, she closed her eyes again.

Dreams of her mother's arduous training filled her sleep. Her resentment for the days upon days of pain her mother had inflicted on her while growing up still clung to Kiana. *This dream was no different.*

"Get up, daughter. It is time." Her mother had never failed to wake her before the sun had risen.

The young Kiana reluctantly listened. She hated her mother, and they were not on good terms. She had longed to be a normal child.

After the session with her mother, she ran to her father with tears in her eyes and embraced him. Though he was a warrior of commanding presence, she knew the soft, quiet man would comfort her. "Father, Father. Why does Mother punish me so?" she asked, gazing up into his violet, gold-flecked eyes.

"It is for your own good, Kiana, my little rose. It is in preparation for your survival in this harsh land. To be Otsoa, if you so wish."

"I understand," she trailed off, sniffling. "But, it hurts, Father."

He stroked her black hair gently. "I-I know." His voice cracked momentarily. "Please, my rose, try to bear with it. Hold the pain dear to you and keep it as cold as steel. Do not let the fire of anger cloud the dance. Then, like the hurricane's eye, make your mind at peace within...yet unleash a raging storm about you! Use it against your enemies."

Kiana's dream moved to a moment later that night when she overheard her father and mother speaking.

"Our child has no time to heal from her wounds before you inflict another upon her. I beg of you to give her a moment's rest. Time to recuperate."

Her mother gave a whispered hiss, "She needs to be strong so no *man* may reign over her." Her mother paused, then said, "Though, I accept. *For you,* the star of my night. For the freedom you gave me. Our daughter will have a day's rest after every second training day henceforth."

Having that day rest allowed Kiana to improve further and faster. Her muscles had time to heal, and her reflexes began to sharpen. Soon, the arrows stopped striking her. She was ever grateful to her father for fighting for her, for appealing to her mother.

She had always felt worse when he was the one disappointed in her. When she had been disobedient to them both. He would never shout or physically hurt her, but she knew when he was upset with her. She spent more time with her father, learning from him about leading people and delegating tasks and jobs to the different peoples of their Otsoak. From harvesting yams to shoveling shit, she learned how to run the encampment. Her parents, Otsoa of separate valley segments, were not often together. One or the other was typically away on patrol or a raid for supplies. Even if both were in the valley, their duty to their Otsoak, to their people, came first.

At intervals, she wished her parents had been farmers, tanners, or some simple profession in a peaceful Aurulan township or Xamidian coastal city. She used to love to hear stories about people from the outside world, people brought into the fold. About the shining cities on the ocean to the east, the vast forests and mountains to the west and north. Stories of beasts and powerful magi. She had been born in the valley; she knew nothing else.

However, as she aged, these thoughts of leaving the valley faded. She began to feel pride for her people and grew out of her childish dreams. Without her mother's oversight, she started training independently, taking it upon herself to become stronger. She cared for the people here, and she would protect them. She had set her sights on something else, striving to become Otsoa and surpass her mother. *One day, I will take up the name of First.*

Kiana opened her eyes. It was pitch-black and cold. Her body was shivering from the drop in temperature; night had come to the Burning Sea. She pushed herself to her hands and knees, wincing with pain in her left arm. It was too dark to tell if she was still bleeding.

She figured, since she did indeed wake up, she was not at risk of dying from blood loss. She should keep moving, keep making distance away from the valley. Using her sword as support, she struggled to her feet.

"Rest more, she-wolf!" a voice cackled in the darkness.

She spun about, shakily raising her sword in her good hand as best she could. She saw nothing—no glowing yellow eyes, no dark shapes looming over her.

"Truly, you should rest more, or you will be dead," a sibilant voice said matter-of-factly.

Then she saw small glowing green eyes blink open a slight distance away. *Just out of my sword reach,* she noted.

"Come closer, demon, and fall upon my blade," she growled weakly, stepping toward the glowing eyes.

"Not good, not good, stupid she-wolf. Chance to kill you while sleeping, I had." The luminous eyes bobbed around and blinked in front of her.

She stopped in her tracks; *it was true. If it wanted me dead, I would be.*

"Then, Primus tell, why haven't you done so?"

"Fill her mouth with sand; I could have. Or eat her feet off. Mmm, yes, *delicious* feet. Content with another lick, Kogs will be. Wait till stupid she-wolf is sleeping once again."

"Licking my feet!" She blanched, feeling suddenly nauseous.

"AHHH! It reads my thoughts!" The thing squealed, and the eyes disappeared into the dark.

"Wait!" she called out. "Come back." There was only silence in response.

After waiting a few minutes to see if the creature would emerge, she decided it would be best to keep moving. Traveling at night had its benefits. For one, it was frigid and less dehydrating than walking in the hot sun all day. She would find shade in the morning and rest once again. After another few days' walk, she should come to a water source where they had previously made camp on the road.

"Where is it! Stupid she-wolf!" she heard a cry some distance away, "Can't lose the human. Masters will not be pleased!"

She heard a pattering sound on the sand in her wake. *This thing was sent to follow me.* Ignoring it, she continued forward.

"Sneaky, she-wolf thinks it can escape the great, magnificent Kogs!"

"You realize you speak your thoughts aloud, demon?"

"Blasphemy! It uses sorcery to penetrate me! It's a witch! A witch, she-wolf demon. If anyone is a demon, it is this evil human female."

She stopped walking. She felt something bump into her lower legs. Another squeal. She slowly turned around. She saw a small, lizard-like humanoid creature with a simple, tattered shirt made of some reed or fibrous plant at her feet. It cowered, holding its hands over its eyes.

After months of battle against the Daanav, a talking lizard did not surprise her much. *Was it trying to be invisible in the dark?* She bent and poked it gently on the top of the head, brushing a wavy tuft of red fur cresting its head in a mohawk. At her touch, it jumped back.

"Cursed! It can see me even when I have cast my greatest invisibility spell!"

I'll play along. "Who goes there? I thought I felt something."

A clicking sigh of relief came from Kogs. She watched it wringing its small clawed hands together mischievously. He began to cackle softly. "Kogs is too great for the likes of the witch-demon, she-wolf pup."

"Must have been the wind," she said to the air about her. She turned and continued walking. Kogs followed behind her, continuing to talk to himself and belittle her. Keeping the act up, she pretended he was not present, which led to her learning a few things about the creature named Kogs.

"The masters take poor Kogs away from his prosperous, growing grub farm. Very rich was Kogs back home. Ah yes, Kogs miss the smell of the fat blood flies in the morning; it is such a tasty breakfast. Kogs' handsome mate, Gaks, always enjoyed fishing in the river every morning near our farm. Oh, what has become of my Gaks? Kogs prays to the masters he is unharmed. Little Avendicaticarius too."

His masters had taken him from his home. Where that home was located, she could not quite figure out.

"Kogs is tasked to follow the stupid witch-demon-she-wolf pup. Follow her back to others of her kind. Tell the masters, and Kogs can go home to his Gaks, they say. Yes, yes, soon Kogs will be home with his beloved Gaks. After the master's murder, all the witch-demon-she-wolf pup's village and find where the deep gate is."

"The deep gate?" Kiana finally spoke, keeping her tone naturally nonchalant.

"It is the way back home. Well, not Kogs's home, the masters' home. They took Kogs from his home somewhere else, and Kogs must go through the masters' home to get there. Kogs thinks. Kogs not sure." Kogs did not seem to notice that he had responded to her question.

"I pity you, Kogs. Far from home, away from your mate—it must be terrible."

She heard wet sobbing behind her. "I miss my Gaks," Kogs sniffed. "And my grubs."

She stopped and turned around again. The little lizard man rubbed his eyes, not watching where he was walking. *Poor thing,* she thought. She crouched down in front of it. "There, there. Did you want me to help you get home, Kogs? Get home to your Gaks?" She reached out and patted the creature's head.

It looked up at her, big reptilian eyes watering, and nodded repeatedly.

Perhaps I should slide my blade across its throat and eat it. Yet already, Kiana had learned more about her enemy in an hour than in many months of fighting them. Also, one couldn't help but feel empathetic for the thing, being forced here against its will, just another victim of these strange creatures, the Daanav.

"All right, Kogs, I'll get you home."

"What a kind *stupid* witch-demon, she-wolf pup." Kogs paused, angling his head in surprise. "CURSED! It has cursed me. Poor wretched Kogs! Sorcery and testicles! CURSED!"

Kiana watched the moon slowly creep through the sky as she carried on, as Kogs slung vulgarities in her wake.

Chapter Nineteen

FORMULATE

Simon yawned and stretched. Developing the right mixture for the sandstone blocks took a day and a half. A day and a half of no sleep at all. Twenty percent sand. Thirty percent was a silver-tinge ground-up shale. Twenty percent random crushed stone and the remaining thirty percent water.

"Skrull's boiled balls," Simon cursed as the mixture seeped through the bamboo form. "Too much damn water! Get another load!" he shouted at his men. "Let's try it again!"

His men, also quite fed up, having attempted this process numerous times over the last day, grumbled and retorted.

"Give it a rest, ya!" one of his men retorted irately. "Let's have a break? Ya, boss?"

"We are this close, Ilan." Simon held his fingers up in a pinching motion. "We are going to succeed this time; I know it."

"You can succeed by sittin' your pretty little arse down on my lap, ya." Ilan grinned wide at him, revealing a dark gap where a tooth should have been. Laughter rippled through the other men.

By the Primus's teachings, only a man and a woman could partake of one another. Dagad was far from the capital of Aurulan, so many did not bother to follow these teachings. *Myself included. Really, what kind of all-powerful being preaches to love all beings yet orders Skrull to take any sinner to hell who disobeys His dogma?* Simon's mother, Teresa, was a devoted follower of the Primus and would take Simon to the temple twice weekly, saying the same prayers monotonously, 'I accept the Primus as the creator of all beings.' Simon would say the word and act the follower, only to keep his mother happy. *I faked it until her deathbed to not break her poor heart.* Not long before his mother's passing, he knew of his attraction to both men and women. *Yet another secret kept from dear Mother.*

"If we get this damned mixture right now, I swear on my life. I will sit on your pretty little prick," Simon finally answered, realizing his mind had sidetracked into the realm of theology.

Religions aside, many of his workers were openly engaged with those of the same gender as themselves. He often caught them heckling passing guardsmen or younger errand boys who strayed too close to their work sites. For the most part, they would direct their fervor at *Simon.* Even the men with wives or other women as their only partners would join the jeering.

Ilan raised his eyebrows. "Little? I'll show you little, ya!" Ilan turned to the workmen, "Well, you heard him, boys? Let's get this damned block done, else I'll lose my chance at sir boss's delicate arse, ya?" He stretched, rubbing a hand over his stubbly head of chestnut hair.

Simon eyed the man with amusement. Then, with a sigh, he returned to his makeshift headquarters. Once they had figured the mixture out, there was still a plethora of work to do. *Ilan would have to wait.* Though Simon didn't think ill of the idea, he could use a bit of pleasure in this fool's pit of an undertaking tasked upon him.

Back to it, he thought. Now, there was the organization of teams: a group to mine the rock out of the cliffside, another to crush it into stones and dust, and more to haul the sand, crushed stone, shale, and water to the building site. Instead of creating the sandstone blocks and moving them to the wall, Simon had built forms where the wall would be placed. Using bamboo strips cut vertically down the center of the shoots, they tied them together to create crude forms for the mixture, leaving the blocks with many crescent-shaped divots along the outer sides. He also added uncut lengths of bamboo inside the form as extra reinforcement for the blocks. Roughly, the blocks were a man's length if he lay beside it, by an arm's length deep and high. Mixing the four parts in a few large clay urns and pouring them into the forms was time-consuming, as one full pot did about a quarter of the mass of the block.

The four Otsoa had presented themselves to Simon the day after the First had left him to his work. The Fourth Otsoa had arrived early; he was an elderly man with a long gray beard and a mustache curled up slightly at each point. The single silver ring tied to the base of his beard stopped the long hair from blowing up into the man's face. Slouched somewhat over, the man leaned on a tall bamboo staff as he walked.

He arrived first and hobbled over to Simon's makeshift headquarters.

"Good day, Builder," the man greeted him cheerfully. "You certainly have your work cut out for you."

"Good day to you as well," Simon said, smiling. *Thank Hettra for a civilized individual,* he thought. "This will be the swiftest wall ever built, says I, Simon Meridio of Meridio Enterprises. Who am I pleased to make an acquaintance on this pleasant day?"

"Gaspar Haytham, Fourth Otsoa. Here to serve. What would you have my people do?"

"There will be a variety of laboring positions that need filling. I fathom we can divide the burdens up by Otsoa. Since you are the first to arrive, you have the pick of the piglets, as they say."

"Who says this?"

"Never mind that. We need miners, sand gatherers, haulers, and mixers. We will be going day and night, so you must provide me with enough people to cover that time frame. Can you provide ten fresh bodies every four hours?"

"Indeed, I will have your able-bodied people gather and cart sand in from the dunes, whom I can rotate out when needed," the old man answered.

"My thanks to you and your people, Fourth Otsoa. I leave the task in your capable hands."

"Please, call me Gaspar, if you will." He smiled amiably. Then he nodded and began inspecting Simon's workers, mining the rock face and chopping bamboo shoots.

Simon watched Gaspar mingle with the men, going to each individual and speaking with them one-on-one. *Getting to know the boys, was he?* Then, a sudden impact on his upper back sent Simon sprawling forward onto his drawing table, knocking some papers off.

"Sheep slave! Where is your lover? The camel."

Mittal Gohra, wonderful. Simon figured the man was roughly the same age as himself. Turning to greet him, Simon put on a playful grin. "He is having a nap by the stream bed." He pointed and saw Marigold's head among the bamboo shoots, awake and chewing on something. "Ahem, well, he was napping."

Mittal hooted. He had a neatly trimmed mustache of short black hair on his upper lip. He slapped Simon's back again.

Gods. He must be in high spirits after his promotion to Sixteenth. Taking the unfortunate Kiana's spot. "Mittal Gohra," Simon said.

Mittal shot him a glare. Pale scars marked the man's face and forearms through his tan Xamidian heritage. "That is Sixteenth Otsoa to you. *Slave.*"

"Of course," Simon cleared his throat, bowing his head slightly. "And who are these other two that accompany you, Sixteenth Otsoa?" He gestured to the two silent individuals standing patiently behind Mittal.

With a grunt, Mittal launched into an introduction. "Behold my elders, the Seventh, Howler Thien, and the Thirteenth Otsoa, Rojas the Keen."

Simon studied the two Otsoa, particularly the Thirteenth, *Kiana's father.* The man wore baggy gray robes; his face and head were covered in wraps. Only his violet, gold-flecked eyes met Simon's own, giving him a sense of unease. *The same eyes as his daughter.*

He altered his focus to the other figure, an oddly crouched individual with tight-fitting brown-and-tan clothing and tufts of fur poking through parts of their clothing. Simon identified a woman's breasts and hips, yet their face was covered in a full-grown beard that ran down their sinewy neck, limbs, and back, making them almost beast-like. There was an impressive bulge in their leather shorts. They gave a broad smile, exhibiting yellow pointed teeth, as they noticed Simon taking them in.

Unable to hide his surprise, Simon stuttered the last feature he had taken in, "Did you sharpen your teeth?"

The next thing he knew, Thien had dashed toward him, mouth wide as if to tear out his jugular vein. They stopped a hair's length from his neck; Simon stood frozen.

A wicked fanged smile, possibly a snarl, spread across Thien's canine-like face. Thien closed their mouth and gave Simon a few sniffs. "I smell *fear*, Builder," they hissed through their teeth.

Simon tried to hold in his trembling, but his curiosity overcame him. "But how is this possible? Are you half-beast? Or have you made yourself look like this?"

Thien stood up, out of their crouching position. They were two heads taller than Simon when at full height. "I smell your eagerness for knowledge overpowering your fear." They smiled down at him, fangs dripping slightly with saliva. "There is a story of why we are like this, but I will only say we were born this way. For now. If you prove yourself worthy of Hasiera, perhaps I will tell you that tale."

Simon nodded his head repeatedly. "Thank you, Thien, you are truly fascinating," he said eagerly, eyes slowly slipping down their body, hovering on some fantasized regions.

Thien smiled wryly at Simon's unhidden ogling, then stepped back a few paces.

"What number Otsoa are you again, Thien?" Simon said, shaking his head. *Hettra's tits,* he thought, *why is it that if I'm not thinking about work, the first thing that comes to mind is sex. Is there not more to life? Am I nothing but a deviant?* His wife, Saudett, was akin to him in this; he even struggled to keep up with her libido. Another reason for their *expanded* relationship.

"I am Seventh."

"What do you need from us, slave?" Mittal interjected. "Can you get to the point?"

"Ah yes, well, if you three had been on time, you could have fought over the favored job of farming sand, but that has fallen into the hands of the lovely Fourth." He gestured over to his men working, old man Gaspar still chatting with them. Simon frowned; the men had gathered around Gaspar and seemed to be listening to him speak. He contemplated shouting at them to get back to work but thought he'd rather stay on the Fourth's good side.

"What other tasks do you have for us?" Thien hissed.

"Mining the cliff and crushing the stone from it. Hauling the crushed stone and water to the building site. Or mixing and pouring an exact amount of the sand, stone, and water into forms to create the wall material—"

Mittal cut him off mid-sentence once more. "My Otsoak will take on the task of mining."

Thien and Simon looked at Rojas, who stood with arms crossed, making no move to speak. They looked back at each other.

Thien shrugged. "And I the hauling."

Simon nodded in agreement. Then he looked back to Rojas, those flecks of gold in his violet eyes. Simon's thoughts trailed back to Kiana. Her dancing blade, her mischievous and comforting aura. *Her body*—hidden within robes.

"Mixing," a low, earnest voice touched Simon's ears.

Skrull's balls, Simon, focus! "Thank you, Rojas, for your people have taken on the most difficult of the four tasks. But with all your help, we will make the Valley of Hasiera an impenetrable fortress for generations to come."

"A fair speech, boss! Touched my heart, it did."

"Ha, so noble he is, that Simon, ya."

"I be tearing to my eyes, says I."

His workmen had crept up, now paces behind him, laughing at this heart-wrenching moment.

"Get back to work, you idiots!" Simon yelled. "Naurr! By Skrull's hell, Naurr! Where is that blasted man? Show these fools some manners."

"Like you showed your camel some manners last night, eh, boss?!" said one of his crew.

Simon picked up his stool and threw it at the hagglers. It bounced a few feet harmlessly before them, and they laughed and scattered back to their workplaces.

He turned back to the Otsoa, shrugging. "It is hard to find good help in this day and age."

Chapter Twenty

HYPOCRITE

"Fucks to the desert," Jude cursed under his breath. "Fucks to the heat. Fucks to the fucking sand. And fucks to my chaffed, sweaty arse!"

Nearly a week into the wasteland, Jude thought of reporting the girl dead. He would only be paid half his standard fee, but it might be worth it at this rate.

"Why in Skrull's fucking name is this little girl walking across this bloody hellscape anyways?!" he exclaimed to no one.

"As I said, the nomads attacked Dagad and took a handful of peasant laborers and materials. Nothing of value. That bitch's husband was one of the lucky bastards who got nabbed. Now she's gone after him to die by his side. The red-haired girl's family and the bitch must have made some sort of deal to go after him," Ryon spat in disgust. He was riding on Jude's right-hand side, fumbling in his saddlebag. "This is a fool's quest," Ryon continued as he retrieved a vial of black powder. "The captain should have demoted her for insubordination rather than promote her."

Jude watched as the man snorted a powder pinch and continued droning on. Jude pushed Ryon's vocalization out of his mind. *Greens must have hooked Ryon on grit as well.* He sat silently as they trotted along.

The caravan the two crooks had come up with on such short notice was of adequate size. It seemed Zalias Ershya, the underhanded green-clad merchant, or "Greens," as Jude liked to call him, was on the brink of leaving when Jude had accosted him. A few carriages had simple iron cages covered in thin linen sheets. Zalias was not overtly trying to hide the prisoners inside; he had to water and feed them regularly to not let his "goods" die off. *I imagine once the caravan approaches a city, the bastard would drug up the captives with more grit to keep them quiet and put a heavier covering over the cages. At least, that is what I would do.*

Last night's stop for the evening had left the caravan guards antsy. Many looked at the cages or strode past to peek through the sheets. Jude imagined they would typically *use* their prisoners on the trip. Greens must be keeping them at bay because Jude had threatened to report him. *It honestly makes me fucking sick to think about these helpless people. Perhaps I should extort this Zalias Ershya, "honorable merchant," once this is done. If I threaten to report him, should he not send me a portion of his monthly earnings. On the other hand, I could just kill Greens for being a despicable stain on the Earste Lân.*

"Ha," Jude muttered. "Quite the hypocrite that would make me. The poor young magi I capture, never to see their families again. Who are not only used for their magical competencies. The sleazy bastard Ebras Corb must use each to his cock's content. At least I don't have to see it, out of sight or mind, as it were." He grumbled under his breath, "The fucks to Corb. The fucks to Greens. The fucks to fucking Ryon and this fucking desert." He grimaced bitterly. *I will stick a dagger in Ryon's throat if he does not shut the hell up about his hatred for this woman of his.*

Although...Jude's plan to find the bandits might happen to kill two birds with one stone. He planned to light a massive fire that would cause a smoke signal for all to see and bring the Skrull-fucking bandits to him.

He hated low-life scum: these nomads, Greens, Ryon, and the like. Most of all, he hated himself. *The fucking bastard I am.* The Lan was infested with them, yet he was part of it. He dreamt of sitting in his garden in Nidhaut, listening to the bird song, minding his own business, and drinking some of his own unique mix of tea. Thistle, nutmeg, anise, some ginger, and a few other bits and pieces, all grown in his modest garden. *Perfection.* Tossing in a bit of this and that, whatever he felt for at the moment, it never turned out the same with each brew. He hummed to himself, remembering the pleasure of it all. *Ah, to be home, at peace, with nothing to worry about.*

"You're suddenly in a good mood, Huntsman. What's this humming about?" a nasal voice asked to his left.

His mood instantly fell once more. Jude glared at Greens, which made Greens flinch back in his saddle, his jewelry jingling about him. "None of your damned business, you damned pock wart on Skrull's scrotum."

"No need for profanities, Huntsman. I was just curious how you plan to find your little lost child in these gods-forsaken lands." Greens waved a hand, displaying the vast sea of sand.

"Give it a few more days, and you will see," Jude said.

From his right side came Ryon's voice. "Care to enlighten us on your master plan?"

"Nay."

From his left: "Do you plan on doing circles in the dust for months until my stock is nothing more than bare bones?"

"*Your stock?*" Jude bent a brow at the brightly dressed merchant.

Greens coughed nervously.

As of yet, Jude hadn't mentioned the caged captives.

"Don't act the fool, Huntsman." Ryon came to Zalias Ershya's defense. "You are not so blind. If anything, you should acknowledge it so the rest of us can get our fuckin' pricks wet."

Jude's closed fist collided with Ryon's face, sending him toppling head over heels backward off his horse and landing with a crash of his heavy armor. He groaned and pushed himself up as the two stopped their mounts and looked down on the man.

"Gods! Fucks!" Ryon spat as he kneeled in the sand, holding his nose and mouth. Jude could see blood trickling down the man's hands.

"I may take innocent young people away from their loved ones, but I won't abuse a helpless child," Jude spat, beating down the rage inside at his own hypocrisy.

"They are not *all* children," Greens whispered.

Jude turned and heard a yelp as Greens spurred his horse on and out of his reach. He sighed heavily and kicked his horse into a slow trot to continue with the caravan train, leaving Ryon in the dust. One of the carts with the covered cages had caught up to him, a slight murmuring from within. He felt his anger build up, took a deep breath, and found himself back in his garden, sipping tea. *Mmmm, the bliss.*

CHAPTER TWENTY-ONE

STRIFE

Two weeks slipped away as Saudett and company trudged through the desert, Hata guiding them onward, following her sense of where people had traversed the sands beforehand. Still, the going was slow. Dusk was nearing as they approached a rocky outcropping.

"Might be some water here. Either way, a good place to spend the night," Kaplan stated as he swung down from his mount and walked his horse the rest of the way toward a rock-strewn crag.

The others followed suit and dismounted. The horses whined and pulled back against their reins. The light dimmed as they entered the area, and a horrid smell reached them. Surveying the area more closely, they could make out mounds of rotting flesh, corpses of horses, and people. Flies buzzed about in droves.

Saudett watched Kaplan motion them to stop. He slowly made his way onward alone, pausing, lifting his foot like he had stepped on something. Crouching, he put his fingers to the ground and touched it, bringing the two fingers back up to study it.

"What is it?" Saudett called.

"Some sort of tar, which has been covered in a layer of sand; hence why I didn't notice it at first," Kaplan pondered aloud while waving the rest of the troop forward.

There didn't seem to be any immediate danger at present. Saudett walked up to Kaplan's side to examine the strange substance. "Never seen anything like it before. Like pine root tar, but more visceral?"

"I feel something strange in the sands," Hata cried urgently. "It's coming this way!"

"Quick! Move the horses into the gorge! Keep them together. We don't want them running off. Hata, where is it coming from?"

"That direction!" Hata pointed back to the direction they had come but at a slight diagonal. "It does not feel like horses!"

"Form a line and follow up on Hata's attack." Saudett barked. "Let's see what we're up against!"

Baal hefted two massive pickaxes in each hand, growling in anticipation. The others brandished their weapons.

Kaplan pulled a handful of arrows from his quiver and stuck them in the ground before him, notching one, surveying the growing darkness.

Saudett approached Hata and whispered, "Just like we practiced, Hata. This is the *real* thing. Do not hesitate." She gave her a quick embrace, then moved to join Taryn in a two-man phalanx, spears at the ready.

Brena nodded to her daughter and rapped sword against shield at the ready, looking over to Hata. The two spear women were flanked on each side by Brena and Baal; Hata stood in the center of the formation, with Kaplan slightly back and to their left.

Silence fell.

Let's have it, then. Saudett steeled her resolve.

Teras protect us. Hata breathed as the silence held. *What is happening?*

Then, a screech pierced the haze, and three lumbering figures charged toward them out of the gloom. Two smaller creatures dashed around to each side of the group.

Hata began to hyperventilate.

"Baal, Brena, the flanks!" Saudett ordered. "Hata, the most enormous wave you can muster for the three in the middle. Slow them down!"

An arrow whistled past, striking one of the giant beasts in the chest. It screamed and slowed momentarily before renewing its charge. Then, another arrow pierced its leg. A *hiss* and a *thud* as another caught it in the side of the neck. With a gurgling scream, the hulking creature fell behind the other two.

Hata gathered her will and summoned as much sand as possible before her friends. A massive wall surged upward as she strained, teeth clenched. The barrier of sand blocked the group's vision of the three abominations. Then, with a scream, she unleashed the wave.

"Now!" Saudett shouted as the group sprinted after the wave in a counterattack.

The hound-like creatures met Baal and Brena first, simultaneously, ahead of the hulks.

The creature lunged up at Brena to meet her, and she charged through, lifting her shield to receive the impact. Its clawed fore-feat hung onto the edge of her shield as she hefted it and slammed the shield and creature into the ground. Brena swiftly pierced her sword into its belly in a fluid motion as it landed. She held it down with her shield arm, then twisted the blade free and stabbed it repeatedly.

The creature attacking Baal hesitated. Seemingly intimidated by Baal's size, it did not try to lunge at the massive man but instead chose to bite and swipe at his legs. Baal roared in frustration as the hound dashed in and out. Staying out of his reach, though the creature did not make a scratch on the man. Then it ran in again, and Baal swung down in a rage to meet it. His pickaxes sunk deep into the rock-strewn earth. As Baal grunted and struggled to free his weapons, the creature took the opportunity to sink its teeth into Baal's calf. It hung on tight with its jaws.

Baal began to laugh. He stopped trying to remove his pickaxes from the ground, grasped the monster's head between his hands, and *squeezed*. Its eyes bulged, its grip on him loosening. Then, with a sickly pop, Baal crunched the creature's head in his hands, brains and black matter mushing through his fingers.

Everything felt like it was happening in the same instance. Two of the hulks did not stumble, breaking through Hata's wave of sand like a gust of wind. The third, who had taken three of Kaplan's arrows, seemed to have halted and did not emerge from the dust from the wave's explosion.

Her head spinning with the chaos, Hata could hardly follow what was happening. She couldn't decide who she should help. *I am useless,* she thought. In a frozen state, Hata watched a hulk lunge toward Saudett with an overhead swing from its massive arm. Saudett nimbly sidestepped and thrust her spear into the bloated chest. It roared grotesquely and swiped its other, clawed hand out at her. She danced back, and an arrow struck the creature in the shoulder. It reeled in pain. Saudett dashed in, leaping high, her spear piercing through and out the back of the massive monster's grotesque neck. Using her descent from the leap, Saudett pulled her spear free with a spin, black blood showering her as she did so. The creature tilted unsteadily, then fell onto its back.

Only one left, Hata breathed in relief.

Taryn moved in. Her long pike gave the woman plenty of space out of the last creature's reach. She was slowly backing up and circling the abomination. After each missed swipe, the hulk roared in frustration, and Taryn would counter and stab into its boiling flesh, never seeming to make a killing blow. *Was Taryn toying with it?* With countless wounds bleeding black, dripping into the sand, the creature's assault slowed. Taryn had circled back to where the wave had struck the three hulks.

"Enough of this then," Taryn shouted, a cocky grin on her face while she moved in to deliver the final blow.

They all seemed to be handling themselves. Saudett, Brena, and Baal had dispatched their foes, leaving only Taryn. The group all quickly turned, moving to aid the Tulu woman. Hata relaxed.

Then she saw a silhouette in the dust behind Taryn, the dust *her* wave had created.

"TARYN!" Hata cried.

In that same instance, huge claws ripped through Taryn's midsection, her legs crumpling as her torso tumbled through the air, blood spraying, gore, guts, intestines stringing out, hands still clutching the upper half of her spear that had likewise been severed.

Hata screamed in rage as the creature lumbered out of the dust. Her fear was overcome by guilt and hatred. *THIS IS MY FAULT!* Hata walked toward the two beasts, hand outstretched, thousands of sand marbles floating around her. They whistled out from her as she advanced, still screaming. Her vision blurred.

Saudett watched in awe and terror as Hata ripped the two remaining hulks into pieces, the sand projectiles moving so fast her eyes could not follow. They punched through flesh and bone, bursting in a black mist out the other side, with hundreds of small detonations. The first creature fell, in tatters, to the onslaught and began dissipating into the dirt. Hata put her hands together, the ground shook, and a massive rock spike drove up from the earth before her, screwing the last hulk into the air on a diagonal stalagmite.

It hung in limbo for a moment before it began to deliquesce, the black clumps of flesh falling and rolling down the stone.

Chapter Twenty-Two

SUBSISTENCE

"We're almost home," Kiana murmured aloud so Kogs could hear her.

"Good, good, yes." Kogs cackled to himself. "Soon, the masters will slaughter the stupid witch-demon-she-wolf pups, evil peoples."

This had been going on for a few days now. Kiana would reassure the little lizard that they were almost there, and he would cheerfully plot her people's demise. Her wound had stopped bleeding but ached excruciatingly. Luckily, she had found some water a couple nights after the attack and recuperated a bit, though she was now starving, and contemplated seeing what Kogs tasted like. Her stomach grumbled at the thought.

"A monster within you?" Kogs asked. "Witch-demon-she-wolf pup?"

"We may not make it home at this rate. I haven't eaten a thing in days."

"If it doesn't go home, Kogs will be punished. They will hurt my Gaks!" he exclaimed. He began rummaging in his small pockets, pulling out some beetles and bugs. He held them up to her in one hand. "Here, take these. I was saving for later. They are the sweet kind. Very good."

She eyed the bugs dubiously but figured something in her stomach was better than nothing. She plucked a beetle between her fingers, closed her eyes, and popped it into her mouth. With a crunch, the innards of the beetle squished onto her tongue. She gagged as she slowly chewed the beetle; it tasted bitter and off. Solid pieces of the insect's carapace were getting caught between her teeth. She swallowed the remainder. She took what was left of Kogs's offering and downed them as quickly as possible, trying as she might to not chew.

Kogs nodded in satisfaction. "I will find more; we will feast!" With that, he scurried off.

She paused but didn't move to stop him as she sat cross-legged in the sand and closed her eyes. *This would be a chance to rest.*

Pain shot up her hand; the wooden sword fell from her grip. She was in another dream, a memory from her past.

"Pick it up."

"Can we not stop for a bit?" She looked down at both hands, blistered and bleeding through the linen wraps.

"Pick it up."

"Mother, please." The pain burned into her shoulder where her mother's wooden sword stung into her, tears welling up. She grabbed her sword, jumped to her feet, and charged her mother, screaming. Disregarding the stances and the steps, she swung in a blind rage. Breaking the dance, she attacked and hit nothing.

Another smack to her hand, and her sword went soaring once more.

"Your anger will get you killed one day..." her mother's voice faded.

"I hate you!"

Kiana opened her eyes to find many bugs in her lap, most still moving. Scorpions with their tails and pinchers ripped off, beetles, and larvae. A variety of other types of insects. *Who would have known the desert was so full of them?* Kogs sat before her, keeping the critters from escaping into the sand. The ones Kogs had given her before had at least been dead. *These are still squirming.*

"Many thanks to you, Kogs. This will give me the energy to complete the journey home. Then, in turn, we can focus on getting you home."

"A simple, simple task for grub farmer Kogs. Many bugs; just must know where to look." He paused, head tilting back and forth. "How will it get Kogs home?"

"First, I'll start by killing every last one of your masters."

"Haha!" He cackled. "The stupid witch-demon, she-wolf pup has gone mad; it has. There are thousands of masters! They will slay or steal everyone in this land." He paused again, head dropping sorrowfully. "Just the same as Kogs's home."

"Not in this land. Even if my people fail, others will fight. The Earste Lân is full of kingdoms, kingdoms thriving with peoples. Many people, from many faraway countries."

"Why doesn't it ask these kingdoms for help?"

She blinked. *Why didn't we ask the kingdoms for help? Because we are strangers, outcasts, bandits, thieves, and murderers. That's all the realms would see.*

"They will not come until the enemy is at their gates. Most humans care only about themselves; we offer aid if we get something in return. Few are genuinely compassionate."

"Ah, like how Kogs only cares for his Gaks and his farm. Like this?"

"Aye, we are the same."

Kogs bobbed his lizard head in agreement. "Come now, demon-she-wolf pup, finish your meal." He squealed to himself. "Because most of her meal," he paused for an awkwardly long time. "Most of her meal is fat juicy mealworms! KEEEH HEH HEH!"

Naurr and Simon were taking turns overseeing the operations. If Naurr was asleep, then Simon was awake, and vice versa. They went day and night; the Otsoak teams had come together well. The first layer of the wall on one side of the valley was complete, and another was almost halfway across. They had left a single space in the wall for a makeshift gate, which for now would have movable bamboo stakes tied together to form a barricade, giving the nomadic people a choke point to focus their defenses on. The second layer of sandstone was already up to Simon's chest. One more layer of stones would make it difficult to reach the top while standing at ground level.

He would be satisfied to complete three layers of stone before the Daanav attacked. Preferably four, but three would at least give him some comfort, knowing a human being could not hop over the wall effortlessly. *Still, those monsters were massive, and the hounds could leap. It needs to be higher.* He would also have to construct some scaffold for archers to stand behind the wall. If he lived to see it, he would add another layer of sandstone behind the first, a platform for a walkway behind the first layer of the wall.

Perhaps he would even build large square towers at each gate for heavy defensive equipment. *A ballista, perhaps?* Or even large stones or boiling oil to throw down upon the enemies. After that, he could design some more infrastructure for the camp. Roads and aqueducts. Solid homesteads. *Oh, the possibilities.*

Simon's thoughts were broken by a shout from one of his workers. "Boss! Boss! You're going to want to see this, ya!"

He saw Ilan Bronwen rushing toward him.

"We've hit a cavern in the rock. Looks like the water stream goes deeper into the cliff!"

The underground pool...the place where I am to drown. Wonderful. Simon coughed nervously and said, "Well, what are you waiting for, Ilan, my man? Lead the way."

"Right. You still owe me a sitting, ya know." Ilan lasciviously said. "We finished the blocks on the next attempt, ya."

"Aye, and I will hold up my end of the bargain. Let's deal with this first; come now."

Simon followed behind the dust-covered worker, noting the man's tight leggings showing off a toned, rounded buttock. He grinned at the thought. *If I'm not thinking about work, I'm thinking about sex. Hettra's sagging tits, Simon, get it together.*

Ilan grabbed a torch from another bystander and went to the back of the cavern. They had carved out a good thirty paces into the cliffside at a slight angle upwards. A small hole, maybe the size of a melon, had broken through near the back. Simon could hear water trickling on the other side.

"Let's make this hole a little bigger, shall we? Then we can see where it leads," Simon ordered.

"That's what *I'll* say, ya boss?" Ilan said, chuckling at his own joke.

Simon stared at him impatiently.

"I mean...right away, boss! Hoof! McKay! Get your arses up here, ya!"

Two burly individuals hustled up with large pickaxes. They looked to Simon for instruction. He nodded at the hole, and they began hammering away at the rock without a word. Chunks broke away, and maybe half an hour later, the gap was large enough for a man to crouch and squeeze through.

"That's good for now. We'll go check it out first. If it's worth it, we can make the opening larger. Ilan, you're with me."

Ilan, brandishing the torch, bent and vanished through the opening.

Simon composed himself and ducked in after him. It took a moment for his eyes to adjust as it was much darker without the sun's backlight at the cave's entrance. They now only had the torch's light to guide them. The stream of water flowed from his right to his left. He assumed if they followed the water to the left, it would lead them to the waterfall on the cliffside, so they needed to go to the righthand side.

"Let's see how far we can follow the stream. Right behind you, my man." He patted Ilan on the back, giving his shoulder a slight squeeze.

"What are we looking for, ya?" Ilan asked curiously.

"Does not your curiosity motivate you enough?" Simon answered. "To see where this mysterious river is coming from. What could its source possibly be?"

"It's groundwater that managed to find a way up, ya. Same concept as digging a well, sir boss, sir."

"Oh, the formality, Ilan. *Do* keep that up. Ahem, and obviously, it is groundwater!" Simon cleared his throat. "Anyways, we'll just have a look, then make our way back. Who knows? Maybe there are some gems or some such treasures buried here. Either way, it's a moment's respite for me. I reckon, for you as well."

"Lot of good gems will do us out here in the arse of fucking nowhere. I'd trade some gems for a romp and some damn ale, ya."

"Are you always in such an exceptional mood?" Simon asked.

"Oh, I'm just a fountain o' fucking cheer, ya," Ilan paused. "IF I HAD SOME DAMN ALE AND A ROMP!" His shout echoed through the cavern.

"I will inquire with an Otsoa about acquiring some beverages of the sort. Leave it to your ever-so-thoughtful chief engineer. I have your best interests at heart."

"If you say so." The man shrugged.

They continued; the minutes stretched by. At times, they could walk alongside the stream; at others, they needed to duck down or wade through the water, which was icy cold. Slowly, the stream became broader and more profound; they could only swim to follow it further. The walls at the sides gave them no handholds to help them along. Ilan was struggling to keep the torch out of the water. They came to a point where the ceiling above them ended. Simon put his head under and could barely see the tunnel continuing into the underground rock. *The only way forward is down.*

He resurfaced. "All right, let's head back."

"About fucking time, ya," Ilan murmured. "You owe me for this one, boss."

"I do indeed. As for that *romp* you keep shouting about. Shall we conclude our agreement now, as it were?"

"Eh? Here and now?" Ilan's soft brown eyebrows rose.

"We did just have a bath of sorts. Of course, I'll do whatever needs to be done to keep my man's morale up. I think I'll de-robe and scrub a bit first. I'd advise you to do likewise." He gave Ilan a once over. Most of his men were well-muscled construction workers, Ilan among them. He was rather attractive to Simon, though somewhat filthy from working all day and night. Simon grinned playfully at the man.

"Right." Ilan began to remove his wet clothing.

After they rinsed themselves thoroughly in the cold water, they followed the stream back until they found a suitable spot of dryer land.

"What do you have in mind?" Simon inquired curiously.

"Let me show you." Ilan rested the torch against the side of the cave wall carefully, then descended to his knees in front of Simon.

"Hettra's tits," Simon moaned.

Ilan stopped.

"Ahem, what?" Simon sputtered in surprise.

"Already?" Ilan grinned mischievously.

"It's been far too long since my last encounter, as it were."

"You owe me a seat, ya."

"I do indeed. Lie down then, my man."

Ilan did not hesitate.

Simon was tingling with anticipation.

They both moaned as Ilan grasped Simon's waist.

"Gods, Ilan," Simon murmured as he hunched over the man.

Sometime later, they exited the cavern together, Ilan chatting Simon up about this and that. Simon thought to himself, *Ilan is in a much better mood than the journey into the cave.* Ilan rejoined the others at the cave entrance and started working again as if nothing had happened between them. Simon nodded. *The way it should be, have a bit of pleasure and return to business.* Then, he returned to his makeshift tent to focus his mind on the tasks at hand.

I need to try and swim up the stream further. Perhaps we could fashion some sort of light that would function underwater or possibly have someone on a rope that we could pull back in if things went ill in the dark. Simon needed to find the source of this damned dream. He needed to find some ale...and he needed a *real* bath.

CHAPTER TWENTY-THREE
REGRET

Jude ordered the caravan to halt while he rode for nearly half an hour. He gazed back in the direction he had come. The desert sky was always clear blue, but smoke snaked through it, billowing upward.

"The bandits should be able to see this from leagues away." He grinned at his genius. *Bringing the bastards to me is much easier than galivanting aimlessly across these Skrull-forsaken lands.*

He began heading back toward the caravan. They were just over a week into their journey since leaving Dagad. They had been traveling roughly due east since the beginning. He figured they'd wait another day or so before circling back. If they weren't attacked by the nomads by then, he would call it off and report the girl dead. *Fucks, I can't perform a miracle, you know.* He had done the best he could.

When he had finally informed Greens and Ryon about his plan earlier that day, the two were far from pleased.

"I could lose everything!" Greens cried in disbelief. "I will take my stock ahead while you fools enact this senseless plan!"

"Then who would I have to give me the guise of an honest merchant caravanner?" Jude asked.

"Aye, I say this is rightly fucked. I'm heading back to Dagad," Ryon stated.

"Who will I have to protect me from the merciless nomads?" Jude paused. "If either of you leave now, I will use this." As Ryon began to turn his horse about, Jude held up a small yellow glass marble from his pouch.

Ryon halted his horse and looked back.

"What's this?" Greens asked. "Are we to be afraid of a pebble?"

"This here will call upon two members of the Council Aerie to instantly appear at my position," Jude lied. *This is a simple flash bead.* "Where I will then inform them of your illegal grit trade. Oh, and Ryon, as an officer of the law, involvement in said illegal grit trade operations will, unfortunately, be," he sighed regretfully. "*Execution* on the spot."

Ryon paled. Promptly turning his steed around once more, he began preparations for the smoke signal. Jude listened to Ryon shouting orders with calm satisfaction. *Yes, do as you're told...scum.*

"I don't believe that that rock can summon anyone or anything. I think you're bluffing." Greens eyed him suspiciously.

Jude shrugged and kicked his horse onward. "Halt the caravan; begin burning the ferns. I will ride that way to better determine if the signal is adequate. Do not think for a moment about running off. As one man on horseback, I will find you and your cartful of slaves in no time. If I am forced to do so, you will rue the day you crossed me." He galloped away around the closest dune, Greens stuttering in his dust wake. *If I was in their shoes, I would slit my throat during the night. Thank Skrull, I'm dealing with damned idiots.*

On returning to the caravan, he caught something from the corner of his eye to the north. Very faint, he could make out a wisp of dust cresting a far-off dune. *Riders?* As he continued, the cloud slowly grew. He caught the glint of sunlight flashing on steel. *Riders.* He kicked his horse into a full gallop.

"Fucks be to Skrull." *Time to make haste,* he thought. *I must make it back before the nomads reach the caravan.* Before Ryon and Greens decided to mount a defense of their precious goods. The smoke signal had wrought results far quicker than Jude had anticipated.

Hata held Taryn's limp upper body on her lap. The dead woman's clouded eyes looked up at her, a look of shock frozen on her face.

"I couldn't save her. I couldn't do anything." Tears streamed down Hata's cheeks, dripping down onto the cold face of Taryn.

Saudett gently placed a hand on Hata's shoulder. "You did all you could. It's not your fault."

Hata pulled her shoulder away from Saudett's hand. "It is my fault! I should have killed them all with my first attack! I'm not strong enough!"

Saudett looked to Brena and Baal for support. They stood together nearby, watching their daughter. They did not move to aid her.

"You could say the same for all of us," Kaplan interjected. "I could have shot at Taryn's foe instead of Saudett's. We could have all attacked the same one instead of taking them one-to-one. You can never be certain to know what will happen in battle; there are too many factors to account for. The only way to anticipate these things is through years of experience and honing your skills. Also, there is always a slight factor of luck involved."

Hata looked up at Kaplan, sniffling. Saudett followed her gaze toward her parents. The two nodded solemnly to her, Baal's arm wrapped around his mate.

"If you are going to fight, you must be prepared to face death. That of your own and those around you." Saudett approached Hata again. "We're safe now. Come here." She put on a weak smile.

Hata put her arms out as Saudett approached, reaching for her.

Saudett went to her, pressing Hata's head to her shoulder.

"To be honest, Taryn got herself killed," Kaplan stated.

Hata's head shot up.

"Kaplan!" Saudett warned.

"She was too full of herself, toying with the beast. She failed to remember the third creature."

Hata opened her mouth to say something, then stopped.

The group silently agreed that Kaplan was correct.

After a few minutes, the others cleaned up the mess and tended to the horses. Brena finished stitching and wrapping the wound to Baal's calf with clean linens. Kaplan carried both pieces of Taryn's body away to be buried.

Saudett knelt and stroked Hata's red hair through her fingers, whispering in Hata's ear, "We all make mistakes; that is how we learn to better ourselves. On my first trip across the Burning Sea, as a new caravan guard, I let someone very precious to me die."

Hata's eyes widened, "You did?"

"He was my mentor; he taught me how to fight and live. Along with many others, he helped raise me in the absence of my father and mother. He died because of me the first time he took me out into this desert."

"*No*. Because of you? What happened? What was his name? Where were your parents?"

"Slow down, Hata. I will tell you the tale." Saudett paused and sat down next to Hata. "His name was Ismael Kaur. My parents were the leaders of a reputable caravan guard company out of Al'Jalif, part of Xamid, on the eastern side of the Burning Sea. They made their livelihood away on the road. They also believed it was far too dangerous to bring their child.

"Ismael oversaw the training of recruits for the company at our estate grounds. When I was young, and quite frankly alone and bored to death, I would pick up a stick and copy the soldiers in the courtyard. I would mimic their moves and watch as they sparred with one another. On one such day, as I was imitating them from a corner, Ismael promptly walked over, grabbed me by the shoulders, and placed me in the line of men and women training.

"Ismael never treated me like a child; he ensured I got the same training and punishment as everyone else. Most of all, he spoke to me like an adult. His example made the other soldiers treat me like another recruit, not the house leader's daughter. They would joke around and treat me like one of their own. They were my true family. Ismael was more of a father to me than my own."

"He sounds like a good man. A good family. I'm sorry your true parents were not as present in your life." Hata looked at her with a mix of happiness and concern. "I don't know what I would do without mine." Her head turned to eye her mother and father, who had begun to dig a grave for Taryn.

"Thank you, Hata. Your parent's love for you is clear, but they also let you make your own decisions, which greatly benefits you."

Hata nodded in agreement. "But what happened to Ismael?"

"Yes, yes, where was I? The tale of the man I consider my father. When I was nearly thirteen summers old, my parents left on a typical journey to Aurulan and back. It should only have taken a few months at most. We waited days, weeks, and months...four months went by, then a fifth. We heard nothing. Half a year went by.

"I foolishly acted out and proposed a search party. I had rarely even left the estate, never been with the caravan, or ventured through this wasteland at that point in life. Yet, I was *angry*. I needed to find my parents; I needed to find my mother. I gathered two dozen recruits and informed Ismael we would leave at dawn. He did not protest; he looked upon me with sadness and empathy. He wanted me to be happy.

"I regret going into that desert with Ismael; he truly loved me. He had watched me grow up, and I threw his life away to find two people who didn't think twice about not being in their daughter's life." Saudett's voice cracked with those last words.

Hata snuggled in closer to her. *Who is comforting whom now?* Saudett thought as she paused for a long moment, composing herself, thinking back on that time.

"We wandered for weeks on end. I had not the slightest clue as to what I was doing, relying on Ismael for direction. He suggested we head for Dagad to inquire if they had been through town and ensure they were not somewhere in the Aurulan Kingdom to the west. We made it to Dagad but to no avail. Not a soul had seen them in over half a year. The last time anyone recalled her parent's location, they had departed into the desert to return to Xamid, which lined up with the previous caravan they had escorted. Thus, our company resupplied and headed back out into the desert."

"During that time, Ismael tried to guide me and teach me. Things like how to look for signs of water in the desert or where to find snakes and lizards for eating. But I was too stubborn and bitter, not in the mood for schooling.

"He would say, 'Look, Saudett. Under the rock, here you may find creatures sheltering from the sun's heat.' I would respond disinterested, urging our caravan forward. Each time I acted this way, he would remind me that patience was a virtue if one wished to live long in the Burning Sea, as one never knows when one may find oneself alone out here. But I did not take what he said to heart. I wasn't alone; I had him and the other recruits. I was determined to find my parents and told Ismael that now was not the time to learn.

"When he told me that he believed we would need to return home soon without my parents. I raged. In a fury, I rode off, away from Ismael, all alone, for hours and hours. Finally, when darkness had fallen, I couldn't keep my eyes open any longer. I tied my horse to a dead tree and curled up underneath it. I awoke to a warm fire and a blanket over me later that night. Ismael sat humming a tune, two lizards roasting on stakes by the fire. When he saw me awake, he handed over one of the lizards without a word. We sat in silence for a long time before he finally spoke.

"He told me my horse had run off because I did not use the clove hitch knot, he had taught me. I looked around in shock, not noticing the animal had flown. Ismael's horse was grazing on sparse brown grasses near the dead tree. He pointed to a broken branch on the tree where I had tied my horse. Furiously, I demanded to know why he didn't stop it. He told me it had been long gone before he arrived. Then he stated, 'In this place, you should not solely rely on me to rescue your little green arse whenever you find yourself in need.' His face was cold as iron.

"At that point, I noticed we were alone; the others had not followed Ismael. 'Where are the others?' I had asked him. He told me that he had sent them back to the city and that we would move to catch up with them. At that moment, I burst. My blood was boiling, and my ears and neck burning. 'What about my mother and father!?' I screamed. But he was as calm as could be. He said we would continue looking for three more days, then head home to rejuvenate and reconsider our options.

"I wouldn't have it and decided to look for them without him. He just stared at me silently, with sadness in his eyes. As I was ready to leave, a howl broke the night air. Desert wolves. Ismael stood up immediately. He told me the wolves wouldn't hesitate to attack us if they were hungry enough. He hoped it was a loner. But moments later, we heard multiple howls breaking out all around us.

"Ismael cursed, and I asked him what we should do. He told me to take his horse and ride due east without hesitation. He said, 'Do not stop; do not look back.' I remember it like it was yesterday. At his words, tears filled my eyes. My throat began to close, and no words came out. He reassured me that he would be fine, then hoisted me into the saddle. He said, 'Wait until my signal, then go full speed. Don't look back, little fox.'

"Finally, finding my words again, I begged him to stay and fight by his side. I would do anything to save him. He reached up and put a hand on my cheek. His last words were: 'Know this, Saudett Aanya Kafilah, I love you as I would my own daughter.' His eyes shone red in the night, glistening with tears in the firelight.

"Before I could answer him, the snarls and growls of countless wolves erupted just paces away from us. Ismael glanced left to right and hefted his spear. 'Go!' he shouted and slapped my horse's hindquarters. The horse took off. I turned and saw a wolf leaping at him and his spear tip flashing in the firelight. That was the last time I saw Ismael Kaur, and I never told him...I never told him that *I loved him too*."

Saudett collapsed into Hata's arms, and Hata embraced her. Hata's eyes were burning red with emotion as she stifled a sniffle. "That is heartbreaking, Saudett. He loved you so very dearly. I'm so sorry. Thank you for telling me this. It helps. I need to go talk to my parents." She squeezed Saudett tightly one last time before standing and going over to Brena and Baal, who embraced her on arrival.

Saudett sat in silence. After sharing her regretful tale, she felt utterly alone at Hata's abrupt departure. A flash of anger filled her. *I pour forth my heart, and you just leave me?*

She took a deep breath, shook the thought from her mind, and instead reflected on her childhood, remembering Ismael. She was genuinely grateful he had been a part of her life. *I learned so much from him and would not be the woman I am today without his nurturing kindness and sacrifice. Thank Hettra for Ismael Kaur's time in my life.* She put a thumb to her lips. Then she stood and made her way to the rest of the group to help with the burial of Taryn Drel.

CHAPTER TWENTY-FOUR
DECEIT

Jude arrived at the caravan minutes before the horde of hundreds of nomad raiders. They outnumbered the caravan guards two to one, at the least.

"All the gods be fucked," he cursed. He didn't want the two forces to engage one another. "Put down your weapons! There is no need to fight!" he shouted, trying to calm the caravan guardsmen preparing for a defense.

"No! I'll lose everything! Fight, you bastards!" Greens countered, joining him in the center of the already organized barricades. "I'm the one paying you! Not this whoreson!"

It seemed Greens and Ryon had already assembled a defense and set up the wagons and crates of supplies in a defensible square pattern. Smoke still billowed upwards from the massive bonfire in the center. A third of the men made ready with crossbows behind the makeshift barricade. Another third was on foot, with long pikes reaching out. Ryon led a cavalry, readying for a counterattack against the nomads.

They're surprisingly organized, Jude thought. *This is problematic.* He would have to rectify that problem so they could be taken prisoner and returned to the nomads' camp. He flipped open a pouch on his belt and fiddled with some marbles. The crossbowmen were the biggest threat to the nomads, as they could fire indefinitely from the safety of cover into the columns of horsemen. He pricked his thumb on the tip of his belt knives and coated one of the marbles in blood. He waited until the nomads rode in for the attack.

The column of archers on horseback spilled around the barricade like two snakes slithering past on both sides. Greens retreated to one of the covered wagons.

Arrows whistled and thudded into the carriages and makeshift barricade with resounding *thunks*. The crossbowmen answered the volley. Nomads screamed and fell from their saddles, only to be trampled by other horsemen pursuing too closely.

A guardsman slumped over a crate, an arrow jutting from his head.

An archer on horseback took a bolt to the shoulder and plummeted from his steed; he managed to roll and push himself to his feet. At that moment, two footman caravan guards charged the fallen bowmen and stuck him on spears.

The two footmen turned, *too late*, as a dozen nomadic cavalry closed on them. A spear pierced the skull of one with an explosion of gore behind the impact. The other took the full brunt of a stallion's chest, crushing him into the ground.

Men screamed on both sides; riders fell.

Jude watched as Ryon began to bring his cavalry around from the opposite side to meet one of the columns of nomadic warriors.

Jude rode up behind the frontal barricade and flicked the marble nonchalantly between some crates.

"Keep it up!" he called from atop his mount. "Don't stop firing; take the bastard-sons-of-whores down!" He moved his head a fraction as an arrow whistled past it. He turned his horse. "I move to join the mounted counter-assault!" he exclaimed so all could hear through the chaos.

He turned and rode some fifty paces away; then, twisting in his saddle, he looked back at the barricade. There was commotion there, the soldiers staring and pointing to the sky. He followed their line and saw the massive flaming sphere descending directly toward the barricade.

"Fire magi!" he shouted as the blast sucked the air from his lungs.

The explosion created a shock wave that thudded through the ground and air. Jude's horse whined and reared under him as he struggled to keep it under control. The barricade and the dozen soldiers were hurled in burning pieces of flesh and armor, scattering in all directions. Chunks of charred gore, fabric, and debris rained down on them. Only a blackened smoking crater was left in the sand.

The nomads poured through the opening in the barricade. Jude dismounted calmly, putting his hands up in surrender, indicating those around him to do the same.

"We are no match for a mage of fire. Let us at least leave here with our lives," Jude reassured those around him, who then began dropping their weapons as they kneeled, their hands above their heads.

"Perfect," he whispered. *All is going according to plan.*

The nomads quickly corralled them into a group and stripped them of their weapons. Jude managed to conceal most of his daggers from searching clumsy fingers. His pouches of magic-infused marbles escaped untouched.

Ryon's countercharge had been quickly routed, with no backup from the supporting barricade crossbowmen, and they were rounded up to join the group of people on foot surrounded by nomads.

Ryon and Greens made their way to his side. Ryon's eyes were wide with disbelief. "What are the chances that something like that would fall from the sky and strike precisely on our defenses? If I do say so myself, one of the gods must have it out for us."

"Fool," Greens hissed, "this is the Magnus Huntsman's doing. He is the only one who even interacts with the magi. He threatened us with the marble, remember! He must have more tricks up his sleeve."

Jude grinned wickedly at Greens. "Very perceptive of you. I did indeed summon that fireball. Perhaps, due to the fact you two deranged imbeciles were in the middle of fucking my Skrull-damned plan!"

Greens sunk back.

"For Skrull's sake, I should have sided with the Huntsman from the get-go," Ryon grumbled.

"Shut up, you twit," Greens shot back.

A woman on horseback dismounted and approached. She wore the simple brown-and-tan linens of the nomads. She had brown skin, the slightest crinkle of frown lines across her forehead, and slightly graying black hair peeking from her hood. Her eyes were as dark as chocolate. Her mouth and nose were covered.

"I assume you three are in charge of this lot, as you are the only ones among it still speaking aloud."

Jude spoke up before Greens had a chance. "You are indeed correct. We are traveling merchants on our way to Al'Jalif, the Jewel of the East. We bring many precious goods. My friend here." He waved toward Greens. "Specializes in the very rare dealings of young human slaves to do with as you please."

Her eyes studied Greens with ferocity, looking him over with a furrowed brow. She raised a hand, and two more nomads approached. She then looked at the covered carts behind them.

"Take this one away; separate him from the rest of them," the woman ordered. "Tie him to the back of one of these cages once we've emptied them of their so-called *goods*."

"This man is full of lies! They are his! He is the one who captured them! Enslaved them! He summoned the fireball!" Greens hollered as he was pulled away toward the wagons.

Her eyes met Jude's once again. "You were responsible for that?"

He tried his best to look shocked. "I've never seen such a thing like that in my life. Where could it have come from? We assumed you had a fire mage in your midst."

"If only that were true," she sighed, shaking her head.

"This one," Jude nodded to Ryon. "Is a member of Dagad's military constabulary force and has had a hand in overlooking the capture of these young people and the induction of grit to incapacitate them."

Ryon's mouth opened, dumbfounded. "Wha—what?"

She waved her hand again, and Ryon was promptly ushered off after Greens.

"Thus, I am to believe you are the saint among this trinity of do-gooders?"

"I met this caravan in Dagad a week ago, as they were the only ones readying to leave at my arrival from west Aurulan. Everyone else hesitated to depart due to a recent attack on the town. I did not realize they had people under those coverings until a few days in. I wanted to turn back right then and there, but they threatened to kill me if I did so or told a single soul about their business," he lied easily, summoning tears to his eyes in an instant. "I was truly an utter fool. Alas, I am a coward who only cares about himself."

She sighed again. "Unlock the cages. Get those people out of there."

Jude exaggerated a mournful bawl, looking about anxiously, "Primus, grant mercy on us! What are you planning to do with us?"

"We will offer the slaves two options. First, we will offer them enough provisions to continue or return to where they came from. Secondly, we will offer them a new home."

"A home?"

"Yes, a home."

"Is this offer accessible to all of us here as well?"

She studied him closely.

"Let me be honest with you. I'm quite fatigued with travel, the months on end. Back and forth, forth, and back. Walking, riding, bumping along in a wagon. The same scene day in and day out. I'm prepared to settle down, start farming, and have a garden. *Have a family.*" It wasn't all lies, minus the family part.

Her eyes softened. "I was in the same situation many years ago. Yes, the offer is open to all. Let me warn you, though, it will not be such a peaceful existence. We face a far greater threat than you are aware of."

He tilted his head at that comment. "I can handle a blade when needed. At any rate, the prisoners may be too narcotized to make coherent decisions for themselves. It may be better to nurse them back to health first in your homeland and then offer them this choice."

"Folks brought back to the Valley of Hasiera do not carry the opportunity of departing it. *Ever*," she said flatly.

Jude blinked at that.

"Our home is a secret place; we mean to keep it that way. I understand it is difficult to ponder, and I recognize your hesitation. This is your only chance. You have one hour before we ride."

He nodded.

"Your name, Merchant?"

"Jude Nelon." Pausing, he thought, *should I have given a fake name?* He shrugged inwardly. *Once I capture the girl, I will never see these bastards again.*

She returned his nod, turned to her horse, and began barking orders to her kin.

She seems like a strong woman, yet perhaps too kind. That kindness is a likely way to end up dead one day. "I am surrounded by fools," he muttered.

Chapter Twenty-Five

FIRELIGHT

People. Kiana could make out the dimness of the firelight in the distance. She hoped it was a returning patrol of Hasiera.

"What is it? Is it the demon, she-wolf pup's home?" Kogs questioned enthusiastically.

"It could be," she whispered hoarsely. She stumbled toward the glow. Her stomach was tight with hunger, and her body was weak from exhaustion. Her mouth was dry, her lips cracked and bleeding, and she could hardly speak. The bugs had nourished her, but she had not had water in days. Kiana pushed on.

"Show yourself!" Kaplan yelled into the darkness.

Saudett was pulled from sleep as Kaplan jumped to his feet, the scimitar flashing from its scabbard. The others were rousing about her. There was silence for a long moment. Then, Saudett heard a strained whisper as a woman stepped into view of the firelight, her clothing tattered and bloodstained. Her body was cut and bruised. She stood momentarily, swayed, and then collapsed into the sand.

Kiana opened her eyes. Sweet, warm water touched her dry, cracked lips and parched tongue. She fumbled her hands to take hold of the skin and gulp down the water.

"Slowly now. Slowly," a warm voice whispered.

Her vision blurred. The hands holding the skin were soft yet stern, guiding her own, steadying her so she did not drink too much too quickly. She blinked up at the face of the woman. She had long blond hair in a thick braid, the wrinkles of smile and laugh lines, and thunderbolt tattoos jolting up her neck. *Hettra sent me an angel from the heavens.*

The woman pulled the water skin from her hands, putting it aside. She gathered something warm from a wooden bowl, steam drifting from it. It felt as if Kiana had not smelled a thing as savory in all her life: a stew with a mix of meat, roots, spices, and potatoes. Her mouth began to water.

"Are you able? Pace yourself," the woman asked gently.

Kiana nodded and cupped the bowl in her hands, then sipped, scooping chunks of vegetables and meat into her mouth with her fingers. She finished the bowl quickly and finally took a moment to gather her surroundings. Five people sat around a campfire, *staring* at her. They were quite an odd, mismatched group of individuals. The *angel* moved to sit next to a behemoth of a man with a fire-red beard and shaven head. The same thunderbolt tattoos as the angel, but cresting his head. His teeth gleamed in a grin...*or was it a snarl?* It was difficult to tell.

A short Xamidian woman sat glaring at Kiana; she had a soldier's short-cut black hair. Next to her sat a young, red-haired girl dressed in plain clothing. Lastly, another Xamidian sat nearby, hooded and black-bearded; it was hard to discern other features. Another soldier, she gauged by his poise.

"Who are you people?" Kiana asked questionably. "And why, in Skrull's name, are you all in the middle of this hell they call the Burning Sea?"

"I would ponder the same question of you, woman," the short Xamidian answered. She sat stiffly as if ready to strike at a moment's notice.

"I suppose it is only fair, as you all did save my life just now." Kiana paused to think for a minute. "My caravan was attacked nearly a week ago by something I have never seen the like of. Fiends, beasts out of children's nightmares. They slaughtered everyone. I was the only survivor, by luck, being trapped under an overturned wagon." *It isn't that far from the truth,* she thought.

"Surely, you are mistaken. The demons must have slaughtered your caravan full of filthy brigand scum," the soldier woman said bluntly.

Kiana frowned slightly; *she couldn't know.* "What are you talking about? I am merely the daughter of a humble merchant."

"The skin around your eyes is much darker than the rest of your face, indicating you spend some time out here with your mouth and nose covered, akin to much of the nomadic raiders that attacked Dagad several weeks ago." The short woman's eyes burned through Kiana, through her *lies.* She was angry, and she had seen right through her.

Kiana sighed. "Yes, I'm afraid you are correct. I am a *filthy brigand scum*, as you put—"

In a flash, the woman leaped over the fire toward her, spear in hand, leveled for Kiana's neck. A broad, curved sword flashed up in front of her, catching the spear on the flat of its blade.

The hooded Xamidian man stood between them, holding the spear woman in check. "Think before you act, Lieutenant," he hissed. This is our one opportunity to get your husband back."

"Move, Kaplan! Let me end her life; we will find him either way with Hata's pow—"

There was a *thud,* and the short woman went down. The red-haired girl yelped and rushed to the downed woman. The bulky bald man stood over her, growling.

"Why did you do that?!" the red-haired girl yelled.

"Hata," said the angel. The red-haired girl, *Hata,* looked at the angel's serious expression, taking a moment, then nodded in understanding, plainly hiding something of value.

"I regret our harsh methods of attacking the village; there was too much bloodshed. Please, if you see fit, let me explain everything." Kiana surveyed the surrounding area, the same area where her Pack had been attacked during the night, the first time Simon had witnessed the Daanav. A mound of fresh earth was not far from the fire, a broken spear shaft jutting from it. Someone had died recently; *one of their companions?*

A moment later, the soldier woman groaned and sat up. "Skrull's hell. You could have held back somewhat, Baal. Your point has been taken."

"Friend Saudett was filled with blood rage. Need to calm down." He cracked his knuckles, ever-smiling with teeth bared.

Saudett groaned again, holding her head, then turned her attention to Kiana again. "And so, Primus tell, how do you find yourself alone in the desert? And how have you survived it?"

"Let me start at the beginning." Kiana sighed. "It looks like you may have already had a run-in with the Daanav that ruled the night in the Burning Sea."

"Daanav? That's Xamidian for 'demon,'" Saudett answered inquiringly. "And aye, we have. We lost one of our members to their attack at sundown."

"How many were there?" Kiana asked.

"Three of the larger ones and two smaller hound-like creatures," the male Xamidian, Kaplan, answered flatly.

Kiana's brows rose slightly. "And only one of you died? I am astounded." Only the young girl Hata sat up a bit straighter at that comment. "These monsters are the reason we attacked Dagad. We had a contact in Dagad find us a team of builders to help us fortify our home to mount a defense against the Daanav. We received word the team of builders was working just outside of Dagad for a few months. We took that opportunity to make our move to capture them. Fortunately, the Daanav have yet to sniff out our sanctuary, but it is only a matter of time. It gives time for your builders to complete their work."

"Who was your spy in Dagad?" Saudett asked with a scowl.

"I will not say; we may have need of them in the future."

"And I may kill you now if you do not tell me," Saudett spat.

The hooded man tried to reason with her. "Lieutenant Saudett, threatening her does not get us anywhere. She gives us a reason to cooperate against these monsters, these *Daanav*, and it sounds like the brigands were desperate and had good reason behind their attack. Though they could have taken a more peaceful approach."

"No, Kaplan! *They killed Yakeb!* I will not forgive them." Kiana could tell the woman was holding herself back from lunging at her a second time. Saudett's knuckles whitened around her spear shaft, teeth grinding.

"We feared if we approached civilization, we would be mocked, scrutinized, or, worse, arrested or executed as brigands. And why not? That is precisely what we are. We judged that taking what we needed was safer for our people. I don't know who this Yakeb was, but I deeply apologize for your loss."

She saw tears glistening in Hata's eyes as she watched Saudett seething in anger. Hata reached out a hand and touched the soldier woman's arm gently. *She cares deeply for this Saudett.* Saudett's face flushed sharply with anger toward Hata upon her touch, then visibly relaxed when she saw the girl's face.

Saudett gave the young woman a weak smile in return. "I'm sorry, Hata." Saudett took a deep inhale, calming herself further. "You are right, Kaplan Mir, *as always*. It is better to be mutual allies than to walk into this one's camp empty-handed. Perhaps we could even use her as a prisoner in exchange for my husband."

Kaplan Mir grunted. "What would stop them from riding us down on sight to take their prisoner back?"

Sensible man, this Kaplan Mir, Kiana thought before saying, "If we do this peacefully, I could bring you to our home unharmed, but our leader has one rule, which he has never broken. Once you have come to the Valley of Hasiera, you can never return to the life you once led."

"So, the people you have captured can never leave?" Hata questioned.

"Just so. Perhaps I can aid you. Try and find a way for you and your husband to escape." *It's impossible, and I won't allow it.* "Who is he? They shouldn't make as much fuss if he's just one of the simple workmen. Perhaps they may not even notice he is gone."

"My friends and I will be quite conspicuous within your camp." Saudett nodded toward Baal and sighed. "And I'm afraid whatever fortifications your people are working on, my husband oversees it. His name is Simon Meridio, chief architect of the builders you captured."

Kiana's eyes momentarily widened in shock. *Simon's wife.* Her mind rolled with thoughts of the charming man, ideas of teasing him further upon return to Hasiera. Perhaps settling down with him. With him by her side, *husband* of an Otsoa. *Yakeb?* She remembered Simon's father had been slain by the First. Sorrow and empathy filled her for the couple. She understood now why the woman was so enraged. Kiana's voice cracked as she finally asked, "Who was Yakeb? The man you seek vengeance for?" She tried to act as if she did not know, eying Saudett.

"He was my husband's father." The woman paused. "Whoever was responsible for his death will have my answer with a spear through the gut. They will die slowly and painfully."

"Saudett, was it?" Kiana asked curiously.

"Aye. For that matter, what is your name, woman?"

"Kiana Ahmadi, Sixteenth Otsoa of Hasiera."

"Formally, I am Saudett Meridio, Lieutenant of the Shepherds Eye Rangers."

Kiana waved a hand to the rest of the group. "Your friends?"

"Aye," Saudett turned her head to Kaplan. "Sergeant Kaplan Mir, Shepherds Eye Ranger." Then she pointed to the two Vouri. "Baal and Brena Vasara, to whom I owe my life."

Baal grunted in response.

The edges of the angel Brena's mouth curled slightly into a smile.

"Lastly, the daughter of the Vasara House, Hata, could not leave her parents unguarded on this journey." Saudett nudged the girl playfully.

Hata smiled shyly.

Kiana nodded. "My pleasure, and my thanks to you all. Your bond together will aid you in the difficult tasks ahead. I fear we have trying times to come. Let me tell you how I came here alone in the desert." She explained the attack on her Pack and how they split their forces, some to take the prisoners and goods back to camp, while the others sacrificed their lives to stop the Daanav. She was careful to leave Simon's name out of her reiteration.

When she reached the point of the story where she had awoken alone after the battle, she called out loudly, "Then the great and mighty Kogs offered to escort me home! He should come out and introduce himself." There was silence.

The others looked at her dubiously.

"Too much sun, this one has," Baal said.

Great, they think I'm insane.

After a moment, they heard a scuffling in the sand. Two green eyes blinked into existence, reflecting the firelight.

"Has the she-wolf demon come home? Shall I return to the masters and call forth their destruction?!" Kogs squealed from the darkness at the edge of the firelight.

"Not yet, Kogs. We need to talk about saving Gaks and getting you home first. We can't do that if you go back to your masters. Come, sit by me, Kogs."

He slowly emerged into the light, his green eyes flashing. "Is it safe? How will we save my Gaks?" He went over to where Kiana sat and plopped down next to her.

"What is that thing?" Hata asked curiously.

Kiana glanced around. The others eyed Kogs suspiciously, sizing him up. After their run-in with the Daanav, she imagined a small talking lizard was not surprising. According to her father, many strange creatures existed in the Earste Lân. Besides Howler Thien's peoples, the Volkinn, she had only heard the stories of satyrs, centaurs, and dragons. Or even lamia, the half-human, half-beast creatures. Kogs was of a similar vein.

"Ah yes, he is a—" Kiana started.

"Is lizard. Looks tasteful," Baal grunted, licking his lips. "Add to stew?"

Kogs jumped back to his feet and covered his eyes. "It deceives poor Kogs!"

"Wait!" Kiana touched his head gently but firmly to stop him from running away. "Shh, it was but a jest. Calm yourself, Kogs." The lizard let out a strange clicking purr as she stroked his red mane of fur.

Baal gave a deep laugh.

Kogs uncovered his eyes and studied Baal suspiciously. "Big one is...funny?"

Baal suddenly laughed again loudly, and Kogs flinched in fright.

Kiana stifled her own laughter. "Apparently, he is. Let me introduce you to our new friends. This is Kogs. He was sent to follow me back to the valley and report to his masters, the Daanav, on its whereabouts. Kogs was taken from his home to serve the Daanav, and he taught me much about them. That the sunlight will kill them, slowly but surely. It would seem the demons are not just mindless beasts. They can hide underground, fusing with the earth. Lastly, they are looking for something. What was it they were looking for again, Kogs?"

"The masters speak of the gate, a doorway home! That is all little insignificant Kogs know. Kogs is not great enough to know more. Just find the filthy humans' home and tell the masters, they say. Masters want to slaughter filthy humans. That is Kogs's place."

"If Kogs doesn't tell the masters, then what happens?" Hata asked.

The small lizard man swayed to one side. "Then they will hurt my precious Gaks."

"But they are looking for a gate to go home?" Hata queried again. "If they can't go home, how can they hurt your Gaks?"

Kiana tilted her head; *how had she not thought of that? This girl is quick-witted. Qav's luck was that I had found these people when I did; I would be Kahytul fodder otherwise.*

Kogs swayed to the other side, then grasped his head. Shaking it back and forth in a fit. "Ah! The masters lied to Kogs! They are using poor Kogs. They can't go home to hurt my Gaks. Lies!" He began trembling.

"It is true, my little friend," Kiana said. "Therefore, when we return to *my* home, I hope you will help us rather than tell the masters where we are. And we will try to think of a way to save your Gaks while we are at it."

Kogs stood up, sticking his chin up and out. "I will help the she-wolf and new filthy humans." He paused, eyeing Baal up and down. "Please don't let the funny big one eat me."

Baal brandished his teeth with a low growl at the lizard man. Kogs covered his eyes as Baal's deep laugh echoed into the night air.

CHAPTER TWENTY-SIX

PRINCIPLE

Simon came to the end of the underground river, where the walkable passage could only be traversed further by swimming underwater. *I just could not leave it well enough alone. I must reach the end!* Taking a deep breath, Simon submerged. It was pitch-black; he touched the wall and the ceiling of the underground tunnel, moving forward. A minute passed, and his lungs began to burn. Then, another minute, just as he was nearing his limit, his fingers broke the surface ever so slightly. He pushed his mouth toward a small divot in the ceiling, a pocket of air, and just enough room for his face. Cold air filled his lungs, and he rested, his hands holding himself up by the cracks in the rock above him.

He took a few minutes to breathe deeply and compose himself. *Push on or turn back?* Taking another deep breath, he went under again and forward. After another few minutes of fumbling through the dark, he came upon another air pocket, his head fitting in the space entirely. He realized suddenly he could vaguely see his surroundings now. He took another dive; a dim light began seeping through the tunnel ahead. He swam hard now that he could see the direction he needed to travel. Moments later, he was under the light. It shimmered on the ripples above. Something wrapped around his leg like a bony-fingered hand. *Gods.* Then another and another. They began to pull him downward. He fought to break free, to swim upward toward the light. He screamed, and water filled his lungs. A *familiar* feeling. A *terrifying* feeling.

His eyes shot open as he coughed and vomited the water out of his lungs. He squinted at the brightness of the sunlight trickling through his tent, his eyes adjusting from the darkness of the underwater cavern. Looking up at the ceiling of his small shelter, the maroon and tan fabrics waved gently from the breeze outside. His sleeping linens were soaked as if he had been underwater just now. *Perhaps I should start sleeping naked if I become drenched every time I close my eyes.* He stood up and stripped the soaked clothing off.

He picked up a moderately fresh loose linen shirt and baggy trousers from a woven basket next to the fur and leather mats he slept on. It was time to relieve Naurr of his shift of overseeing the building operations. The workers and Hasieran had gotten into a good rhythm. They only needed direction at the wall site to pour the next sandstone and place the forms. He pushed his tent flap aside and exited. The warm sun fell on his face. Marigold was tied to a peg near his tent, lying with his head gently resting in the dirt. He crouched and rubbed the camel's head.

"Good morning, sir. A beautiful day is underway."

The camel lifted his head, groaned sheepishly, then curled his head back and into his side.

"Not a morning camel indeed," Simon muttered as he started.

He began strolling through the camp, making his way to a larger pavilion area open on all sides. The smell of fresh flatbread and a curry of some delicious-smelling spices met his nostrils. Nearly two dozen men and women sat on woven mats or hides, eating and speaking. *They are in good spirits.* He quietly found a place in line for the foodstuffs and listened to small talk.

"It's reassuring having that sturdy wall built up. I feel doubly safe compared to before the Builder arrived," he heard an older woman saying.

"We be having a right fortress when he's done with it. He is a handsome lad, too, though a bit scrawny for my liking. Alas, I heard he is with one of his crewmen," another middle-aged Tulu woman replied to the first.

Word gets around quick. Simon felt his face burn red at that.

"Who told you that?" the elder said.

"He had a go with one of his own workmen! The man, Ilan, has been bragging about the deed. No wonder they be working so well together; they get to tug on each other when they be done with all that wall building."

"Heh, I'd enjoy a go with those workmen myself. Those hardened bodies, all filthy and sweaty like."

The two women giggled together for a few moments. "Well, do you be thinking the Builder only fancies the men?"

Simon came to the head of the food line. He filled a bowl with brown rice and curried meat, holding a piece of flatbread in his mouth as he hurried to the opposite side of the pavilion, away from the conversation. He sat chewing his food thoughtfully. *These people of the valley were quite open about...well, everything.* He had heard and seen some sounds in some of the larger shelters at nightfall, catching glimpses of silhouetted carnal pleasure, many bodies tangled amongst each other.

Simon had always been interested in men and women, but it didn't blossom until he married his wife. Saudett, from the progressive eastern country of Xamid, was much more entwined in that lifestyle. She encouraged him to explore and reassured him she would be there. That she loved him always. The first time another man had been with him, his wife was right there with them, the three enjoying a euphoric, connected embrace.

The Auru, the people of Simon's ethnicity and religion, were not as comfortable with non-traditional relationships, especially if you didn't worship the proper deities. A husband and wife were guided by the Primus's favor, one God creator of all others. He noted that the gods were less notably present in Hasiera, much like Xamid. Still, he heard many curses at Skrull and his hell or Hettra and her bosoms, which was simply natural profanity.

Simon shook his head; he wasn't one to think about the gods and, quite frankly, was skeptical, even after his bizarre dreams.

Simon's mind wandered as he ate. He considered bringing Saudett here, seeing if they could live simple yet enjoyable lives together and start their family here. He enjoyed the challenge of building up the oasis into a real town, fortress, or whatever else was needed. It made him itch to accomplish it, to bring civilization to this nomadic tribe of people. Bring trade and prosperity. Perhaps the people of Hasiera could stop hiding if they came into the fold of society. *We could be founders of a new state.*

Do I even have much reason to go back home to Dagad? His father and mother were dead. Only his wife was left. Perhaps, after he built this wall, that golden bastard would let him go back and get her.

Ah, yes, I need to kill that golden son-of-a-whore. But how? He smirked; he still enjoyed the image of pouring sand down the bastard's throat and watching him choke to death.

Then there was that Skrull-damned underground pool that would not leave him alone. He knew he would keep dreaming of it until he investigated it himself. *Or, on the other hand, one day, I may drown for real one of these times. If only I could breathe underwater.*

A hard slap on his back and a half-chewed chunk of meat shot out of Simon's mouth into the sand.

"Gods," he coughed. "Why do people *insist* on doing that?"

"Greatest apologies to you, boss, but 'tis my turn to be taking a rest."

Simon looked up at Naurr. The whites of the man's eyes were bloodshot from exhaustion.

"Do not apologize, Naurr, my good man. I should be the one to beg forgiveness. I was caught up in my head once again."

"Not to worry then. Go on. The drudges need the boss's help at the wall. I will go to rest up now." Without another word, the Tulu man turned and trudged away slowly.

Simon felt sorry for the man, working him so hard. He knew most of his men were young; they enjoyed life before the responsibility of a spouse and children became a part of it. He knew Naurr had a son between six and eight years old. Some of his other men must have wives and children back home to which they longed to return. On the other hand, he was sure some of them had joined in the late-night revels of Hasiera.

Simon finished wiping his bowl clean with his bread, then stood and returned it to a basket near where the food was being served.

"Greetings, Builder!" said the older of the two women who had been gossiping about him earlier. "Would you care to join us in the long tent this night?"

The middle-aged women whistled at him.

He felt his face flush. "Ahem, I'm afraid not—"

"Aha! I told you he only enjoys the men!" the Tulu woman exclaimed.

"Let the lad finish!" The younger woman elbowed her compatriot.

"Heh," the older woman cackled. "He won't be finishing you or me, lassie,"

"Ahem," he cleared his throat loudly. "Madam, as I was about to say, the opportunity to bed such an established fine woman as yourself and your counterpart tempt me dearly. Alas! I'm afraid I am too busy overseeing the wall construction for the foreseeable future, and I must regretfully decline." He raised his voice a notch. "*And*, I prefer neither man, woman, or other being over that of another. All that matters is if said partner or partners and myself are attracted to one another. With hope, all are satisfied with the experience in the end."

"Other beings?" the older woman asked, her bushy, graying brows arching inquisitively.

"I think that means he enjoys the company of sheep!" the middle-aged woman whispered loudly.

"Oh indeed! I also heard tell that the man sleeps with a camel," the older lady laughed.

Simon groaned and rubbed his forehead with his thumb and forefingers. "Gods, never mind." He sighed as he turned and walked toward the building site.

"Probably be having the lumps, eh. Who knows what those critters pass on?" the older woman added.

Her friend nodded. "Aye, he should go have a romp with that dog, the Seventh, if he enjoys the beasties so much."

Simon halted at her words. *Of course,* there would be hatred for people who were *different*, even here in this seeming sanctuary of outsiders. He turned on a dime back to the two women. "I'm sure I would enjoy Thien's company tenfold over yours. *Good day!*" He turned on his heels and stomped off, roiling at their chauvinistic views.

The two women watched him go. He did not hear their answer.

"A good lad, he is," said the middle-aged woman. "He'll fit right in here. He will."

The older woman replied, with a smile, "Eh, ain't that the truth."

"But I'll be having a taste of him yet, I tell you!"

The two women giggled in unison.

Chapter Twenty-Seven

SHEPHERD

"We must keep your powers secret from this newcomer, Kiana Ahmadi. I do not trust her." Saudett leaned in close as she and Hata rode near the rear of the column of travelers. Kiana and Kaplan had taken the lead. Kiana's little lizard was perched on the rear end of her horse, a hand shading his eyes as he surveyed the passing landscape. It was oddly convenient that Kiana had the use of the late Taryn's steed. *Qav's luck to her.*

"Of course, Saudett. But still, I think she is kind," Hata answered. "She seems to generally be worried about her people. She's just trying to do what's right for them."

"She may be doing right for her people, but she does not factor in how it has affected those they have killed and stolen from."

"Joo. I agree, but Kiana did look genuinely troubled by the news of your father-in-law's death."

Saudett snorted. "She could be putting on false airs, so we lean toward sympathy. I would have a mind to aid the demons in finding this little village of hers if not for Simon being there."

"By Teras's mountain, Saudett, I beg you, don't be like that. You must give them the benefit of the doubt."

"I disagree. These people, these *murderers,* could have at least tried to speak to us. Try to hire Simon or plead with the Shepherds Eye to aid them in the fight against these Daanav. Instead, they kill senselessly and take what they want."

"Sometimes, people don't think straight when angry and distressed."

"What would you know? You're just a child!"

Hata's shoulders slumped, her face falling.

"I'm done talking about this," Saudett breathed.

"Fine," Hata answered meekly.

"Fine." Saudett kicked her horse, leaving Hata behind, frustrated by the girl's stubborn naivety. *She needs to grow up; she's too young to know any better.*

As Saudett approached Baal and Brena and their small wagon, she decided not to get between them but bask alone with her thoughts for a moment, so she hung back. Saudett would be a fool to think about going into Kiana's camp any other way than peacefully. If thousands of nomadic people lived there, it would be impossible to sneak in and find Simon. It would be like searching for a specific grain of sand in a sea of it. *Yet,* if they were building fortifications, she could perhaps use the nomads' tactics against themselves. They would be working near the outskirts of the camp.

I could hide and watch for a moment when Simon was at the wall, but I do not know the lay of the land. It could be flatlands as far as the eye could see, all around their little dung heap they call home with nowhere for her to hole up. I should question this bandit more, pretend to be interested in her people, and so forth so I can gather information subtly from her.

Hata rode by her, dust kicking up into Saudett's face. She coughed and squinted to see Hata rein in beside the bandit woman. "Skrull, take the lot of us," she grumbled. *The girl's loose tongue will be the end of her.* She was about to ride up and intervene, but a voice stopped her.

"Let her be, friend Saudett," Brena spoke. "She is capable of making her own decisions."

"I'm not so sure she is," Saudett scoffed.

She heard Baal give a low growl.

"You do not control our daughter," Brena said flatly. "You became her first companion in friendship and more. And with our family. She looks up to you. You tell her that you 'love' her. If that is true, you must guide her gently. But you must allow her to be who she is. Mistakes and all."

"I'm only trying to keep her safe. She could give up her secret to this heathen. The same situation made your fist hold my words just last night, Baal."

He grunted.

"We understand, friend Saudett," Brena said, studying her. "We just ask that you don't take advantage of her because she is powerful."

"If not for her," Saudett breathed. "We would wander this desert to no end. I am truly grateful to her."

"Grateful our family chose to keep our word and join you to find your husband instead of returning to the North Iron Belt to the aid of our kin, the Vouri? To face the unknown threat that has pushed our people from our homeland?"

Saudett was stunned into silence. A long moment stretched on, the three solemnly trotting along. *They knew.* Then she finally spoke, "I'm truly sorry. I should have told you. I was afraid of precisely what you speak of—that you would have taken Hata away, and I would never see my husband again."

Baal laughed, "Vouri never break-word. *Friends* never break-word."

"By the honor of Teras. Now you know for next time," Brena smiled gently.

Saudett bowed in thanks, her lips trembling. "I am unworthy of such friends."

Baal landed a *light* punch to her shoulder. "Is good. Baal like killing ugly dog-beast."

Saudett flinched at the impact but chuckled slightly, "Skrull, take me. I haven't even had a moment to think about those gods-forsaken things."

"The large ones seem simple to combat in a small skirmish and with long weapons. In a sizable force encounter, they will decimate the foot soldiers. A line of pikes may be able to hold them, but I fear their bulk and weight may break the line."

Saudett raised her brows as she did not expect such a strategy from Brena. "With Qav's luck, we can avoid any larger engagements."

"Unlikely, since we are to join these nomads in their defense," Brena answered, a severe expression on her face.

"What in Skrull's hell are you talking about?" Saudett hissed. "We are not joining them! We are to acquire my husband and leave immediately."

"Then you will die." Brena's blue eyes held her own, unwavering.

Saudett grimaced back at the woman. "How so?"

"If the nomads catch you stealing off with him, they will kill you. If not, the *Daanav* will kill you in the desert, or the desert itself will kill you. We will not aid you in *thieving* him back; we will help anyone in need. It is better to offer a trade. We will fight for them, and once the beasts are dealt with, they will give up your husband." Brena's tone was cold as ice.

Baal grunted in agreement.

"It could be years before the threat of the Daanav is destroyed. We have no idea where they are coming from or what they want," Saudett pleaded.

"Then we will wait. We will build. We will fight."

Saudett shook her head in disbelief. *This is where Hata got her stubborn goodwill from.* She sighed heavily, "Have it your way." She slowed her horse to a stop and let the two continue together. She sat in silence, staring blankly. Grains of sand whispered and rolled gently across the dunes. *I am all alone.*

The young woman, Hata, pulled up alongside Kiana at the head of the group.

"Hello, Kogs. Hello, Kiana Ahmadi. How is your wound?"

The blonde angel had cleaned and dressed the wound to Kiana's left arm with the utmost care.

"It is tender but healing. Your mother's grace blesses me." She studied the tall, red-haired girl. She undoubtedly wasn't all that younger than Kiana herself. "Hata, was it?"

"Do we trust this one?" Kogs hissed.

"We trust all our new friends, Kogs," Kiana reassured.

"Kogs still don't trust the big one."

"You'll get used to him, Kogs," Hata replied. "He's simply a big muscle head. He is as cuddly as a hibernating Mountain Bear in a North Iron winter." She smiled playfully.

"Generally, bears are quite irritable when woken from hibernation. No?" Kiana laughed.

"What is bear?" Kogs's head tilted to the right.

Hata's face scrunched up in amused confusion. "They are akin to large furry dogs."

"What are these dogs?" The lizard's head bobbed back to the left, his red mane shaking.

"It is a four-legged beast, man's best friend. You know, like a pet," Hata urged.

"Ah, it's a pet, like Kogs's cute little Avendicaticarius. He is a blind mole beetle that digs up grubs on Kogs's grub farm. Oh, little Avendicaticarius, such a pretty mole beetle. He must be keeping my lovely Gaks company."

"Avendicaticarius? Quite the name for a pet." Kiana stifled a laugh with her hand.

"Yes, very simple name," Kogs said, then continued to murmur about missing his Gaks and pet mole beetle.

"At any rate, Hata, what brings you to converse with this wretched bandit?" Kiana inquired.

"I just wanted to get to know you and understand your actions. How did you end up in your tribe?"

"It's not much of a story, I'm afraid. I was born into it. My father was one of the first to come to Hasiera. My mother was an outsider who came to the oasis in her early third decade, where she met my father."

"What did she do before?"

"She keeps her past behind her; she only looks forward. I know it involved her fine-tuning skills in combat, as she is a dangerous woman. A stern woman."

"She passed her knowledge on to you? How to fight?"

"Indeed. I would train with my mother every day. When I was young, she was hard to be with; she beat, bruised, and bloodied me. I truly hated her and still resent her for those days." Kiana sighed. "I don't know why I'm speaking to you of this, whom I have just met. I don't know the lot of you."

"Now and again, it can be painless to empty your heart to a stranger who is willing to listen."

This girl, she is so kind. Kiana smiled half-heartedly. "Perhaps."

"Would you be the woman you are today had your mother not done what she did?" said a man's voice.

They turned to look at Kaplan, who had kept his distance from the two but had seemingly heard everything.

"Eavesdropping is not welcome, sir." Hata frowned at the man.

He shrugged. "Well?" he asked again.

Kiana hesitated, thinking for a moment. *Was he right? Would I even be Otsoa right now if not for my mother?* She would doubtlessly still be dreaming of leaving Hasiera and exploring the world. Her life could have been very different. "I don't know," she murmured.

"The answer is no. You would not be in this place at this time, doing precisely what you are doing now, if not for the influences of your childhood. You would have made different decisions and taken different paths. The past sculpts you, but the future is full of potential; it is what *you* make of it. You said so yourself moments ago, 'She keeps her past behind her; she only looks forward.' Indeed, it is a valuable way to look upon life."

Gods, who are these people? Why are they making me think so much? They sat awkwardly as Kiana's mind retraced to her childhood. Instead of regretting all the things she could have done, she reflected and began accepting each moment as a part of her.

Her mother's difficult training. Her father's wise words. Hasiera. Her people. The Otsoa.

Kiana could not change her past; she could only accept that all the hardship her mother brought upon her had built her into the warrior and the *woman* she had become. Her father's level-headedness and teaching of governing people had taught her the skills to manage her Otsoak and command her units.

"Kill the filthy, lying masters, Kogs will. That will change Kogs's future, yes." The little lizard was rubbing his hands together, furtively whispering to himself.

"Yes, you are indeed correct, Kogs. We can determine *our* future," Kiana whispered back. Then, speaking louder, she said, "Our new friends are quite virtuous, are they not, Kogs?"

"Yes, yes, virtuous," he answered, still preoccupied with his musings.

"Do you still train with your mother these days?" Hata inquired.

"Now and then, we will spar together, though it is far less frequent now with both of our roles as Otsoa, not to mention the threat of the Daanav."

"Do you see each other outside of these sparring matches?"

"Not often. We live separately in our sections of the valley."

"Your mother may enjoy these sparring sessions as her only means of connecting with you, like my mother and I enjoy cooking and sewing together without that brute of a father interrupting us." Hata giggled.

Come to think of it, we only really speak during our sparring matches. Kiana brought her mind back to one of those moments and let the memory overtake her senses.

Sweat was dripping from Kiana's brows and soaking her back and chest that day. Like most sessions, she had felt like she was always on the defense. She tensed and darted under a swing of the wooden sword, parrying a second, catching a third, and holding it momentarily while her mother conversed casually.

"My daughter, have you met a suitable companion yet? Would you like to share any men or women in your life with your dear mother?"

Kiana pushed the blade away and began her assault. A thrust.

Parried.

She flowed into a spin, a strike low on the opposite side.

Her mother effortlessly hopped over the blow, her sword darting out in a jab instantly, catching Kiana on her shoulder.

With the momentum of her spinning attack and the strike to her shoulder, Kiana lost control and spun backward, face-planting into the dust.

"Your movements are too grandiose, my daughter. You must be quick and watch for tender openings to bite. Remember the dance."

Kiana grunted while pushing herself to her feet. "No, I have not met someone to form a bond with. I am more than satisfied spending my nights in the long tent."

Her mother clicked her tongue in disapproval. "You will end up pregnant, with no one to aid you on those long sleepless nights, with a helpless babe crying at your tits."

"I drink the elders' potion every morning. I will not become with child." Kiana's voice rose.

"Nothing is certain."

"AND I would anticipate that if I were to bear a child, my ever-caring mother and father could provide some assistance for their only daughter!" Clenching her jaw in anger, she burst into an attack once again. Kiana sent a flurry of blows at her mother; each being met in kind. Left, right feint, into a jab.

Her mother countered once, sword weaving through Kiana's attacks to find her sword hand, and the weapon flew from her grip. Then, her mother leveled her own at Kiana's neck.

"Your father and I are both Otsoa; we do not have the privilege or the time to be caretakers of our daughter's infant. You can make your own choices, and choosing to risk bringing a child into this world alone is your own. You will face the consequence of raising it yourself. You will not abandon it and miss every moment you could have had together!" There were tears in her mother's eyes. Kiana couldn't remember the last time she saw tears in her mother's eyes.

"It's getting dark." Kaplan's voice snapped Kiana back to reality.

She looked around to regain her bearings; Kaplan and Hata had dismounted and were readying to make camp. "This looks like as good a spot as any," Kiana said.

"Wait. I feel something," Hata piped up, then looked back to her approaching parents and the sullen soldier Saudett bringing up the rear.

Kiana couldn't resist. "What do you mean, you can feel something?

Hata waved forward the three behind them. "I'll explain later; no sense hiding it now." Once the others had joined them, Hata spoke quickly, "I can feel movement ahead."

Saudett's eyes met Kiana's. The woman narrowed her eyes at her, then grunted, "How far?"

"I believe they haven't noticed us. The monsters are moving crosswise in our path. On the opposite side of that dune." Hata pointed.

"Can we avoid them?" Kaplan asked.

"I will need to focus." Hata gave a quick nod as if to reassure herself.

"All right, try and lead us away from any movement you feel. We will be on the lookout for a place to camp." Saudett ordered. "No fire tonight."

She is a natural leader. Kiana could see the woman's soldier instincts take over.

It was slow going. The group's pace was halved as they followed Hata's lead, the girl now walking in the sand, Saudett close at her side once more. After an hour and a bit, Hata breathed heavily and leaned against the other woman.

Finally, Saudett spoke, "That's enough. We will have to make do with the base of this dune. Hata cannot go on any further."

"I can," Hata murmured in reply.

"You still have to be vigilant during the night, Hata," Saudett paused. "The *entire* night."

Hata's eyes widened in realization.

What is this power of hers? Kiana pondered.

"You will have to try and sleep on the cart tomorrow during the day going forward," Saudett said, tenderly brushing the red hair out of the girl's face. Hata flinched slightly.

Exceptionally friendly to this young woman, this married woman is. Kiana shrugged and began to help the others make a light camp, easy to pack and go at a moment's notice.

"The rest of us should take shifts staying up with the Sunstone," Kaplan added.

They all murmured in agreement.

Sunstone?

So began a restless night for most of the group except Baal, who snored peacefully on his bedroll. Saudett took the first watch alongside Hata, sitting apart in silence. Hata sat cross-legged on the ground, her hands on each side in the sand with her eyes closed, her brow furrowed in concentration. Saudett wanted to speak with Hata but was unsure of what to say. *I am still frustrated with the girl. I bared my soul to her, and she walked off. And Hata is obsessed with this nomad woman.* Saudett was also uncertain if everyone was asleep and did not want them eavesdropping on their delicate situation. Finally calming herself, she summoned the courage to speak after a long time. *I need to apologize.*

"Hata," Saudett began.

"Lieutenant, get some rest," Kaplan interrupted, ready to take the next watch.

"Ah, alright." Saudett stood, looking down at Hata, still intensely focused on her magic. She turned and left the two to their devices. She unrolled her bedding a slight distance from the other sleeping bodies. The cold desert air sent a chill through her. She curled up, knees to her chest, wrapping herself in the woolen blanket. She felt the sudden need to vomit.

"Simon," she murmured. "Where are you?"

Hata opened her eyes as Saudett walked away to bed for the night. She was relieved Saudett hadn't spoken to her during her shift. Saudett's words pained her. *Calling me a child means Saudett thinks I'm lesser than herself, and I'm still upset with Saudett's treatment of Kiana Ahmadi. The woman isn't taking the perspective of the nomadic people into account. She's just filled with rage and vengeance.* It was like a different side of the warrior woman had surfaced; she was usually very calm and collected. *It hurts so much to see Saudett like this.*

Hata felt a ripple in the sand around her. She sucked in a breath.

"What is it?" Kaplan whispered, the hand on the hilt of his blade.

"Shush," she raised a hand to tell the man to wait. "Hold on a moment." Hata closed her eyes and focused on the sensation. She felt numerous heavy dragging feet moving aimlessly through the sands. *Teras protect us,* Hata thought. She sighed in relief as she realized the hulks were moving away from them in a northerly direction.

"They are leaving. We are safe for now," Hata whispered to Kaplan.

He did not release the grip on his scimitar. "Strange that we have not been attacked once more. Is it not?" he asked suspiciously.

"Is it? I am doing everything I can to ensure that does not happen." She felt suddenly exhausted.

"My apologies, Sunstone. It is in my nature to be ever skeptical; it has been ingrained in my soul."

Hata smiled; he was the only one who referred to her as the Sunstone.

"And why is that?" Another voice joined them; it was Kiana Ahmadi. As she sat down next to them, she carried the lizard man, Kogs, cradling him like a babe, ever stroking his tuft of head fur.

"I would not bore you both with the story," Kaplan answered.

"We have all night." Kiana shrugged.

"Please, if you would, Kaplan, sir," Hata implored. "It will help keep me from drifting off."

"If you insist." He took a deep breath and began to speak.

An almost strange enthusiasm overtook Kaplan as his words transported the listeners to a bright, magnificent city: the sun dancing on the sea in the horizon, the sound of gulls in the distance, beautiful colorful sails of catamarans dotting the waves, and shining gold-and-silver tear-drop-shaped domes of a massive palace on the waterfront. They felt as if they were walking, or instead, *running,* in Kaplan Mir's footsteps as he began his tale in Al'Jalif, the Jewel of the East.

Chapter Twenty-Eight
Wish

Kaplan ran as fast as he could through the crowd of people dressed colorfully in bright silks and fabrics in the bustling Market District, clutching a loaf of warm bread under his arm.

"Stop that boy!" he heard a voice shouting behind him.

People stared down at him as he ran. He saw the looks of disgust on their faces, the loathing. *They hate me.* Most looked on, ignoring the merchant's pleas to stop him. The good thing about the rich was they would never go out of their way to involve themselves with a filthy, homeless street urchin.

"Halt!" He saw the glint of silver scales ahead, the pointed helms of the city watch. He turned on a dime, ducking under a slow-moving wagon, but the sound of metal-clad footfalls grew close on his heels. More shouting. Noticing an alley ahead. He made a beeline for the opening, retreating into the safety of the winding back streets. Jumping over a pile of filth, he glanced over his shoulder. He collided with another body, the bread flying from his grasp.

He heard a yelp. "Ah!"

He scrambled to his feet. A young girl came face-to-face with him, with tattered rags hanging loosely on her gaunt, wiry frame. Her wide brown eyes took him in.

"Get out of the way. The guards are coming!" He looked about frantically for his bread.

"Looking for this?"

He looked down into the hands of the girl before him, the loaf broken in two, clutched within them.

"Stop right there!" The guards came crashing down the alley, pushing through the rubbish.

"Come on, let's go!" He grabbed the girl's shoulders and spun her around, nudging her gently to run ahead of him.

She did not hesitate. Quicker than Kaplan expected, she bolted in front of him. He was hard-pressed to keep up. She led him, twisting and turning through the alleys, past the shit-stained walls, where slaves discarded the refuse out of the back windows of each homestead. Though he had never seen her, she seemed to know where she was going. He supposed that Al'Jalif was too large to see every orphan child in the Market District.

After many minutes, the sounds of chase died down, then vanished. It seemed the guards had given up.

"Hold up, you!" he called.

She slowed to a trot, then stopped and turned, nonchalantly taking a large bite from one of the loaves.

"Those belong to me!" he growled, moving closer to her, trying to grab the broken bread from her hands.

She deftly avoided his efforts. "At least one belongs to me, as I saved you from losing a hand back there."

He snorted. "If not for you, I would have been halfway across the Jewel by the time those oafs caught up."

"Should have been looking forward and not back then, silly boy."

He frowned. The girl smiled and took another bite of the bread.

"Have it your way. Keep one. Hand over the other half."

Her eyes sparkled with amusement. "Here you go." She held out her hand with the uneaten piece. As he moved to grasp it, she laughed and thrust the half-eaten one into his stomach, dropping it. Dumbfounded, he bent over to pick up the now-squished piece of bread. When he stood up, she was gone, her giggle echoing down the alley. His stomach grumbled. He shrugged, sat down, and ate what was left of the loaf.

"You aren't going to chase me?" she called inquisitively.

"Why? To use up my stamina?" he answered flatly. "It's simpler to return to the market and steal another than waste time chasing after you."

She crept back into his vision. "For fun, perhaps?"

He snorted again. "I'd rather eat."

"Pfft, come on, sad little boy, chase me!"

"No." He turned away from her, facing a shit-stained wall, the smell gagging him.

"Fine then; I was *going* to bring you home with me. Nishulk gives all the children a portion of rice curry every morning and night if we give her a gift daily."

"I can fend for myself, girl." His stomach grumbled once again.

The girl put her arms around him from behind and lifted him to his feet.

"What are you doing? Let go of me!"

She took him by the hand and began to walk. He resisted for a moment, then gave in. *I am so hungry.*

They moved through the streets, the bright colors of the Market District fading into dreary tans and grays. The further one moved from the Dhan Ka Mahal, the poorer the city became. The palace and its luminous gold-and-silver pointed pinnacles were located directly on the easternmost side of Al'Jalif, the grounds encompassing a large portion of the oceanfront. It was barred off by a ten-pace tall black iron-grate fence and hedging behind that. The gardens were strictly used by only the hefty Sultan, Jhanda Muzumdar, and his score of wives. Kaplan had the itch to see what lay beyond the fence and hedge, but he could scarcely reach the outskirts of the heavily guarded Manor District, let alone the palace grounds.

"Do you have a gift?" the girl asked.

"A gift?"

"For Nishulk. A gift? If you want food, you must give her something in return."

Kaplan had little on his person: a simple steel knife, tarnished and mostly blunted, and a handful of copper, coming to roughly seven pence.

He had other odds and ends at his rooftop home closer to the Market District but still in the slums. He had found some old books in the rubbish near the back garden gate of a high-end estate. He could not read them, yet he cherished them, *vowing* to learn to read one day.

He held out the contents of his pockets to the girl.

"That may get you a half portion for the lot of them." She began to untie a strip of linen wrapped around her thin, tan ankle. As she finished unwrapping, Kaplan watched as two silver coins fell. "This is the only time I will aid you, sad little boy. Next time, you will acquire your own gift." She grasped one of the coins and flicked it from her thumb toward him.

He snatched it out of the air. "Why are you doing this?"

She shrugged. "A silver coin will fill your bowl to the brim. Come on, we're nearly there."

"Wait, what is your name?"

"Jhuta."

"I am Kaplan."

Night had fallen when the girl led him to a doorway into a dingy-brown sandstone complex on the very brink of the city. One atop another, the many rectangular-shaped buildings were stacked at different intervals, forming roughly equilaterally shaped hills.

Entering the dank interior, Kaplan saw the only light source creep through the cracks on a door on the far side of the room. It took a moment for Kaplan to realize the room was full of children of various ages, lying about in makeshift bedding of mostly rubbish. All were thin and hungry-looking. They stared at him as the girl, Jhuta, led him toward the door.

She knocked once sharply.

"Who disturbs poor Nishulk at this hour?" Kaplan heard a grizzled voice from the opposite side.

The girl answered swiftly, "Jhuta."

"Ah, my favorite. Jhuta. Come enter quickly now."

Jhuta pushed the door open and, still holding Kaplan's hand, pulled him inside and shut the door behind them.

Candles lit the room; sacks of rice covered one chamber wall. A massive pot sat steaming over a hearth, the smoke drifting into a dark hole in the center of the angled ceiling. A timid, gaunt-looking boy stood stirring the pot. On the other wall was another doorway. In the center was a large bed covered in faded and torn silk sheets and pillows of varying colors. The woman on the bed was a thin, frail being with an oversized red silk robe hanging about her gaunt frame. Her aged skin sagged on her face.

"What do we have here?" said a ragged voice that was unpleasant to Kaplan's ears. "A newcomer? Jhuta, introduce me to your new man, will you?"

"This is Kaplan. He is sad and hungry, Sultana Nishulk."

"Kaplan, is it? Are you hungry?" Her loose skin creased as she spoke. "Do you come to poor Nishulk bearing gifts?"

Jhuta elbowed him in the ribs.

Sultana of what? Kaplan thought. He raised the silver coin in two fingers. "I do."

The sagging face smiled a toothless smile. "A full bowl for young Kaplan. A worthy gift for a first-timer indeed. Wouldn't you say, Jhuta?"

"The boy snitched it from a noblewoman at the market. I watched him do it."

"Truly?" Nishulk raised her hairless brows. "You have some skill then, Kaplan child?"

"I do."

"Ha, ha, ha!" The skin wrinkled with her laughter. "Whatever skills you think you have mean nothing here, sad little boy. So, here is the deal: Kaplan boy, if you serve me, give me a gift every day for three years. Then, I will grant you one wish."

He studied the creature before him. "And how would you do that?"

"Come closer. I will show you." She waved her bony-fingered hand, beckoning him forward.

He hesitated; he was better off on his own. What could this woman possibly offer him? *I could buy five loaves of bread with a silver coin.*

He began to turn. Jhuta's arms wrapped around his neck in a headlock. He grasped the slim arms with his fingers, trying to pull away, to no avail. She was strong. She inched him forward until he was at the edge of the large bed. It reeked of stale filth. The sickly woman shifted toward him. Stench wafted over Kaplan.

Nishulk grasped his head with both hands, and Kaplan felt his thoughts being penetrated and scoured through. *Violation.* Moments later, she released his head. Likewise, Jhuta let go of her headlock and quickly retreated toward the door.

Kaplan vomited.

"Clean that up, Bello," Nishulk shouted at the boy, stirring the pot of rice gravy. "Kaplan Mir's greatest wish at this moment. It is but to learn how to read. Ah-ha ha! Well, Kaplan Mir, serve me well, and I will *teach* you."

"By all the gods, that is horrendous," Kiana jumped in. "All this time in the valley, I dreamed of life outside the Burning Sea. Yet it's not as wonderful as I had hoped."

"There is evil wherever humanity makes its home. Be it in your valley sanctuary or the slums of Al'Jalif. Or to the *usually* quiet town of Dagad."

Kiana snorted.

"What happens next, Kaplan, sir?" Hata eyed him expectantly.

"What happened next is...I get some rest, girl." He smiled at her. That was the first time Kiana had seen the man smile.

Brena woke Baal in the early hours of the morning for his watch. Being the last to join Hata, Baal let her lean against him. When he caught her nodding off, he gently nudged her. Finally, a warm glow began to peak from the horizon. Baal immediately cradled Hata in his arms and carried her to the wagon he had prepared the previous evening with blankets and a makeshift covering to shelter her during the day. He gently laid her down. She had already fallen asleep in his arms. He put a hand on her cheek, then kissed her forehead. He straightened, looking to see if anyone had caught this tender act.

Kaplan Mir sat silently cross-legged, watching the sunrise, his scimitar across his lap. With Kaplan's back turned from the large man, Baal could not see him smile for the second time that night.

Chapter Twenty-Nine

FATE

Simon rubbed his eyes. *Gods, I'm exhausted.* The damn dream was happening every time sleep took him. His body was sore from swimming. Every time he made it to the dimly lit cavern at the end of the tunnel, he would be immediately pulled down while fighting upward and lose his breath. *Skrull, take me. I must do something about this.*

Simon stood in front of his newly finished wall.

It is finished on one side of the valley, anyway, and I would use the word "finished" loosely. Yes, there is a sandstone barrier, taller than me, across the western side of the gorge, but only the section near the gate had enough scaffolding for archers to station themselves atop it in defense.

The entrance, as it were, was a simple rectangular wall opening. Simon had ordered the construction of bamboo platforms on each side of the gate, spanning thirty paces. Sharpened palisades provided a makeshift semicircle barring the entrance on the ground. It could be dragged to the side when people moved in and out of the camp.

We need to get started on digging a trench in front. It is not half bad for the month, or so we've been at it. But the enemy could also penetrate their defense by moving their attack to the undefended hillside on the valley's south end. By the gods, Simon needed more time. *What if they attacked from the completely opposite side?* He felt despair closing in on him; this fool's task he had been set to just had too many variables. There was no telling when they would be discovered. His stomach turned with anxiety.

"You've done well, Builder."

Simon's mood darkened further. "First," he answered curtly.

"At this rate, another few months and the valley will be much safer. We are grateful to you and your workmen. Come, let us walk." The First gestured for him to follow.

Simon hesitated for a moment, then caught up alongside the man. He needed to voice his thoughts aloud to someone. *Who better to vent to than the leader of this damned village?* "There is still too much to do," Simon said. "If we were attacked tonight, everyone here would die."

"You are correct. If that were to happen, the warriors of Hasiera would fight to the last." They walked on silently for a few minutes before the First spoke again. "I'm afraid I must ask something more of you, Builder."

Simon bent an eyebrow suspiciously. "Ask?"

"The cavern you have excavated in the cliffside. Could you bar off the entrance and make a shelter for the women, children, and elders?"

"It is not large enough for everyone. The underground river goes a long way into the earth, but it will not be suitable to shelter hundreds."

"Very well; here is my second proposal. Can you dig a path to the surface in the same cavern or along that river?"

"An escape route. Damn, that should have occurred to me. Yes, that shouldn't take long. I'll have my men begin immediately."

"Lastly, should Hasiera come under attack, I want you to lead the non-combatants out. Head south. There is a jungle but a fortnight from here. For the most part, it is uninhabited, though it will provide some shelter, food, and water."

"But...why me?" Simon blinked in confusion.

"I have been watching you. My people have been watching you. Though you may hate me, your kindness to those in need far outweighs my feelings for you. I am selfish. I took you from your home to protect my own. You could have refused to work, even at the cost of your own life. However, you could not leave my people to their doom. I thank you for your compassion, Simon Meridio."

Simon narrowed his eyes at the man. *Is he genuine?* His father's face flashed before his eyes, and he felt his neck heating up in anger.

"Behold." The First turned and gestured a hand for Simon to look.

They had made their way to the south-side hilltops and looked down upon the valley. The sun was beginning to set with a warm orange glow. The shadows of palm trees, tents, and a solid line from the wall stretched at an angle east and south. The river gently shimmered with the golden rays. The valley looked at peace.

The rage slowly drained from Simon as he looked upon the sight. It was stunning, a pocket of the heavens within an ocean of waste.

"I still hope you choke on a handful of sand in your sleep," Simon muttered.

The First smiled slightly but said nothing.

"I will do as you ask," Simon exhaled. "If we are attacked, I will lead the helpless out of Hasiera. If by some miracle we are *not* attacked, and this damned wall is completed, will you release me?"

The First scowled. "None leave Hasiera once they have entered it. Should any fools escape, they are hunted and ridden down."

"You just said I must lead your people out of here."

"Yes, if we are doomed to die at the hands of the Daanav. Otherwise, this is the measure of it. I have kept our home hidden from the outside world, and I mean to keep it that way."

"Skrull's cock up my ass, man! Make up your mind!"

The First Otsoa shrugged, turned away from Simon, and descended the hill.

Now left alone at the top of the hill, Simon looked away from the valley. He began to walk out into the desert, the hardened grass-covered hills slowly browning and turning to sand. The rolling desert dunes reached as far as the eye could see. *I could leave it all behind.* His feet sank into the deeper sand.

His father's image and words appeared in his mind.

"Simon, ensure the main beam is reinforced for load bearing of a second level," Yakeb said.

"Ah yes, Father, I nearly forgot. Thank you," Simon answered, smiling at his father's focused expression as he examined the blueprint of the homestead addition.

"Let me double-check the measurements, but other than that, it looks sound, my son."

Simon rolled his eyes. *The measurements are correct.* "Better protected than pitiful, as they say."

His father scratched some charcoal on a parchment, "Hmm, who are *they?*"

"Oh, never mind. So, Father, I spied on you chatting with Saudett. How do you find her?"

"Carry the seven...oh, yes, Saudett! Yes, Saudett. She is a breath of fresh air with a spirit of flame."

"She is strong-willed, to say the least."

"Yes, much like your mother used to be."

"Hettra's peace upon Mother's soul. If only she could have met Saudett. Think they would get along or butt heads? You know what they say about in-laws."

Yakeb's head tilted. "What do *they* say?"

"Uhm, ah. You know...it's not coming to mind."

Yakeb laughed, "Oh, my son. Anyways, have you a mind to propose to this woman? Ready to settle down? Or are you still young and gung-ho about fooling around with men?"

"From the first time I looked at her, I knew I would marry her."

"I'm proud of you, my son," Yakeb smiled. "Now, this window frame. It looks to be a quarter inch off its mark. We need to redraw the plan."

Skrull's balls...

Simon turned back to Hasiera.

No, I will not leave. I will protect the people of Hasiera. I will finish the damned wall. Then I will kill the bastard First and go home. I will do it for my father.

He started walking down the hill.

Half an hour later, he was at the entrance of the mining cavern, relaying the plan to dig their way out.

"Leave it to us, boss, ya!" Ilan smiled at him.

Simon contemplated having more fun with him, perhaps distracting himself from the suffocation of the looming threat, the weight of the task at hand. Then he shook his head. "Who among you is the strongest swimmer?"

"Well, now, that would be me then, boss," Naurr had snuck up on Simon again.

"You should be sleeping, my good man; it's still my shift for a few more hours."

"Couldn't get a wink of sleep," Naurr said. "I say, my stomach is all twisted. Why do you need a good swimmer? I grew up swimming on the coast of Tal'tulu. Where you needing swimming too, eh?"

"The underground river," Simon said flatly.

"Why in Skrull's hell do you need to do that, ya?" Ilan asked.

"Because I'm sick of fucking drowning in my sleep every night!"

There was an awkward silence among the workmen.

Simon cleared his throat, "I'm sorry, my good lads. I'm very irritable and frustrated now. Please, let me explain." He paused for a moment. "It began the day of the attack on Dagad. That very morning, and many mornings since I've had a dream where I am underwater. A faint light shines above, yet try as I may, it is unreachable. I see another light below, and I'm being pulled downwards. As I lose my breath and suck the cold water into my lungs, I awaken in this world, my lungs still full of the water." He breathed heavily. "More recently, I have dreamt of the passage along the submerged tunnel. There are air pockets along the tunnel. I feel like I am being called to this place, to this underground river. The damned dream has become more frequent since coming to Hasiera. I am literally drowning in despair!"

There was another long pause after his story.

Finally, Ilan spoke. "Why don't we tie a rope to ya? Pull ya out should things go belly up, as it were, ya?"

"Aye, we could do that," said Naurr. "But how in Skrull's mighty hell would we know he needs to be pulled out? First, we need to check if the air pockets in the dream are truth. If so, the air must be coming along up from somewhere, eh?"

Simon held back tears. *The bastards are too good for me, acting like it's no big deal, just another problem to solve. Such brothers. Such men.*

"Come on, boss. Let's see what in Skrull's hairy balls is calling for ya," Ilan gently guided him toward the tunnel.

Simon let himself be led. He wanted to break down; he didn't want to ever feel the water filling his lungs again.

The group followed the stream further into the ground, a few men carrying torches to light the way, some with ropes and tools ready. They eventually came to the end of the traversable underground. From this point on, they would have to swim underneath the surface.

"All right, you lazy drudges, give me the end of that rope and some iron spikes, quick like!" Naurr ordered. "Ilan boy, hand me that hammer of yours."

Ilan quickly fumbled the sizable hammer from his belt and handed it to the out-stretched hand of Naurr.

Naurr clutched the hammer. "I will find the first spot of air to place the nail and tie the rope to. Then advancing until we find the end of the tunnel."

"Come now, this is foolish. Let's head back," Simon urged.

"Don't be worrying now, boss. The boys and I always have your back." With that, Naurr clenched the hammer between his teeth and dived into the water, the rope trailing into the darkness.

"Gods, the lot of you are mad. It was just a dream!" Simon exclaimed anxiously. He would pace if space permitted; instead, he fidgeted nervously with his nose ring.

"Boss, once we kick this dream of yours, I highly recommend visiting the long tent with us, ya. These Hasierans sure know how to partake in earthly pleasures. They have plenty of wine and some herbal concoctions that numb the senses. Plenty of fun to be had. Take your pick: men, women, one or two. Everyone shares; nobody cares. It is quite the establishment, it is, ya," Ilan said with a wink.

Simon sighed, rubbing his eyes. "I'm sure it would be a hoot, my dear friend. If we somehow rid me of this cursed dream, I will take a very long rest, first and foremost."

"Perhaps after that, then, ya?" Ilan asked longingly.

"I'll think about it. Gods know I need a rest, and some more pleasure would be welcome."

With a splash and a gasp of air sucked into his lungs, Naurr caught his breath and slowly waded toward them.

"That there is a long stretch onto the first nail, but with a rope now tied, it should be cutting down on time. I placed the second spike as well, but I ran out of rope."

"Right here, chief." One of the other men handed him a larger coil.

"Eh?! Give me a minute to catch my breath! You hounds!" Naurr crouched down, panting heavily.

"Here, let me do the next nail." Simon tried to wrestle the rope from Naurr's shoulder.

Naurr resisted him for a moment, then let Simon take the coil.

"Not so fast, boss. I'll do the next run, ya." Ilan took the rope, reached around, and pinched Simon's buttocks. "Be back in a jiff, ya." He put a hand on the line already placed leading into the water and quickly disappeared beneath the stream.

Philandering man! Simon smiled, thinking back to their exchange in the cave. *Come back quickly, Ilan.*

This time, they sat in relative silence for a while. Simon tried to think of something to distract himself from the situation. Since coming to the valley, he hadn't had a good talk with Naurr or any of his men. All their conversations that *did* happen were about the work on the wall. If he was honest, even before they came here, all they ever talked about was the task at hand. He looked around at the handful of others, leaning against the walls or sitting and crouching in the cramped tunnel. He wondered what they could be thinking about. He cleared his throat. "Naurr and anyone who wishes to answer, what do you think of our new home? Do you all miss Dagad? Your families?"

Murmurs erupted amongst the men, some in agreement, some more disgruntled.

"Alas, I be longing to see my little boy, Noa, again," Naurr whispered. "And my beauty of a lady, my Cenna."

Simon felt his heartache. "I apologize. I got you tangled up in this mess, all of you."

"It's not on you. You didn't steal us away and bring us here," one of the men replied.

"Yeah, and it's not so bad. There are scores of gorgeous people here. No need to worry about money or your next meal. Comradery, fellowship, some friendly competition between the Otsoa," said another man standing and holding the rope end. "*Gods*, the long tent." He rolled his eyes in exaggerated pleasure.

"It won't last long," yet another added. "Did you see the monsters we are up against? *I did*. If we don't finish the wall, the place will go from heaven to hell in minutes."

"It's true," Naurr said. "We must help these people. I couldn't go home to my boy, knowing I did nothing to help them. The Primus brought us here, and we best not leave them to die."

"I agree with you on that front, Naurr." Simon nodded. "Let's assume we finish the wall before the attack. Let's go even so far as to say the Hasieran people repel or defeat the creatures. I have it from a reliable source that you are never allowed to leave once you come to the Valley of Hasiera."

Expressions darkened on a few of the men, Naurr included.

"Who said this, then?" Naurr asked.

"From the very lips of the First Otsoa himself," replied Simon.

Naurr stood, cracking his knuckles. "We may have to do something about that, then."

There was a moment of silence, then the man on the rope spoke up curiously. "Ilan's been gone for quite a while."

"Skrull, take me," Simon muttered. He had forgotten about him. "We had best retrieve the man."

CHAPTER THIRTY

FORWARD

There must be a thousand of them. Over the last few days, the force of nomads Jude was traveling with had tripled in size. They had met up with other similar-sized groups and were now moving in force for home—the Valley of Hasiera, the oasis in the desert. The company was always alert, ready to engage in battle at a moment's notice. They had been traveling night and day. Sleep for none. Jude had swallowed a magic marble that made the lack of sleep mean little to him.

The nomads had left a tiny detachment with the wagons and weaker drug-induced prisoners to follow in the coming days. Greens and Ryon were left among them. *The bastards.* The last Jude had seen of the two criminals, they were bound at the hands, stumbling behind one of the carriages. Jude smiled and mouthed a silent prayer of thanks to Qav for luck, that the two would get what was coming.

But Jude needed to discover more: *Why is such a large force gathering and seemingly ready for war?* He had not had a chance to speak with the woman who appeared to be the group leader, who had captured Jude and his *friends.*

A small group of freed prisoners and some of the caravan guards that had accompanied them originally had not joined them after the skirmish with the nomads. Instead, they had chosen to make the journey home to Dagad. They had been sufficiently provisioned. A wagon with many goods had been left to them for resale and a chance to start over. Most slaves had been young people in their second decade, so Jude doubted they would be worldly enough to know what to do with the goods and would most likely be taken advantage of again.

He shrugged. *The world is brutal, and those children are not my problem. I've already managed to get them a second chance at life.* His problem was finding the damn red-headed Vouri girl. *But why the fucks are the nomads gathering such an army?* He needed to speak with one of them. He angled his horse to gently drift in the direction of one of the nomads riding nearby.

He feigned nodding off sleepily in the saddle and let his horse get reasonably close to the rider before the man cried, "Hy!"

Jude pretended to startle awake and brought his horse back a few paces from the other man. "Terribly sorry, the heat and lack of rest had me drifting off."

The other man waved a hand in dismissal and stared forward as he rode.

Jude coughed dryly, pulling at his tunic's neckline. "This heat, how far are we from the nearest watering hole? There are a lot of people here in need of it."

Still staring forward, the man pulled a water skin from his saddlebag and tossed it to Jude without looking at him, the water sloshing in the skin.

Jude snatched it out of mid-air and took a long swig. "My thanks to you, friend!" He tossed the skin back. "Can you enlighten me as to why we are gathering such a formidable battalion?"

"*We* are not. *Hasiera* is preparing for war."

"War against whom?"

The man looked at Jude for the first time and gave him a once over, sizing him up. "Against death itself." The man spurred his horse forward, away from Jude.

Jude arched an eyebrow questioningly. "Well fucks then, I suppose we're done talking."

A horn rang out through the scorching noon air.

People pointed to the sky. A shadow flashed over Jude, briefly darkening his vision before gliding swiftly over the sands.

The nomads began to shout, "Kahytul! Kahytul!"

Jude heard a piercing screech as an enormous vulture-like bird wheeled about. It was red-brown, save for its long, thick neck and upper legs of sinewy, rutted gray skin. Massive talons caught the glint of sunlight. People and horses chaotically dashed in all directions.

Jude held his horse steady and watched. The Kahytul flew directly in line with the sun, blinding him so he could not see where it went. Moments later, he heard another screech as the colossal condor crashed into a group of nomads, skidding along the ground, talons ripping through horse and rider. The hooked beak plucked a man up, leaving a trail of destruction behind it. Thundering flaps of its massive wings, the bird took a few running steps before leaping off the ground to continue its momentum. It began to ascend once more.

Jude toyed with a marble in his pouch. The Kahytul was coming around for another pass. He didn't like relying on the spell-infused beads but didn't see much of an option.

The bird came in low, not enough to touch down this time. Arrows and spears arched toward it, most falling short. The bird stayed just out of reach, surveying the area, circling.

"Spears! Archers! To me!"

Jude saw the warrior woman commanding her troops. She led a tight band of spear-wielding cavalry, flanked on each side by groups of horse archers, to make a three-pronged V-formation snaking about the desert. She judged the angle of the next attack the bird would come from and led her force to meet it head-on.

As they rode directly at the beast, about to collide, for a moment, time stood still. The bird screamed, then lunged its maw at the woman heading the column. There was an explosion of sand and dust. The archers on each side unloaded arrow after arrow into the cloud as they flanked about. Miraculously, Jude saw the woman riding out the opposite side of the clash, many horsemen following her, now spear-less. Drawing their swords, they turned and charged back into the fray. The dust was settling somewhat now from the initial impact.

By the gods, they are insane. The Kahytul continued screeching, though it sounded distressed and gargled. One wing hung loosely at its side, and it limped about. Spears bristled from its chest, and arrows pin-cushioned the sides and back of the massive bird. Still, some unlucky warriors were crushed under the mass of the raptor or ripped in half, splashes of blood and limbs bursting into the air.

The leader reached the rear of the raptor; she stood, leaping onto the back of the bird and running up its spine. Nomads hacked and slashed at the legs and belly of the beast. The bird's head turned to see the woman running headlong at it. It screamed and vainly tried to snap at the woman as she ducked and thrust her blade into the pink-gray flesh of its neck, directly below the massive hooked beak. Blood spilled from the wound. The Kahytul flailed about wildly in its death throes, crushing yet more people. The woman rolled down the broken wing, narrowly avoiding the beast as it fell onto its side, another cloud of dust erupting upwards. Then there was silence.

Jude walked his horse, slowly picking his way through the carnage. *I'm surprised at how quickly these nomads dealt with this situation. Remarkable, I expected far more losses.* He made his way to the massive corpse, sighting the commander. She was now instructing her people, directing them to butcher the beast.

"Pluck it. Wrap the feathers; they can be used for fletching and clothing in the village. Start a fire and begin cooking everything you can."

The men and women bustled about at her orders.

"That will feed many for a score of days," Jude said as he approached the woman.

She looked in his direction. "It will, yet at the cost of many. All for a bit of meat to last us a week at most."

"It would have killed far more had you not reacted so swiftly in taking it down."

She grunted. "It is behind us now. I cannot change the outcome."

"No regrets." Jude shrugged.

"Plenty of regrets, but we must make the most of what will come. To never hesitate or second guess."

"Quite the philosophy you live by."

She tipped her head slightly. "And what philosophy does Jude Nelon live by?"

"To take a moment for oneself. Enjoy some tea, and appreciate the gifts of nature. Rest, do not work too hard. We all die anyway. Enjoy the days you are gifted."

"If one is to rest in the future, you must toil with passion and vigor in the present."

"You could work your ass raw only to be gutted by some conscripted farm boy or perhaps bitten by a red-hooded viper and succumb to its venom."

"I put much vigorous effort into avoiding such fates."

"That's what I'm saying, for Skrull's sake. You toil immensely to avoid such things, and the next day, you take a stray arrow on the battlefield or catch the plague on a passing wind. You have no say in the matter; leave it to Qav's cards."

"Fate is our own; the supposed gods in the sky can go have a fuck," she declared, staring defiantly at Jude.

Fucks, woman. Not open to any other opinions, eh? He could tell this conversation wasn't going anywhere, and he had gotten far from the topic he had initially come to inquire about.

"We seem to be set in our ways," he paused. "I never did catch your name?"

"I am the Third Otsoa of Hasiera. My name is my own."

"So be it, Third Otsoa of Hasiera. Can you tell me why this *Hasiera* is gathering such a battle-ready force? Riding day and night? Are we planning another raid on a village on the outskirts of The Burning Sea, perhaps?"

"We would not need such a force as this to accomplish such a task. No, we are gathering for our final battle. A dance with death itself. And I fear we will be too late."

"Why do you people refer to this threat as death itself?"

She laughed, and heads turned to look at her. People seemed surprised at the sound coming out of the woman's mouth. She calmed abruptly. "You are coming to Hasiera, are you not? You will find out soon enough should we make it there alive. *And* if we make it there in time." She mounted her horse, and Jude heard her mumbling, "Why have we not been attacked yet?"

Curse you, woman! In time for what?! Attacked by what? Jude screamed inwardly but held his tongue. As the woman rode away, he turned to the felled bird. Pricking a finger, coating a white marble in his blood, Jude let it rest on the bird's lifeless form for a few breaths. Then he plucked the marble up and placed it into his pouch.

Chapter Thirty-One

GATE

It was dark. Saudett and company had been traveling an hour or two since the sunset. They had managed to avoid the Daanav. Instead of traveling during the day, they moved at night, using Hata's ground sense to avoid the creatures. They could not stay in one place for long. So, when they could, the entire group rested during the day in shady outcrops they could find, which were few and far between in the Burning Sea. Saudett had let Kiana take the lead.

The damned murderer. She noticed Kiana was beginning to bond with Kaplan Mir as they conversed while spearheading the route home. The two made unlikely allies. Perhaps when Kaplan had protected her from Saudett's attack that first night Kiana had stumbled upon them, something had begun to form. *My own companions turn against me.*

Saudett brought up the rear. And she still was very *alone.* Hata was occupied, concentrating on avoiding the monsters. *She has no time for me anymore.* After their minor argument, Saudett felt that Hata may be avoiding her. Saudett longed to see Simon again. *I want to feel loved again. Take him home, and return to our life. I want to be held in his arms.*

Gods. She felt weak and drained. Lethargic. More tired and hungrier than usual. After every sleep period, like clockwork, she would get nauseous and retreat from the group to vomit. *Why is this happening? I let the sun's heat get to me,* she thought. *That, or I am with babe.*

She hadn't bled in some time. It had been over a month since that morning before the attack since Simon had been with her. Typically, they would have taken measures to avoid that. This last time had been different. *Simon's dream left us out of our minds and overtaken by passion.* As her thoughts wandered, she barely realized the others had gathered at the top of a dune before nearly riding her mount into one of them.

"A bit early to make camp, no?" Saudett said to nobody in particular. "And atop a dune?"

Kiana Ahmadi answered, "No, friend. *This night,* we camp in the Valley of Hasiera."

Saudett looked up and then down upon the valley before her. A canvas town sprawled out far ahead, tents packed tightly together yet seemingly organized, many glowing warmly with evening firelight. A torch-lit curving wall cut across one side of the landscape, meeting a cliffside, closing off the encampment to the side directly facing them. *Simon is down there!* She fought back the urge to gallop down into the valley.

"Ha. That was not here before," Kiana murmured in awe.

"What wasn't?" Hata asked.

"The wall," Kiana said.

"If you meet my husband, be sure to thank him," Saudett said, pride tightening within. She felt her emotions swelling and depressing like a squall.

Kiana's violet eyes flashed toward her, then back to the valley. "Indeed. Shall we make our way down? I could dreadfully use a bath."

"What is 'bath'?" Kogs chirped.

"Ah!" Baal grunted. "Bath makes lizards into soup for Baal's stomach!"

"Scree!" Kogs covered his eyes. "Big one is too dangerous. I must go back to the masters; destroy the big human and all along with him."

Kiana interjected, "Now hold on, Kogs, remember the masters lied to you about your Gaks. Our big friend here is merely joking with you. It is only because he adores you."

Baal turned pink and coughed. "Go down now." Without another word, he began descending the dune toward the village.

The lizard tilted his head, "Big man likes poor Kogs?"

"I believe so." Kiana grinned cheekily.

Kogs made a series of clicking noises as he put his head down and swayed it from side to side. If Saudett could tell any better, the noise appeared almost bashful.

"The big dirty human wants to spawn with dashing hero Kogs?" The little lizardman shrugged his shoulders. "Who can blame him?"

Hata stifled a giggle.

A horn sounded in the distance of the camp.

"They know we're here. I had best get down there," Kiana said as she headed after Baal.

"Quickly, everyone," Brena urged. "We should not let Baal approach alone. He may not come to approachable terms with the welcome party and do something rash."

Saudett reined her horse beside Hata's, grasped her hand, and whispered, "I'm sorry."

Hata smiled weakly down at her, "It's alright, Saudett. Let's just go find your husband."

Saudett sighed, exhausted and eager. Wanting nothing more than to see Simon once again. "Aye, Hata." She gave the girl's hand a gentle squeeze. "*Let us.*"

Moments after the *humans* had descended the dune into the valley, another figure approached the peak to look down upon it, keeping in the shadows of the dune. Its lanky arms, too long for its body, grasped the dune's pinnacle, and its long fingers sunk into the sand as it crouched on the opposite side. Its skin was almost stone-like, yet cracks broke the surface of it. A faint yellow glow emanated from the crevices across its body, some dripping with the strange liquid.

The featureless humanoid face raised as if to sniff the air. There was a faint hissing noise as it inhaled. It had a single glowing red eye socket, the same visceral substance forming an eye on one side of its head; the other, a cold black hole. The creature tilted its head, looking down at the growing firelight of Hasiera. Moments later, it was gone, its light extinguished, slinking back into the shadows.

Ilan was gone. Simon held his breath as he pulled himself along the rope underwater, kicking his feet and dragging himself, hand over hand, through the murky darkness. Naurr had gone ahead of Simon, quickly disappearing from his vision. As Simon's lungs burned in his chest, the rope ascended. A moment later, his head breached into a sizable pocket of air.

"You all right there, boss?"

"You are here, Naurr? I can barely see you." The space they were in was big enough for both; reaching his arms out, he could not touch the other man. He could feel the fresh air breezing slightly. *There must be a crack up to the surface.*

"Aye, it should be getting light going forward. There is a shaft of light in the next area."

"It must be dark outside by now. With hope, a full moon will aid us. I'll take the lead this time, Naurr. Stay close to me and be ready to pull us to safety if needed. *This* is the part where I usually drown."

"I got you, boss."

"Very well." Simon took a deep breath and plunged back into the water.

A few heartbeats later, his vision cleared slightly. Simon picked up a faint white-and-green glow ahead. The rope had been pulled down to the base of the tunnel, allowing him to push off the stone surface with his feet. The tunnel itself was slightly declining the entire way. Suddenly, the floor beneath him vanished, and the rope took a tight corner, leading straight down. He could make out green light rippling on the water's surface.

Am I not facing downward? How could there be another water's surface? He was instantly disorientated and could not determine up from down. Looking at what he thought should be up, he did make out a sliver of white light through another rippling surface and what looked like a jagged opening in the rock above. *Are those stars?* He thought. *Is that the way up?*

Simon let go of the rope and began swimming as hard as he could toward the night sky. As he took his first few strokes upwards, something grabbed his ankle. Taunt and *bone-like,* familiar. It pulled him downwards as he took another stroke upwards. Another hand grasped him. He looked down but could only see the green light reflecting off the surface below him. *The surface?* There must be air down there. *Fucks to this.* Simon stopped struggling. He went limp, letting the hands slowly pull him downwards. Simon closed his eyes and concentrated on holding what little air was left. He relaxed. *Relieved.* His eyes shot open as he was suddenly falling through empty air. Gasping, sucking in a much-needed breath. Then he hit the ground. He landed on his back, onto *something soft,* breaking his fall.

Taking a moment to breathe deeply and get his wits about him, Simon stared at the ceiling, where he saw a rippling pool of water and a rope dangling out of the pool down toward where he lay. He suddenly noticed a man's silhouette against the white light through the water's surface above. The shape got larger and larger as he realized it was heading down toward him. Simon rolled onto his side as Naurr's head broke the pool's surface.

Naurr landed with a grunt where Simon had been a heartbeat beforehand.

Simon looked at where Naurr landed and what he had landed on. Horror took him as he realized that it was Ilan's body. His head and neck pushed back at an unnatural angle. He had landed face-first into the rock cavern, his arms crumpled underneath him. A small pool of blood had formed below him. He was cold and white. The life was gone from his eyes.

"By the Primus, why?!" Simon screamed. "Another man is dead because of me. I should be the one! Take me! Skrull, you goddamn bastard!"

Naurr removed himself from the body and slowly moved to Simon. He sat with his legs crossed and murmured a small prayer for the dead man. "Praise be to Hettra for Ilan's life. He gave us a way out of here."

Simon's moans slowly faded; he took a few heartbeats to comprehend Naurr's words. Finally, he took a moment to survey the chamber they found themselves in. The walls around the pool to the ceiling were smooth, slick, flat vertical surfaces. They had no purchase, unclimbable. *The rope.* There would be no going back if Ilan had not brought the line here.

The pool, unnaturally above, was not just a pool; a small stream led to it, winding along with the cavern's ceiling. Simon followed the stream's path leading into a doorway, an archway. Yet the arch was affixed to the roof as well. Instead of doors, green and black glowing clouds, like shadows and the emerald sea struggling against one another. Every so often, sparks of lightning streaked across the unknown surface. The energy source appeared to originate from a large crack in the archway, where a white dagger protruded from the green-black marble stone the archway was made of.

"Skrull's hell. What is this?" Simon murmured. He looked to Naurr, the large man who had fallen to his knees, hands clenched in prayer, muttering in the Tal'tulu language. Simon was taken aback; he did not consider Naurr a religious man.

Simon stood. There was nothing else in the cavern. The stone walls that made up the cave also surrounded the archway. The only exits were back the way they had come or through the mysterious gateway. The dagger, jutting out of the crack, was too high up for Simon to reach. The white of the blade and pommel contrasted brightly against the dark marble. Was it made of bone? He would need a boost up to get it. *Then what? Should I pull it out?*

Something moaned, and lightning began to streak across the shadowy surface more frequently and violently. The clouds began to push outwards toward them; the shape of a figure over eight paces tall, with hulking shoulders, was driving a single massive arm against the amalgamation. The figure looked familiar like one of the bigger Daanav Simon had seen in the desert.

It is trying to breach the gate! The lightning flared again; the creature moaned in pain. Another burst of lightning, then a flash of light. *The hulk is getting through!* Simon heard a crack, and green-black dust burst from where the dagger extruded. *We would be dead men if that thing made it out!*

"Naurr! Let's pull the dagger out! Help me reach it!" He called.

Naurr was now on hands and knees, his head down, not looking up.

"Fucks, man!" He ran to the kneeling man, trying to pull him toward the gate. He didn't budge. "The gods can't help us, Naurr!" Simon looked around madly; Ilan was the only other thing in the room. He dragged the lifeless body and propped it against the wall under the dagger. Lightning flashed wildly; the hulk, silhouetted in the storming portal, was still not breaking the surface tension. The lightning bolts began concentrating on the mass pushing against the storm, and the form winced back.

Hettra's mercy! Now is my chance! Simon tried to stand on the dead man's shoulders, but the body's limpness made it sag under Simon's weight. He reached higher, stretching his hand for the blade. *Just out of reach!* He slipped, falling onto his back, Ilan's body crumpling over. The entire figure of the hulk seemed about to erupt through the gale.

After another crack in the marble and a burst of violent flashes, the monster screamed. Then it was gone. The lightning declined, sparks diminishing as the storm settled.

Simon sighed heavily in relief. "Skrull, take me. What have we gotten ourselves into?"

CHAPTER THIRTY-TWO

HUSBAND

"Hold! Who sets foot in the Valley of Hasiera?"

Saudett and the group were surrounded by horsemen as they reached the base of the dune descending into the valley. Dust clouded their vision.

Kiana shouted in answer. "I intreat you, Ninth Otsoa, Shalasar Kaskin! It is I, the Sixteenth Otsoa! Kiana Ahmadi!"

Saudett watched as a murmur pulsed through the crowd of horse warriors surrounding them.

"Sixteenth no longer, I fear. You were deemed dead in name, protecting the valley," said the Ninth, dressed in dark, almost black wrappings in a nomadic fashion. Yet the jingling of ring mail touched Saudett's ears as he adjusted his saddle to better look at Kiana.

Kiana's face darkened. "And who, Ninth Otsoa, who takes up my station? I will challenge for reinstatement."

"Mittal Gohra," the Ninth answered shortly. "That aside, these matters can wait. Who do you travel with, Kiana Ahmadi?"

"Rangers from Dagad, tracking our scent."

This time, curses vented through the onlooking horsemen:

"Why lead them here?!"

"Should they escape, they will bring the Auru down on us!"

Saudett fidgeted feverously. *I'm so close to Simon. Oh, so close. I need to sneak away to look for him!*

"Silence!" Kiana shouted over everyone. "They saved my life. I owe them a debt. They are willing to aid us against the Daanav."

At first, the nomads gasped, but that surprise soon turned to satisfied whispers.

"So be it," said the Ninth Otsoa, Shalasar Kaskin. "I will notify the First. They will be guests in your tent, Kiana Ahmadi. See that they stay in line." The man wheeled his horse and began riding back to the village, the others quickly following suit. Dust kicked up in their wake.

"That went better than I expected," Saudett heard Kiana mutter to herself.

"If not for the demons, we would be set on pikes atop your new wall." Kaplan half-smiled at Kiana.

"Perhaps," Kiana said. "In any case, it has been weeks since I slept on some furs. I will have water drawn and food prepared. We all need rest; let us make haste."

Saudett and the others did not protest. In silence, they followed Kiana. They walked under the rectangular opening that made up the would-be gate in the wall. Archers atop it kept a close eye as they made their way through, watching as the group strode through the winding paths of tents. Saudett focused on her surroundings, trying to look for her husband. Warm light silhouetted the people through the thinner sections of the canvas. She caught the smell of roasting meat and vegetables and saw people eating together, conversing, and laughing. Pleasurable sounds coming from a tent much longer than most drifted across the travelers' ears. She noticed the people sitting outside, smoking and drinking, were studying the newcomers as they traversed the scene. She kept her eyes peeled, hoping to glimpse Simon strolling through the tents. *Primus, show him to me.*

Kiana led them to a tent that looked much like all the others. "A bit small for all of us, but we must make due."

They tied their animals to some wooden stakes just outside the abode. Kiana held the flap open as they each made their way inside.

"A moment, I will fetch some aid," she said from the entrance. "If you would get a fire ready, there is kindling and dung for burning just outside the tent." Then Kiana disappeared as the flap closed.

"Outstanding," Saudett said with a scowl. "After all this, we get to smell of shit at the expedition's end."

"Better than one more night in the hell that is that desert," Brena retorted. "And Hata can finally rest now."

Baal grunted. "Bookman. Help Baal." As he exited the tent, Kaplan sighed and followed him out.

"I'll go look for Simon," Saudett said hurriedly.

"No. You endanger us all." Brena moved in front of the exit.

"Get out of my way."

"No." Brena's ice-cold gaze kept Saudett in place, that, and the hand on the hilt of her sword.

"Please, Saudett," Hata begged. "Wait."

"I've waited long enough! He is here. I'm so close!" Saudett pointed her spear at Brena. "My husband is more valuable than my fellowship to you. This is your last warning."

Brena unsheathed her sword, hefting her shield at the ready. "Try me."

"STOP!" Hata screamed, reaching her hands and spreading her fingers wide toward the two women. Suddenly, the earth shifted and spiraled up around the Brena and Saudett, tendrils grasping around their legs and up to their waists. They grunted and winced as Hata closed her outstretched fingers slightly, and the earth hardened.

Hearing Hata scream, Baal and Kaplan rushed back into the tent. Taking a beat to assess the situation, Baal spoke, "Is friend Saudett," he paused with a growl, "dishonored?" He placed a hand on the shaft of his massive pickaxe.

"Let me go! I need to find Simon!" Saudett shrieked in frustration. *Why wouldn't they let her go?*

"We should restrain her," Kaplan said flatly. "Can you get her arms as well, Hata?"

"Right." Hata raised her right hand further, and the earth crept up Saudett's torso, then up to her arms.

Saudett struggled, screamed, and hollered hysterically.

After cementing her arms in place, Hata opened her left fist. The earth that was holding Brena was released.

Blinded by rage and unable to lift a finger, Saudett began to wail helplessly. "I'm so close. *Please*. Please let me go," she sobbed. "I *beg* of you, Hata. I need to find him." Her eyes burned as tears streamed down her face.

She could see Hata was holding back her own tears. "I know, I know. It's just a little bit longer, and you will see him. I promise. Kiana has probably gone off to find him," Hata reassured her.

Saudett grimaced at the mention of Kiana and spat venomous words, "We should have left that bitch to die in the desert."

"Then you all would be dead at the gates," Kiana answered as she entered the tent. A couple of nomads carried baskets of food with them. Then they hurried about, quickly getting a fire going and adding oil to a large copper basin. The helpers shot glances at Saudett and her earthen-covered form.

"I take it the lady here wanted to rush off to find her husband, and you all stopped that. Thank you for your concern, but I trust you enough and have faith that my people will stop anything untoward. You can go about the valley as you see fit; just *do not* leave it."

"You heard her, Hata." Saudett urged. "Please let me go find him."

Saudett watched as Hata looked at Kiana and then at her mother. Kiana nodded. Her mother's eyes still pierced icily into Saudett, not catching Hata's silent inquiry. Hata took a deep breath and said, "So be it." She let her other arm go limp to her side. The hardened soil went loose and fell away.

Simon! I'm here, Simon! Saudett pushed her way out of it, heading straight for the entrance. Clenching her teeth, holding her rage within, she shoved her way through her companions and into the night air. None of them said a word to her as she departed.

A moment after Saudett had disappeared, Hata collapsed near the fire. Gently resting her hands on each of her arms, she closed her eyes, exhausted.

Kiana whispered, "Let her sleep. We will bathe in the river, then return here to sup and rest for the night."

Baal sat down next to Hata. "Baal, stay. You go wash up, my pretty ladies." He bared his teeth in his signature toothy smile.

"I can wait until the women are back," Kaplan said.

"*All* the ladies." Baal turned that toothy smile in Kaplan's direction.

Kaplan frowned at the man, then shrugged and walked out.

Brena snorted and left with the others.

Kiana followed.

CHAPTER THIRTY-THREE

HASIERA

Saudett rushed through the camp frantically. "Simon! Simon!" she called. People were exiting their tents to see what the commotion was about. She ran over to one such observer. "Have you seen my husband? He's a scrawny, pale Auru man."

The man looked at her with confusion on his face. "What does he do?"

"He built your Skrull-forsaken wall!"

"Oh yes, the builder! He was last seen at the entrance to the mine, so hears I. That way." He pointed.

"Praise you, my thanks!" she called as she rushed toward the indicated direction.

She felt a chill in her bones. She stopped between two tents and doubled over, vomiting a little of her stomach's contents into the dirt. Shivering, she stumbled toward the cliff face, using her spear to aid her as she walked.

Kiana looked upon Brena's naked form. She was kin to a goddess, with fair white skin that looked smooth and soft. Brena's pale tone contrasted with the black, jagged lightning bolt tattoos that stretched down her body. Kiana longed to touch her. From her neck to chest, the tattoos chained off into numerous other bolts around her breasts, ribs, abdomen, across her back, and further to her inner and outer legs, the lightning serrating to her feet.

Brena's thick, braided blond hair was now untied, and the woman's hair flowed down to her knees. Her hair spread wide about her as she submerged herself in the stream.

Kiana waded in beside her. "You are truly an angel," she whispered.

"Much appreciated, Kiana Ahmadi," Brena replied.

Kiana wondered, "Are you and your husband open to exploring others?"

"I'm afraid we are not. Though you are a beautiful young woman, I am afraid I am not attracted to those of our sex."

"Oh, well, it didn't hurt to try," Kiana mumbled.

Brena laughed. "You are far braver than I. It took me years to find the courage to ask Baal to stroll down the mountain with me. Even then, it was difficult to get it through his thick skull. Thank you for being so forward; it is refreshing. Don't lose that."

"I would be inclined to scratch your itch, Otsoa," Kaplan said, using a woolen fabric to scrub his face and beard.

Kiana snorted. "You must be some twenty summers senior to me."

"As am I," Brena added.

"Does that make a difference?" Kaplan said solemnly.

True, she thought as she surveyed the Xamidian; he was toned and lithe. Scars marked his muscles as they glistened in the low light. His black hair grayed slightly above the ears; otherwise, it was jet black and slicked back from the water. Her gaze fell *lower*; she tilted her head to consider it.

"Perhaps."

A horn blasted in the distance, then another closer and another.

"Hettra's mercy!" Kiana gasped. "An attack! Quickly! Back to the tent!" The trio scrambled out of the water, grabbing and pulling on their clothing, fumbling away from the stream. Kiana and Kaplan waited a moment as Brena donned her chain mail and heavier aspects of her armor, her untied hair sticking wetly to the back of her topcoat. Kiana had left all but the rags she had been wearing from the journey in her tent. She opted to run naked over wasting time with the ripped garments.

Chaos erupted in the camp. Screams and shouts all around them:

"RUN!"

"To arms!"

"The Daanav! They've found us!"

"Gods, take us!"

Many of her people were jumping atop their horses, picketed outside their tents, drawing blades, bows, and spears, and galloping hard toward the wall. Kiana and company dodged and ducked out of the path of the stampeding warriors, narrowly avoiding being trampled to death. Wild war cries now filled the air. Elders pulled children in the opposite direction. Women with babes cried for help.

The trio returned to Kiana's abode; Hata and Baal waited outside. Baal brandished his pickaxes menacingly. Kiana returned to her tent, heading directly for a simple chest in one corner. Flipping it open, she took a boiled leather jerkin, two pauldrons, braces, and leggings and quickly put them on. Donning a thick linen robe atop, she hastily wrapped her head and face in linen, strapped a sword on her belt, and then returned to the others.

"Well," she said as she returned to them outside; they were already mounted, weapons drawn. "It is time we enlisted your aid, my fast new friends."

"Speaking of friends, it would appear your pet lizard has run off," Kaplan said with his monotone, flat inflection.

"Fucks," she cursed under her breath. Her eyes widened; she hadn't seen Kogs since descending the dune toward Hasiera. *Now we're under attack. I should have slit the serpent's throat when I had the chance. Where did he go?*

"Stay close. We ride to the wall. Hi-ya!" She spurred her horse, twisting it toward the wall, the others following close behind her.

Saudett leaned on her spear. Horns had sounded, and the camp behind her was in turmoil. It was plain to see that the monsters had found the valley and were initiating their assault. She stood at the cave's mouth, looking back at the camp. People were heading toward her, clamoring for the safety of the cavern. It would be hard to find Simon once this cave was full of people. She ducked inside into the darkness. There, she opened her eyes wide to get used to the gloom. She found nothing, no one to meet her, not a soul. She could hear voices approaching from outside. She felt along the jagged wall with one hand as she went deeper inside. She began hyperventilating. *Simon must be in the chaos that was the camp.* He could be killed in the Daanav attack. *I am a fool. I should still be back there looking for him!* She turned around just as the first people entered the cave, torches in hand.

One of the older women grasped her shirt as she pushed through. "We beg you, please stay. Protect us! Help us!"

She ignored the woman, pulling her shirt free from the weak grip. Then, she pushed against the oncoming mob using her spear, driving herself back the way she had come.

Seventh Otsoa, Howler Thien, crouched atop the wall. It was a full moon, and they were glad of it. They always felt vigorous on a night of the full moon. They felt their fangs grow slightly as they stared at it, then focused their gaze on the scene before them. They could see everything stretching across the steppe with their heightened senses. The dune was seething with blackened shapes, swaying like long grass in the wind. They could not determine an exact number but guessed a few thousand strong. A roiling mix of hulk and hound Daanav alike. They watched as a wave of the monsters flanked far to their left, headed for the southern hillside that would descend into the valley below, free of the hindrance of the newly built wall. *Ha,* Thien thought, *the demon fools should send their full strength to that side.*

They snarled. The enemy's main force slowly descended the dune, creeping toward the wall. Thien would take their Otsoa, the Volkinn, and deal with the flank. Sniffing the air, the pungent smell of death and decay filled their nostrils. They caught the scent of the First and a handful of other Otsoa approaching from the rear. Returning to the camp, they watched as the First, Fourth, Sixth, Ninth, Eleventh, Thirteenth, and Sixteenth rode up to the inner part of the gate. A host of warriors behind them.

Thien dropped down in front of the First, landing on all fours. Then they stood, tall as the man opposite them on horseback.

"How many, Thien?"

"Near three, maybe four thousand. Hard to say; I can only smell the reek of death on the wind. We must meet them before they reach the wall and fill their ranks with arrows as we hold the line before the gate. I will take my Volkinn and raze the flank on the hillside. When I am finished with them, I will signal for our counterattack on the horde."

"Very well, see to it," the First said curtly. "Ninth, stay on hold with your lance riders. When the Seventh signals, begin your counterattack with them on the enemy's flank."

"Aye, First Otsoa." The man raised two fingers to his chin, then turned his horse while making a fist in the air, bringing a score of riders following him south toward the hillside.

"Fourth. Your archers, see to the wall."

With two fingers to his chin, Gaspar Haytham shouted, "Archers!" A column of archers followed the old man to the wall before they quickly clambered up the makeshift scaffolding.

"Thirteenth, send runners to begin evacuating the people east and south. I doubt our builder has tunneled out of the mine cavern yet. Have one of your runners look for him and tell him east and south. Have them make for the jungle."

Rojas turned his head, and a man sitting a few paces back and to his left nodded and rode off.

"I best set out, too," Thien growled.

The First Otsoa nodded.

Thien crouched down and sucked in a deep breath, flinging their head back and letting out an eerie howl. There was a pause, the wind moaning gently before a single answering howl came from the distance. Then another and another until the night air was filled with the sound. Thien bolted, clawed fingers digging into the earth as they bounded toward the hills in the wake of the Ninth.

The First unsheathed his blade and raised it high above his head. "To me! Hasiera, to me! Brothers and sisters! If you so worship the gods and find your head in Hettra's fine tits, come morning, give thanks! Give thanks; you have not joined me in Skrull's wicked hell!"

"Hasiera! Ah-lai!" A reverberating cheer and coarse laughter bristled amongst the warriors.

"We own our fate, and the *gods* can be damned!" continued the First. "For now... *WE FIGHT!* We fight for our children so that they may live! For our brothers! Our sisters! Our mothers and fathers! We fight for the peace *we* have created! Ah-lai! We fight for *HASIERA*!"

"*HASIERA!*" came an earth-shattering roar from all present taking up the call.

He shouted again, "*Hasiera*!"

They answered once more, "Hasiera! Ah-lai!"

The First Otsoa kicked his horse into a trot, making for the gate. "Hasiera!" he screamed one last time, spurring into a full gallop, the war cries a deafening echo behind him.

The Otsoa answered with the thundering of hooves as a thousand warriors of Hasiera rode out to meet the horde of Daanav.

Kiana and company made it to the wall just as the last riders had vanished into the opening. She could hear the battle clash on the wall's opposite side. She reined in to face the others.

"Hata, you should take to the wall. It will be chaos on the other side. Your parents should stay by your side. If any of those things break through, you'll have to deal with them. Protect your daughter." The Vasara's nodded back to her in agreement. "Kaplan." She looked at the hooded man on horseback, an arrow nocked in his short bow.

"I have your back, Otsoa."

She nodded. "And I, yours." She watched as the Vasara family quickly rode to the bamboo scaffolding abreast the wall and dismounted. She waited until they started climbing before twisting her mount back toward the gate, unsheathing her sword.

Hata pulled herself up the last rung of the rickety ladder. Nearly two paces of sandstone wall provided little cover for those who defended it. She looked onto the battlefield. Two cavalry spears had pierced the enemy ranks, riding diagonally out of the gate, cutting into the wall of the Daanav. The cavalry began to curve back toward the wall in a long arch. Two more cavalry columns, consisting of horse archers, rode parallel along the wall. A pocket of Daanav, cut off from the rest, was filled with arrows as the archers rode alongside. The two lines of cavalry nearly formed a heart shape as one side turned in a wide arch to meet their counterpart, who were cutting their way through the enemy. The left-stranded demons were in turmoil as both columns met and spread wide to ride them down. The left flank of the battle seemed to have a flawless execution of the tactic. Hata could see a man with glinting golden armor in the moonlight at the head of the column. The right flank, however, did not fare so well.

A mass of the hulking demons had thrown themselves at the first column of cavalry on the right, trampling and decimating the line. The cavalry was now cut into two forces, the latter half's momentum at a standstill. The Daanav fell upon the soldiers, now immobile. It was a slaughter. Arrows still whistled in small clouds as the archers of that flank's cavalry tried to back up their kinsmen. As they skirted the wall, the cavalry archers were cornered; the cliffs of the valley's north side had cut them off, becoming detrimental to the nomad strategy.

I need to do something! Hata saw Kiana and Kaplan ride out swiftly, making to back up the crumbling right flank, which was quickly turning into a chaotic man-to-monster brawl.

"I can't do anything from this far away!" she cried.

"Patience, daughter. Look." Brena pointed. "A group of Daanav from the center is heading for the gate."

She looked where her mother had indicated. She was correct. Maybe fifty to a hundred demons, most canine-like entities, had broken straight for the gate. A small group of men and women had replaced the small, sharpened stake barricade in a semi-circle around the entrance and stood at the ready.

"I go down," Baal said with a grin.

"Wait, Father!"

Baal put one hand on the wall, grasping his pickaxes in the other, and leaped over.

"Don't worry, Hata. Your father will be fine. He will truly be in his element now. Let's see what we can do to aid him from here. Remember when you sunk him in the quicksand?"

"Yes." Hata took a moment to remember how she had done that. "I don't know if I can manage that from here. I think I must be touching the ground below." She hesitated.

"Try not to think about it."

"Voitoon!" They heard Baal's war cry as he rushed to meet the Daanav. Nomads manning the fence jabbed spears up and outwards, skewering many hounds as they bound over the barricade. One such hound leaped clear over the bamboo barricade, only to have its head explode in a burst of black chunks as her father's pickaxe tore through it. Men and women fell, overwhelmed, fangs sinking into necks, limbs lopped off as the blade-like bones protruded from the creatures leaping by them.

Baal dropped one pickaxe and grasped a hound by the throat. Then, he swung his other pickaxe, bursting through the torso of another lunging beast. His fist constricted on the held beast's throat as it thrashed wildly, then went limp. He tossed it aside and moved to aid a nearby Hasieran. His eyes met Hata's momentarily as he glanced up at her.

"He needs help," Brena said flatly. "That was his asking."

Hata took a deep breath. *I won't let Taryn happen again!* She let out a scream. Slapping her hands together, she pushed them down on the sandstone parapet, palms spread wide. *I will protect them!*

There was a ripple through the rampart and toward the wooden barricade. Like a small shockwave, it went under the feet of battling men, women, and Daanav. Under the palisade, and stopping at a group of hounds and hulks approaching the barricade. They began to stumble and sink into the earth. The smaller hounds were suddenly chest-deep in the ground, and the hulk's lower legs struggled to push through.

Hata raised her open hands, then closed them tightly into fists. *Die!* The canine heads shook frantically as geysers of black blood sprayed out of their orifices. *Die!* One of the hulks running at full speed as it sunk had its legs ripped out from under it. Its torso careened forward into the barricade, which skewered through its face and chest. *Die!* Others were simply stopped in their tracks, unable to move, screeching in pain. Bone and sinew crushed and cracked under the force of the hardening earth.

Baal laughed loudly. All could hear him over the din of the battlefield. "My daughter!" he shouted. Men and women looked at him quizzically from the wall and lower barricade as he cleaned up a few straggling demons with brutal executions. Arrows filled the cemented hulks, who gave ghastly moans, unable to prevent their fate, until they were silent and unmoving, propped up like strange limp statues.

Kiana cut into a hulk's neck as its arms reached above its head to strike down on a fallen nomad. Blood oozed from the gash as the weight of the creature's arms pulled it back as it fell. An arrow whizzed past her ear into the head of a leaping hound, moments from tearing into Kiana's back from behind. She looked back momentarily at Kaplan and nodded, then refocused on the stage around her. It was pure chaos. All forms of discipline had been thrown to the wind. It was free for all. *I must gather our forces and order a retreat,*

or we will all die where we stand! She scanned the area, looking for someone with a signal horn. She noticed a Pack of nomads on foot fighting some few hundred paces from her. Many bodies and a handful of Daanav filled the void between herself and the group. It was becoming too cluttered for horseback; she dismounted.

Kaplan followed suit. "What is your plan, Otsoa?" he said as he slapped his horse's rear, then returned the bow to his back and unsheathed his bright curved scimitar, grasping it in both hands.

"Signal a retreat." She pointed at the Pack ahead.

"Take my right. Stay close." He sprinted forward.

Kiana was surprised at the man's agility. She closed the distance as he met the first of the Daanav in their path. He flashed his scimitar as a hound looked up from the corpse it was shredding into. Its dismembered head flew through the air. Two more snarled and bound toward Kaplan.

Kiana met one of them.

Noticing her, it changed its attention and leaped headlong at her. She caught the clawed feet and teeth with her blade. It pushed her back with the impact. She rolled onto her back and kicked the beast over her. Continuing to tumble, she found herself on top of it, its claws and mouth still clutching her sword, which was pinned under her. She put her weight on the blade.

The hound jerked and squealed as it kicked and tried to push up against her. Its hind feet managed to scratch through her leather leggings and skin. She ignored the pain. The blade slowly met the back of the demon's jawline, then, with a sudden thump, sunk deep, splitting the mouth wider. The beast stopped struggling. Kiana stood.

Kaplan had dispatched his second foe quickly as well and had continued onward. She arched a brow. *What an efficient man.* She broke into a run after him. Three hulks stood in their path. Already engaged with one, Kaplan deftly removed the hand of the shorter arm of the monster. It roared and charged him with its larger, bulky shoulder. Kaplan fell under the massive weight, disappearing beneath it.

"No!" Kiana screamed.

Simultaneously, the scimitar pierced upwards through the hulk's chest, black blood coating the blade. Kiana took a deep breath. She didn't have time to observe further as the two remaining Daanav hulks rushed toward her. She breathed, *and she danced.*

Blade glided and flashed as she spun and leaped between the two hulks, avoiding massive claws and efforts to crush her. Black blood scattered into the mud as gashes riddled the two creatures. She continued the dance: vertical slash, spin into thrust, pirouette, horizontal feint into upwards slash. The hulks moaned and stumbled. They lumbered weakly, then crumpled over. Kiana exhaled slowly as the two Daanav fell behind her, carved into ribbons.

She looked to where Kaplan had fallen, the scimitar still piercing through the hulk like a battle standard. She scrambled over to him.

"Kaplan! Kaplan Mir!"

A groan came from under the dead beast. "I'm here." He coughed and wheezed. "Help get this thing off me."

Stabbing her sword into the earth at her side and, using all her might, she pushed against the corpse's side.

Kaplan groaned as he appeared, grunting to push the hulk off with his added effort. He took a moment to breathe deeply, catching his breath.

"Did not think I would die like that. Slowly suffocating," he muttered. "I'd much rather be cut down, a quick death for me, by Qav's luck."

She helped him to his feet. "I'll take you up on your offer," she said.

"What? I don't mean a quick death this second—"

"To scratch my itch, as it were," she interjected.

Realization dawned on him. He smiled. That was the second time Kiana had seen the man smile.

"If we survive," he said, chuckling, "gladly." His eyes flashed down her body.

"Shall we?" She removed her sword from the earth. The group of nomads fighting ahead was thinning rapidly.

Kaplan nodded.

This time, Kiana led the way.

Saudett scrambled from tent to tent, calling her husband's name in tears.

"Simon! Simon!" she screamed. "Where are you, Simon?!" She fell to her knees, putting her head in her hands. Suddenly, howls rang on the wind around her, and she looked up. A rush of shadows blurred past her. People. *No.* Animals. *No, they must be people!*

They were on all fours, running by her up the hills to her left. She caught a glimpse of their faces and hands. They were covered in fur, fangs protruding from the upper lips, their clawed hands digging into the earth as they sprinted away. Her eyes followed the strange beings, and she realized a wave of dark shadows was plunging down the hillside straight toward them.

The two forces clashed. Hound-like demons met wolf-like people. The monsters hit them like an ocean wave crashing against a cliffside. The wolf-like people began ripping, biting, and tearing, some using weapons to complement their unnatural speed and senses. It quickly became a massacre, the hound demons falling apart, left and right. A particularly large wolf-person picked up hounds and tore them in half with their bare hands.

Saudett struggled to her feet, stumbling toward the pitched battle, leaning on her spear.

A Daanav hound turned its head to her. Looking for an easy kill, it bound toward her.

She sighed, lifting her spear reluctantly. Simon's face flashed before her eyes, and rage grew within her. *Where is that bastard?!* She lunged, spear reaching forward and down the throat of the beast's open maw. She kicked the limp dog from her spear and began looking for another.

A piercing howl met her ears. The large wolf-man had three hounds on its back, gnawing on it. Yet, were those breasts on the wolf-*man*? She sprinted to its aid. Her spear punched into the back of one of the hounds, mounting the wolf-person. The hound arched its back in agony as it fell off, squealing. She twisted and dug the spear further in before pulling it out.

Then she heard a snarl behind her and spun around to meet the face of a hound with the butt end of her spear, knocking its head to one side. She drove the tip of her spear toward its unprotected head, but it gnashed its teeth and turned just in time to snap up at her spear. It caught the end in its teeth. She pulled and struggled while the hound's forepaws raked against her leg. She clenched her teeth through the pain and jumped, putting her whole weight on the spearhead still in the creature's mouth.

Pole-vaulting over the beast, she twisted mid-air and landed on its lower back with both feet. She heard something snap. The beast released its grip on the spear and wailed. She raised the spear and thrust it down into its back, where she thought the creature's heart lay. She had guessed correctly, for the hound went limp.

A ripping sound behind her made her look back at the wolf-person. They had clawed hands in the mouth of the last hound and were pulling its jaws apart. With a rip and crack of bone, the hound stopped flailing and was tossed aside.

The wolf-person was panting heavily. Its green-yellow eyes studied Saudett for a moment. Then, without a word, it crouched and sprinted into the darkness.

Moments later, a chorus of howls joined voices in the night. Saudett heard hooves pounding into the earth behind her, and then a cavalry was all around her, ascending the hill on which Saudett stood. She turned, trying to catch her bearings, realizing she was on the opposite side of the valley from where the excavated mine shaft had been. Saudett could see the pitched battle in front of the wall in the valley below. She watched as the cavalry, which had just ridden past her, now flanked the horde of Daanav on the south-hand side of the battlefield, forming a long line. She could vaguely make out others among the horsemen, crouching on all fours. *The wolves.* As the flank attack prepared to charge, she noticed the demons had reached the wall near the cliff face on the opposite side of the valley. The pockets of nomads seemingly surrounded and cornered were slowly being cut down.

After a shrill blast of a horn, the line began its charge. Saudett heard a wave of howls and cheers as the force thundered down the hill toward a panicked enemy.

Thien kept pace with the cavalry assault. The Daanav facing them took a moment to rally and began to counterattack the charge. Thien's back burned with pain where the hounds had sunk their fangs into them, but they kept running. They took a moment, in their mind, to thank that short human woman who had aided them back there. A breath of silence before the two forces crashed together. The deafening crunch of man, horse, and Daanav alike, their guttural screams, and the clash of blades to bone filled the air. Thien leaped for the first hulk, clawed hands finding purchase in the fiend's shoulders, and they dug their fangs into the abomination's neck. They tasted the thick, acidic blood in their mouth. They clenched their teeth and tore away, black ooze spraying across their face, their clawed hands sinking deeper into the flesh as they pushed themself away and leaped for their next victim.

Kaplan and Kiana reached the large Pack of nearly a hundred nomads holding their ground on foot. A solid circular formation of spears bristled about them. The circle parted slightly as the two approached an unhindered flank of it. Seeking reprieve in the center of the ranks, Kiana and Kaplan took a moment to recuperate, panting heavily, trying to get a second wind.

"Daughter, you and your companion fought valiantly."

She looked up. "Father. Should we not signal a retreat to the wall? We are surrounded."

"We wait for the Seventh and Ninth to attack the flank; then, I shall call the retreat. We have been slowly falling back as it is."

As she slowly walked along with it, Kiana realized the formation was inching toward the wall.

Kiana heard the horn blast, sounding the attack to the flank. Her father put a hand on a nearby man's shoulder; he lifted his own horn to his lips and let loose three high-pitched, quick bursts of sound. The Hasieran warriors broke rank and ran. A small square of men and women stayed behind to cover their retreat. Kiana knew they would not see those *heroes* again.

Hata watched as the left flank of the horde was hit while the rest of the nomads began to move as one, retreating for the gate. Baal and the others manning the palisade quickly pulled the wooden barricades to the side as soldiers rushed back to safety behind the wall. Many immediately dismounted and joined those in the semicircular outer defense. Hata watched the golden-clad man rein in his white stallion near where her father stood.

"Dawn approaches," he shouted. "Hold the line until we see the sun!"

A cheer went up around him.

Arrows rained down from the wall upon the approaching monsters. On the right side of the wall, Hata could see the Daanav had come to the base of it. She saw hounds leap onto the backs of the enormous hulks and jump again to clamor up and over the wall. There were no bamboo scaffolds that far down the wall and no defenders. The hounds dropped into the camp below, bounding in all directions, some into the tents to wreak havoc, others moving to assault the recently retreated force at the inner gate.

"We should go help down there," Hata exclaimed.

"No," her mother said sternly. "If the main gate is breached, then all is lost. The people will have to deal with the stragglers getting in by themselves. We hold here."

"But what can we do here?"

"What can *you* do? That is the real question, my dear daughter."

Hata frowned. *What could I do? I was able to stop a small group of them, but what could anyone do against so many?* She closed her eyes, thinking about when the magic first came to her and how she had easily manipulated the sand to form the marble pellets. With her eyes still closed, she brought the same image to her mind—only at a size *tenfold*. Her hands moved by themselves.

Sand drifted up from the earth in front of the wall. The spheres grew and grew in her mind. She heard people murmuring, whispering about her, but she stayed focused. *I need more sand.* The spheres began to rotate quickly in place, ever-growing and compacting. Clenching her teeth and sweating profusely, she opened her eyes.

Ten enormous spheres floated in the air before her, spinning rapidly. Her hands were rotating counterclockwise in front of her in the same direction. She closed her fists as if to grab the whirling spheres. Holding them, she twisted her entire body around. The orbs followed her lead and began orbiting like a sling above and around her.

She opened her hands as she came full circle, and the massive projectiles launched toward the enemy force. They shot through the air in different directions, not arching in the slightest and moving fast. They impacted the ground in a sickening burst of Daanav gore. They bounced and rolled through the horde, carving massive lines into the throng. Black violence erupted, and bone and flesh became pulp as the spheres cut through them. Finally, the orbs halted, leaving a trail of carnage in their wake.

A cheer went up around her. People nearby were shouting and clasping each other in joy.

"What was that?!"

"Thank Hettra, it's on our side!"

"An earth mage is with us!"

"Where?!"

"Atop the wall! Look!"

Many people looked up at where she stood. Hata ground her teeth, exhausted and drained from the effort. She wanted to fall to her knees and rest.

A gentle hand rested for a moment on her back. "Be strong, my child. You are their hope." Brena gestured to the people around them.

Hata straightened her back, trying to stand taller.

Someone else shouted, "Dawn is near; the darkness is fading!"

Another cheer went up among the nomadic people.

Hata looked out at the battlefield. The enemy did not seem to take notice of the approaching dawn. *There.* Something strange on the horizon, just past the dune leading down into the valley, from which the Daanav attacked. It was unnaturally dark. She squinted and realized three massive columns of thick blue-black smoke billowed skyward. Then she saw the source of the smoke.

Three colossal creatures crested the top of the dune and began descending toward the battle. Their oval bodies were covered in the same slick black hair as the other Daanav, with six insect-like legs protruding out of them, also wrapped in fur. A humanoid torso mounted the front of each creature, attaching to their bulky, bulbous body at the waist. The torso had four arms: two fused with the massive lower body at the wrists, while the other two were bladed where the hands should be. The scythe-like appendages flailed wildly about the air. Clanging long sickles together over their lurching heads, the abominations slid forward. Thin blue flames covered the entirety of their massive backsides, the blue-black smoke endlessly undulating upwards.

Darkness crawled over the horde of the Daanav... and over the Valley of Hasiera.

Chapter Thirty-Four

Home

Simon blinked himself awake. He sat cross-legged, back against the smooth stone wall, his eyes on the gateway. The moonlight that had been creeping in from high above was gone. It had grown dark in the chamber, the only light a faint glow emanating from the humming portal. Naurr had also drifted into an inadequate sleep, curled up in the corner, still mumbling as if he were having a nightmare.

What should I do? The dagger appeared to keep the Daanav from breaking through the portal. Yet the water in the ceiling was flowing seamlessly through it. *I don't see much of an option. If I climbed back up the rope and into the stream, would I not just be pulled under again?* He felt a twitch in his fingers, like an overcoming need to wrap them around the hilt of that dagger and pull.

So, he had two choices: pull the dagger free or try to penetrate the portal, though he didn't see much good coming out of the latter. He stood and walked the short distance to look at the contraption. The roiling surface sparked faintly off and on, and long arcs of forked energy crept across the clouded surface. It was like watching a rolling storm far off in the distance, yet he could reach out and touch it; he was so close.

He lifted his hand. It shook slightly. *Am I afraid? Or was it anticipation? Excitement? Just a little touch shouldn't hurt anything.* It would prove if option two was viable or not. He shrugged to himself and put his single index finger into the expanse. Like spiders attacking their trapped prey, energy bolts arched across the surface to converge on his finger. Pain shot up his hand, arm, and neck, and then his vision went white as the power filled his skull. He was blasted back from the gate, sliding along the floor. His vision faded from white to black as he lost consciousness.

"Boss! Boss! What happened to you, boy?!"

Simon opened his eyes to see the figure of Naurr standing over him. Simon's head was throbbing. There was fog in the air. He smelled something...roast pork? *I wouldn't mind some pork right about now.* No, it was smoke. He looked down at his left arm. His linen shirt had burned away to his elbow, and jagged white marks scored along his arm. *Sizzling.* Vapor rose from the grooved lines. He felt a burning pain all along his arm and neck.

"By the gods, what happened?" Simon murmured.

"The thunder woke me. To see you flung across the room like a sack of wheat. What did you do to cause this now?"

"I—I touched that *thing*," Simon stammered, waving his good hand toward the portal. "The thing!"

"Are you going utterly mad, boss?"

"Well, I couldn't bloody well wait on you and your crazed mutterings to get anything done around here!"

"The Primus sent these here demons to punish humanity—"

"Don't be ridiculous!" Simon cut him off. "Naurr, come, man." He stood, holding his limp left arm with his right hand.

"Well, then, boss. *Please* tell me why in all the *fuckin'* hells they are here then."

"I don't know. I don't understand the science behind magic and whatnot, but come on, enough of this god and that god horseshit, Naurr. We must get out of here." Simon stumbled toward the portal. "Pfft, the gods," he scoffed. "Why would they even bother?"

"The Primus's plans are beyond our understanding, eh?"

"If you say so. Anyways, it looks like we can't go through the portal. Help boost me up to grab that dagger."

"What dagger?" The stocky foreman arched his head.

"What dagger? You truly have gone mad, my good man. That one," Simon said, pointing directly at the protruding blade.

"'Tis just a crack in the archway."

Simon shook his head in disbelief. "You truly cannot see it? A white-pommeled dagger is jutting out of that crack!"

"'I don't understand the science behind the magic, eh." Naurr shrugged his shoulders mockingly.

"This is even more reason for me to acquire that dagger! Only I can see it! By Skrull's burning balls, it's calling me!"

"I thought you don't believe in the gods and their mingling of fate."

"Just help me, *please*," Simon sighed exasperatedly.

"Or, I could be climbing my way out and getting help to pull you up, along with leaving this here demonic device to its will. Don't try to fix what is not broken, eh?"

"It is obviously quite plainly broken. The thing is malfunctioning in some way. Hence, the cracks and damage to the frame are caused by the invisible dagger. Things are becoming clearer by the minute," Simon said, brushing his good hand through his matted hair impatiently. "I must pull it free."

"You're going to right kill us then," Naurr mumbled as he followed Simon.

Saudett slowly descended the hill, watching as the horde, with seemingly renewed vigor from the darkening clouds, pushed their assault. With the appearance of the smoke-spewing behemoths, the charge on the left flank had lost momentum. They were circling, now in full retreat, Daanav hard on their tail, moving back up the hill toward the unprotected side of the valley, their numbers significantly reduced. As for the monster horde, it looked unending.

The defense at the single hole in the wall was slowly being pushed back. Hounds leveraged their larger counterparts to mount the battlement and drop into the unprotected camp. Some began to attack the archers directly. Saudett lost sight of the battlefield as she descended into the pavilions behind the wall. Not a moment later, two hounds were rushing toward her. She gritted her teeth and charged.

Spinning her spear about her, she arched it over her back; coming around, its tip caught the first hound across the face, leaving a large gash over its eyes. Following through, she planted the butt end of the spear into the earth, throwing both her feet into the chest of the second hound. It went sprawling onto its back. She grabbed a curved dagger from her ankle brace and fell on top of the downed beast.

"*Where!?*" She stabbed the monster. "*Is!*" She stabbed again. "*My!*" Black blood sprayed across her face. "*Husband!*" She stabbed again...and again...*and again.*

"First Otsoa! We need to take out those smoking giants!" Kiana yelled, jabbing her blade forward into the chest of one of the hounds, trying to breach the lines of nomads.

Except for the First, all other Otsoa were on foot, fighting man-to-beast, holding the horde back.

The First was yelling orders from his saddle just behind the front line. "Hold! Hold the line!" he called out, not heeding or hearing Kiana's words.

"Father!" she exclaimed pleadingly.

"Easier said than done, my daughter," her father grunted with exertion as his morning star arched down on a Daanav face, crunching inwards with a sickening thud.

"I'd have to agree with your father!" Kaplan added.

A burst in front of them, and a massive sphere of earth ripped through the Daanav, straight toward one of the gigantic blue-burning fiends. The monstrosity reared up just in time for the globe to cut narrowly past it, though two of its long legs were torn off in the process, black blood gushing forth. An unearthly screech rose above the battlefield, and the smoker fell, unable to support itself with its remaining apparatus.

Hata fell to one knee, exhausted. She heard a clamor to her right. People were screaming as a long-limbed humanoid creature tore through the crowd of archers. It was like nothing she had seen yet, its skin stonelike and crackling with power, its single fuming eye fixed on her.

Hata stood unsteadily, using the wall's edge to support her. She raised a hand, and a few dozen smaller projectiles formed before her. As a man fell after the creature's clawed fingers crushed his head, she let the marbles fly, and they whistled toward the monster. The Daanav roared in anger as some of the projectiles met its flesh. But it didn't slow down. Instead, it began to charge toward her. She looked around, realizing her mother was nowhere in sight. *Teras give me strength.*

Someone pushed her behind them. An older man. He stood hunched in front of her. "Run, girl, it's here for you. Fourth Otsoa, Gaspar Haytham, will buy you what time he can."

She stared at the man's back. "Why me? Why is this happening?"

"RUN!" he shouted and shoved her with a bamboo quarterstaff. The weapon began spinning in his grip, and at the same time, a dagger flew out of his other hand directly at the oncoming beast.

Hata lost her balance, taking a step back into mid-air. She fell from the wall. Hata closed her eyes and imagined the earth catching her like a warm blanket. She was on her back when she opened them again, looking at the black-blue sky.

Hata quickly got to her feet, looking at the wall top. She saw Gaspar's neck clenched in the fist of the lanky abomination. Three daggers protruded from the beast, two in its right leg and one in the lower torso, dripping with strange glowing blood. The eye turned unnaturally down to look upon her as Gaspar's body twitched in death. His head slowly detached at the neck, and his body fell with a sickly thump to the wall, landing on the edge of it with a crunch and tumbling over to fall near Hata's feet.

Hata felt rage building inside her, but she took a deep breath to calm herself. She turned and *ran*, hearing and feeling an impact rattle the earth behind her. *It's following me. Where are you, Mother?*

"Voitoon!"

Kiana watched as Baal and Brena burst through the throng of Daanav. Baal's large gelding screamed wildly as it trampled the hounds beneath its hooves. Baal's dual-fisted pickaxes tore through both hounds and hulks, detonations of gore surrounding the man as he pushed on, with Brena in his wake, sword flashing, Daanav falling. The monsters flinched back at the sudden onslaught of the two Vouri. They were headed straight for the injured smoking behemoth.

The nomads around them gawked in stunned silence for a moment before Kiana shouted, "After them! For Hasiera!"

They rushed after them, many on foot, others from behind the gate who were still mounted.

"HASIERA!" The First Otsoa screamed as he rode out after the Vasara's.

Kiana saw his golden blur.

A cheer rose once more among the warriors.

"They ride to their deaths!" Kaplan shouted nearby.

Kiana could not remove herself from the line she held, as the Daanav were still pushing hard against it. She caught glimpses of the warriors cutting their way back through the horde. She could vaguely make out the form of the injured smoke demon moving sporadically in the distance. Roars rang over the field. She saw blue flames through the chaos. Moments later, there was an ear-piercing shriek, and she watched as that blue light vanished.

Hata ran. She stumbled over fallen tents and bamboo poles, glancing backward. The lanky, one-eyed creature limped after her. *Why is this happening?* She needed time to recover and regain power before assaulting the monstrosity again. She ran on. *Leave me alone!* She heard screams all around her; many people had not fled. She ran by the tents they saw on their entry earlier that night. Silhouettes of the Daanav hounds tearing into bodies within them, blood splattering across the inner canvas.

She ran on, looking over her shoulder once more. The thing chasing her vanished as thick darkness fell all around her. *Where did it go?* She tripped over something and fell flat on her face.

"Eeep! She-wolf friend!"

"Kogs! What are you doing here?!"

"Poor Kogs was hiding from she-wolf because the masters came. Blame Kogs, she would."

A guttural, growling voice came out of the darkness behind them. "Slave! You were to find the sand wolves' homes and bring us to them!"

"No! Please, Master! Kogs is sorry! Kogs begs you."

"We will feed upon the Moreas Lân and all the Kadal! As soon as we are finished with these insignificant humans that hinder our path." Its voice was a terrifying, rasping snarl. The single eye glowing in the darkness was fixed on Hata.

"Die now, human!" The glowing eye rushed toward her.

Simon sat on Naurr's shoulders.

"Perfect. Just a little closer now. Steady."

"Hurry it up, will you, boss. I don't need your sweaty balls on my neck any longer than necessary."

"Quite right. A little to your left. Got it!" Simon grasped the pommel. A voice and an image filled Simon's head. *The pact is fulfilled. You are the bearer.* The vision of a hooded figure standing over Simon as a babe came to mind. He pulled as hard as possible, grunting with exertion. The dagger inched outwards. He watched as lightning burst up his arm again, yet it did not hurt this time.

"Boss!"

The energy began arcing off Simon's hand and arm, blasting into the ground around them.

"Boss!" Naurr cried. "Simon!"

Naurr's voice sounded distant in Simon's ears. With a scream of his own, Simon pulled, using his feet to push against the marble of the archway. The dagger came free in a detonation bursting with white light, and the two men tumbled backward.

The sound of an explosion and a single shaft of luminescent bright white light shone into the northern sky. Both armies froze and gazed upon it. Moments later, the Daanav went berserk, ripping into each other and anyone nearby and scattering in all directions. Many ran back into the desert, while others savagely tore through the nomads' defense.

Some stood motionless, and a moaning cry rose from the horde of monsters.

"By all the fucking gods!" Kiana screamed out. "What is wrong with them?"

"I don't know!" Kaplan called back to her.

"This is our chance! Push the attack!" Kiana charged forward. She felled her blade on a kneeling hulk, indifferent to the incoming attack. It died before her.

The nomads of Hasiera sallied forth, pushing their advantage in the chaos. Daanav doubled down in a blood-seeking fury and countered the nomads' assault. Others died where they stood, unmoving, as the nomads finished them off.

The dripping, glowing red eye halted paces from Hata's face, looking up at the white light beam. It gave an ear-splitting shriek. "The gate! The way is shut! It has been shut! We can no longer feel him. We are lost!"

Hata watched as the abomination raised its arms, readying to bring them down upon her. She raised her hand, and the earth began to creep up the creature's legs and solidify. Hata kicked and pushed herself away from it. Its sharp claws descended in a blur to where she had been a breath beforehand.

"We are trapped here!" wailed the one-eyed creature. "In this forsaken Lân—"

A spear suddenly pierced through the back of its skull and out the single eye of the screaming monster.

"Fucks if you are."

Hata heard Saudett's voice behind the limp torso propped up by Hata's magic. She released the hold, and the Daanav slumped down. Hata saw Saudett, covered in blood and wounds, propping herself on the spear stuck fast into the demon's head.

Then, Saudett slumped over weakly.

Tears blurred Hata's vision. "Saudett! I'm so sorry!" She ran to the wounded woman. "I have been terrible to you. I'm so, so sorry!" She held Saudett up, supporting her with her shoulder.

"It's fine, Hata. And no. I was the one being terrible. How could you love someone like me? I *used* you to try and find my husband and nothing else."

Hata shook her head. "No, I don't believe it. You are a good person, Saudett. I know it. You showed me the way; you cared for me. You became my friend, my lover." She paused, wiping tears from her eyes. "I love you."

Saudett coughed blood and wheezed, "I love you too, Hata, but from now on, only as a dear friend or sibling. It can't be like the way it was before." She groaned in pain. "Put me down here."

Hata lowered the woman to a seated position against a stone.

"I realize now Simon is the only one for me," Saudett said as another coughing fit took her. "I am nothing without him."

Hata blinked back tears. *It is better this way. But I still care for her.* "Saudett, we can talk about it later. You're hurt. Let me go get help."

"I think it's over. I—I just need to close my eyes." Saudett leaned back against the rock. "Saudett! Wake up! Saudett!"

Simon blinked. He glanced at Naurr, who was silently awestruck at the gateway. The gateway, where the once black-and-green dark liquid had boiled about, was now a rigid white wall of shining light. The gateway to the Daanav's world was closed, and a new doorway was open. *How in all the gods' names do I know that?*

His left hand was full of a tingling sensation. He looked down at the dagger, the blade, and the pommel made entirely of bright white *bone* clenched tightly in his fist. *An Iban'mael binding blade? What? Iban'mael?* Simon closed his eyes, rubbing them. *Gods, that is bright.*

Jude Nelon observed the scene below them. Pure chaos. Like nothing he had ever seen, the massive horde of strange dark creatures assailed a half-walled field of tents in the gods-forsaken middle of the desert. *Fucks.* A light pillared up into the air to his left, some ways off from the valley. *By the Primus, and I thought I had seen things.* He wished he was home in his garden, making some tea. The Third Otsoa sounded the charge. *Fucks be to me.* He could do nothing but be swept along with it. *Fucks!* He clenched his teeth and rode.

He saw many creatures fleeing into the desert on the undefended sides of the valley. The force he was with began to wedge, aiming like an arrow directly at a massive burning insectoid. Another group, led by the Otsoa herself, was driving toward another such fuming beast. They crashed through the monsters on the ground, many not putting up a fight, and quickly cut them down. Others frenzied, leaping for riders as they came within reach.

Jude thumbed the white marble he had prepared. He rode hard, staying as close as possible to the center of the charging formation. His daggers were not suitable for mounted combat. He bit his lip hard to draw blood as he approached the burning beast. He began to bring the marble to his mouth but was forced to grab the reins with both hands before getting a drop of blood on the marble. They had come up too fast on the flank of the massive burning beast. Just as they were to hit, it turned sharply to meet them. Its large, thick tree trunk-like legs flung horses and riders away, crushing others who slid under its bulbous main body.

Jude pulled his reins firmly in the opposite direction, only to be face-to-face with a deformed, multi-armed humanoid torso. Its upper limbs were bladed like a hideous praying mantis. It twisted its grey-skinned, *nearly* humanoid face almost ninety degrees and fixed its eyes on him, the bladed arms reaching out toward him. Jude flung himself off the right side of his horse. He heard the steed scream as the blades sunk into its back, where Jude had been sitting a moment before. Rolling onto his feet, finally bringing the marble to his lips... *it was gone.* He looked around frantically. The beast continued its attack downwards, tearing the limp horse in two, gore trailing behind the two halves. Then, it advanced toward him.

Jude backpedaled, quickly releasing a dagger from his belt and firing it off in one swift movement while fumbling in his pouch for another marble. The blade harmlessly bounced off the creature's head. Its sharp arms came down on Jude for a second time. He lunged forward under them. The monster screeched in frustration and began to raise its mass to crush him. Jude fumbled his hand on something hard in the sand. *The white marble.*

The monster descended upon him.

A long heartbeat passed as Kiana saw the massive burning creature crush the black-clad figure under its weight, a cloud of dust and sand spraying from under it, obscuring her vision. Another heartbeat, and suddenly, there was a second explosion of dust.

A raptor's scream and the massive form of a Kahytul came into view. It was locked in deadly combat with the burning beast, the Kahytul's wings fiercely beating. One taloned claw dug into the humanoid torso of the demon as the other snapped off one of its scorpion-shaped legs. The colossal vulture soon suspended the beast some twenty paces skyward with its thundering wings. One arm of the limp humanoid torso was flailing wildly, cutting into the Kahytul's chest, leaving long gashes streaking red.

Kiana watched in awe as they roiled and battled for what seemed like an eternity, rolling through the air as one, blue fire and smoke burning both the abomination and bird alike. Finally, the Kahytul closed its beak on the head and chest of the humanoid torso as one of its long-bladed arms sunk deep into the bird's chest. They plummeted earthward.

Fucking monsters. Jude had picked himself up and patted the sand off. *Fucking desert.* Then, he looked up at the carnage above him. *They're falling. Right fucking here.* He turned and ran as fast as he could.

The two monstrous beings crashed into the ground with the deafening impact of cracking muscle, bone, and earth. A black-and-white cloud of smoke and dust detonated outwards, encompassing those onlookers who still stood in awe of the spectacle.

Jude had jumped out of the way just in time, covering his head with his hands as he tumbled to the ground. Coughing and sucking in a mixture of smoke and sand. *I can't breathe!* He grabbed another marble from his pouch, blue-and-green shades dancing across it, and coated it in his blood.

A moment later, the marble expanded into a water bubble full of air, which sat neatly on the ground before him. He stretched his head into the air pocket. As one would think, it did not burst but gently let his head breach it. He breathed deeply, coughing while trying to catch his breath. Typically, he would have used this spell for a prolonged period underwater, but this would have to do. He took another deep breath; it smelled like a warm ocean breeze. He turned to lay on his back, slowly breathing in and out, waiting for the dust and smoke to clear.

CHAPTER THIRTY-FIVE

BREATHE

Kiana had her arm under Kaplan's shoulder. He had taken a wound to the leg and was having difficulty standing. She watched as the last burning creature fell to the charge of the nomad reinforcements led by her mother's Otsoak. A handful of other Otsoa must have joined her in the desert. The Daanav were dispersing back into the wasteland as the smokescreen in the sky gave way. As the first rays of sunlight broke through, a cheer resonated. Kiana found herself crying out along with them.

Hata sat with Saudett's head in her lap. *She looks so peaceful. So pretty.* Her brow had constantly been furled over the last few weeks. *It is nice to see Saudett's face at rest.* The slight rise and fall of her chest as she slept. Hata had found some relatively clean strips of cloth in a nearby fallen tent to wrap her friend's wounds in and managed to get some water down her throat through fitful coughs of wakefulness. Hata sat in the morning light, gently stroking Saudett's hair, thinking about how far they had come when Saudett's eyes shot open abruptly.

"Simon!"

Simon felt different, *empowered*. Knowledge of things he had never known filled his mind. Thoughts of an advanced magical world: mathematic equations, knowledge of strange beings and languages, the knowledge of spellcraft, and plane-to-plane travel. *So much knowledge.* Shaking his head, he pushed the thoughts aside, focusing on the present. The door was still shimmering white, but it seemed slightly fainter, not so blinding. As he walked toward it, a hand fell on his shoulder.

"Boss, we'd best be getting on," Naurr said. "Look."

Simon turned to see what the man was looking at, following Naurr's gaze upwards. The pool and the stream leading to the portal were gone. The rope Ilan had brought was dangling from the hole in the ceiling.

"Oh gods, what have I done? Does this mean Hasiera will no longer have a water source?"

"It does seem that way, indeed. Let's leave the damned door for now. We can come back after we have taken a bit of rest. Hettra's tits, I am starving to death as well. Come on up, boss, hold onto my back then."

"No need, my man. I can help us with that." Simon uttered a word in another language he had never known and waved a hand. "*Afléotan!*"

The two men began to drift upwards.

"Skrull, take me!" Simon yelped. "Where did I learn how to do that?"

"Skrull taking me!" Naurr cried. "You be demonic like now too?!"

"Nonsense, my man. I seem to have acquired some seemingly godly new powers," Simon said, waving as if to brush off the other man's words. They both stopped, suspended in mid-air for a breath, then began to fall.

"Afléotan! Afléotan!" Simon yelled, waving his hands madly.

Inches from the ground, they stopped once more.

"Please stop moving your hands around there, boss."

"Quite right," Simon cleared his throat. "Where were we?"

The two men floated up, using the rope as a guide until they found themselves back in the connecting tunnel above. Once it was safe to do so, Simon waved his hand, and their feet touched down gently.

"Well, what do you think of your new boss, my man?"

Naurr looked at him tiredly, saying nothing.

"Come now, let's go." Another strange new word came to mind, and he patted Naurr on the back. "*Strangung*," Simon muttered under his breath. He felt power ripple through his fingers and into Naurr's body.

Naurr's slumped back straightened, his shoulders raised, and his step quickened.

A few minutes into their trek down the tunnel, they were met by panicked nomads pushing their way toward them.

"Primus, protect us!" a woman shouted.

"It's the Builder!" shouted an elderly man.

Simon grabbed the arms of the man. "What in Skrull's hell is going on here?"

"The Daanav! They have come."

"What?" *The valley is under attack!* Simon pushed through the column of tightly packed people, inching down the tunnel toward that gateway portal. "Go no further than the drop coming up. We will be back for you all!" Simon reassured people as he ushered them by making his way toward the mine entrance. "Come on, Naurr, we need to help!"

"Aye, boss!"

They slowly, anxiously found their way to the entrance hole. The column of hundreds of Hasierans snaked its way into the earth behind them. A few of Simon's workers had made a makeshift barricade over the hole.

"Boss! You're alive. The foreman too! Where's Ilan?"

Simon patted the man on the shoulder and said, "I'm sorry. I'm afraid he didn't make it, but his sacrifice will not be in vain. What's going on here, Francis?"

Francis was ragged, a cut on his arm soaking his shirt red. "The Daanav breached the wall and began hunting through the valley. We saved as many as possible, but..." Francis nodded at the barricade.

Simon peered out between the planks and recoiled in shock, turning and vomiting horribly at the visceral scene before them. It was a massacre. Women, children, and the elderly who had not made it to the tunnel in time. All that remained was a pulped mess of gore. Limbs and heads strewn everywhere gave little evidence to identify the bodies. It was a mass of broken, tangled, and bloody forms. Intestines, blood, and feces were scattered along the floor, trailing out of the cavern. The stench of death filled Simon's nostrils.

He stumbled forward blindly. *This is my fault!* Because he hadn't finished the escape tunnel in time. *My wall failed? By the Primus, is the entire camp gone? Were they wiped out in the span of my one night away?* He gave a guttural scream of *rage* at the top of his lungs.

A Daanav hound leaped from among the corpses toward him.

"*Windan,*" Simon muttered as he slashed the dagger through the air. The Daanav split down the middle as a blade of high-pressure air sliced through the beast. Simon lowered his head. *Dead because of me. Like my father. Like Ilan.* His eyes found the white dagger in his hand. Slowly, he lifted the blade to his neck.

Naurr caught his hand. "Don't."

"There's no point, Naurr; they're all dead. We failed. *I* failed. I'll never see Saudett again. I am finished with this life."

"Nay. Look there, see."

Simon saw two silhouettes in the cave mouth. Two women stood, darkened by the light outside. He couldn't make out who they were. He took a few weak steps forward. One of the figures broke away from the other.

"Simon! *Simon!*"

Simon fell to his knees as the voice came to his ears. "Sau—Saudett?" he questioned, his voice cracking. "Is it really you?"

His wife embraced him, burying his head into her midriff. She squeezed him tight. "Gods, Simon, I thought I'd never see you again!"

"I—I had given up hope," he mumbled into her as her hand caressed his head.

"I told you to be careful that day you had that fucking dream. That day, you were *taken* from me."

"I'm sorry, my star. I was far from careful. Naurr warned me of the dust cloud approaching Dagad, and I brushed it off. I was taken from you. My father was *killed* because of me. I'm a fool."

She held him tighter and said, "Your father is at peace beside Teresa. One day, we will visit their grave together." She paused to look at him. "My foolish husband, your hair and beard have grown and are a total mess. Oh, foolish father of our child." She took his hand and placed it on her belly. She was covered in dry, crusted blood.

Simon, in tears, choked out, "What? Are we having a child? By all the gods on this forsaken day, I am to be a father?"

"*Yes.* You are, Simon," Saudett mumbled, nodding through her tears. "You are going to be a father." She knelt so their faces were inches apart. "Next time, I promise, I will come for you sooner." She put a hand on his cheek. "*I love you,* Simon."

He coughed, half laughing, half crying, nodding repeatedly. "I love you...*Saudett*. You are everything to me."

She pulled him in for a tender kiss.

The battle is over. Kiana exhaled. The Daanav were vanquished, many fleeing and disappearing into the dunes as the sun came into whole light. She sat back against the wall. Kaplan sat at her side. She wanted to explore this newfound relationship with this man, Kaplan Mir; they had fought for life side by side. She sighed deeply. Perhaps tomorrow they could enjoy one another. Her muscles were sore; she was bruised and bloodied. She could barely move.

"Look, here come our companions of the Vouri," Kaplan nodded toward the throng of people before them, some celebrating while others sat or lay resting like themselves.

Baal and Brena emerged from the crowd. They were covered head to toe in the Daanav's black tar-like blood. Baal's teeth gleamed as he saw the two seated against the wall.

"Voitoon! Friends!" He roared as he approached. "Great destruction we wrought this night." He crouched low at Kaplan's side, putting a massive hand on his shoulder.

Kaplan winced in pain, squinting one eye. "Skrull take you, Baal." He pushed the man's massive hand away.

Baal laughed. "You fight well, book-reading man."

"I say the same of you and your mate." Kaplan nodded at Brena. "It looked like you single-handedly took down that burning fiend. Is it true?"

Brena smiled faintly. "It is the Vouri way to overwhelm and crush one's enemies. Even when odds are stacked against them."

"Ha, well, you both did us, the Hasieran, a great favor," Kiana replied. "We are forever in your debt."

Brena shrugged slightly. "Stretched the muscles a tad."

"Shall we feast?!" Baal hollered.

"It may have to wait," Kiana consoled. "I think we all need some rest, especially that daughter of yours. We couldn't have done it without her and her power."

Brena began to look around. "Where is that daughter of ours?"

"Hmm." Baal's laughing and jolliness stopped instantaneously. He grunted and jogged off into the encampment. Brena followed closely on his heels.

Kiana was too sore and unable to stand. A few moments after the two Vouri had departed, she gently put her hand on Kaplan's. He took it and entwined their fingers together; they said nothing and sat silently, dozing off, leaning against each other.

"Daughter. This indeed looks to be a suitable companion."

Kiana's mother's voice woke her gently. She looked up. Her father and mother stood side by side, looking down on her. A bald man wearing black-studded leather stood a few paces behind them; Kiana noticed him fidgeting with the many pouches on his belt.

"Well, I am so grateful for your blessing, *Mother*," Kiana muttered a sigh. "You arrived just in time to claim all the glory."

"The battle was over with the beacon of light's appearance. It seemed to have thrown the Daanav into disarray, even with the demonic dark veil cast by the burning beasts."

Kiana nodded in response.

"I'm still trying to comprehend this all. It is truly mad," Kaplan murmured.

"Much prefer gardening over the participation in strange fiendish wars," the balding man said, affirming Kaplan's statement.

"Who might this be, Mother?" Kiana asked.

"It's a bit of a tale," her mother replied. Then, she turned to the man and said, "Come to think of it, I heard a report that you were responsible for destroying the other burning beast. I'm sure we witnessed the Kahytul materialize out of nowhere to battle the burner mid-air. Such a coincidence that we had met one such a Kahytul only a few days back." Her mother stared hard at the black-clothed man.

He shrugged indifferently. "I'm afraid my daggers were no good in a cavalry charge. I, unfortunately, held back while you all rode on. Stabbed a few defenseless wailing beasts, but that is all."

The group studied him suspiciously.

He shrugged again and pulled something out of one of his pouches. "You wouldn't have happened to have seen a young red-headed Vouri around here?" Not waiting for a reply, he touched an object to his lips, which Kiana noticed were bleeding slightly. The next moment, the man was gone.

Kiana scrambled to her feet, wincing through the pain. "What?! Where is he?!"

"*Sorcery.* The bastard must have been the one to summon the fireball and Kahytul alike! Skrull, take me. I was blind," her mother cursed.

"Hata!" Kiana exclaimed. "He's looking for Hata!"

Kaplan was also on his feet now. "Quick, into the camp! We *must* find her first."

Jude Nelon smirked as he followed the group of four through the gate into the heart of Hasiera. *What fools,* he thought.

Chapter Thirty-Six

SAND

As they rushed through the tents, fear once again gripped their hearts. The camp was in ruins. Pavilions were toppled; bodies lay exposed to the sun, entrails streaming across the mud-slicken earth. People were wailing and screaming in the wake of the destruction. Scars of black ooze remained where Daanav once stood, those who had succumbed to battle or the sun.

Kiana, Kaplan, and her parents made their way through the multitude of mourning people. Finally, they came to the stream that ran through the encampment. There, they found the First Otsoa on his knees.

"It's gone. My people are doomed. How could this have happened?" he muttered aloud, his golden helmet lying loose beside him.

They slowly approached the First and what was left of the stream. It was mud, some shallow pools here and there, where water evaporated as the day's heat rose. In places, the earth was starting to crack.

"How could this happen?!" he said louder. "*The builder.* He went into the cave last night. The underground river. *He never came out.*" The First paused for a long moment, then stood, the golden helmet rolling in the mud of the drying river. He stalked along the dead stream toward the rocky cliffside.

Kiana and the rest followed quickly, trying to keep up with their injuries. The First and Third quickly outpaced the wounded Kiana and Kaplan, Kiana's father holding back and staying near the slower duo.

"I could have stayed here and protected these people." Saudett looked about them at the massacre. "I was standing right here; they begged me to stay."

"Then I would be dead now if you had not shown up when you did. You couldn't have known this would happen," Hata said. "Look forward, not back."

"I suppose, Hata." Saudett smiled weakly. "I would save you over a thousand desert bastards in a heartbeat."

Hata flinched at her words, looking around at the bodies of helpless dead people, particularly the elders and young.

Silence filled the cavern.

Simon studied both women momentarily before coughing, "Ahem, fear not! Many people took refuge in the tunnel, my fair maidens. Speaking of fair, my love, who is this young lass who accompanies you?"

"This is Hata Vasara. So, she is named the Sunstone, as we've come to call her. She's the only reason I am here. I couldn't have made it this far without her. She was the pillar on our journey, and I genuinely appreciate and care for her."

Simon smiled faintly. "A love of my wife is equal to the love we share and is welcome. We are in your debt, Hata Vasara, the Sunstone." He paused, looked at her quizzically, and a thought came to him. *Sunstone is a Ryk Lân power source.* "That's an odd title. How did you come about it, if I dare to ask?"

Hata was blushing at the introduction of herself. "I—"

She was cut off as a man dressed in black-stained golden armor entered the cavern with a sword drawn. He paused and surveyed the strewn bodies in the cavern. Simon watched as the horror on his face turned to fury.

"*Builder!* What have you done?!"

Simon clambered to his feet. "Well," he stammered. "I suppose...I suppose I am responsible. All of it. For the death of these people here. For not completing your escape route in time. Or the wall, for that matter. For the loss of your valley's water supply." Information flowed from a hidden source. "For the nullification of the Daanav's purpose in coming here to Hasiera. To put it in layman's terms, I cut off the Daanav from their home in the Skaad Lân and opened a gate to another. Unfortunately, this also cut off the much-needed water supply from the Skaad Lân—"

"Then you are no longer needed!" the golden man bellowed, sprinting toward him.

Saudett and Naurr moved to protect Simon when his hands moved on instinct, the mysterious bone dagger tracing a line through the air.

The golden man was flung back by an invisible force. Simon held the blade out in the last position he had outlined. The golden man groaned as he was pushed to the ground, waves of invisible force pressuring him downwards. Simon strolled over to the man and knelt next to him. Grabbing a handful of sand mixed with blood in his other hand, he leaned next to the golden man's ear. "This is for my *father*," he whispered.

He used the dagger to prop the man's mouth open, the blade cutting into the First's tongue and between his upper and lower teeth. Simon let the sand trickle into the man's gaping mouth. *Slowly.*

The golden man, the First Otsoa of Hasiera, began to choke on the mixture of his own blood, the blood of his people, and the sands of the Burning Sea, the very earth he had cultivated. He could not move. He shook violently, but the magical force held his head and limbs.

"What's going on here?!" a woman shouted.

Simon saw a middle-aged nomadic woman rushing toward him. At that exact moment, he heard Saudett call out.

"Is it you, *Mother?*"

Then came a scream that was abruptly cut off. Simon saw a black-clad figure with his hand over Hata's mouth. Suddenly, a bright light momentarily engulfed them both. He heard a roar as a massive bald brute of a man rushed through the fading light, but it was too late. He listened to another blonde woman's guttural cry of agony.

Simon turned his gaze back to the man lying before him, still sputtering and choking. He held the man's stare and watched as the life faded from the golden man's eyes.

EPILOGUE

Hata could hear countless crows cawing above her. When she opened her eyes, everything was a blur. Only faintly making out two figures standing and murmuring above her. She watched as one of the figures handed the other something, then heard more muffled voices. The receiving figure soon departed her vision. Hata pulled at her wrists and ankles, but they were bound by metal cuffs. They felt almost hot on her wrists. She tried to feel for the earth, the stone, the sand, and anything around her. But she felt *nothing*.

The figure approached her and bent toward her. She could vaguely distinguish a man's face, jet-black slick hair, and goatee.

"Well, my dear fledgling, we'd best get started," the man said.

The man put something to her nose and another hand over her mouth. The powder was sucked into her nostrils and into her lungs, and she felt a warm, tingling sensation overcome her. Her mouth began to water, and she wanted more. She needed more. *It was wonderful*.

CLAIM YOUR FREE NOVELLA

Greetings,

Thank you for reading. I hope you enjoyed this story and hope you wish to follow the Sunstone Saga of Hata, Saudett, Simon, and their companions on their journey into new Lân's. If so, please sign up for my reader group newsletter. I send out a monthly update on my progress on upcoming books in the series and any special offers or events I may be attending.

If you sign up for my newsletter, you will receive a digital copy of my novella *Caste of the Mountain*. A prequel story following Baal, Brena, and Hata before the events of *The Shepherds of the Sunstone*.

Go to www.nicolinodel.comto sign up and receive your FREE digital copy!

EARLY ACCESS

If you wish to support me further and are interested in reading the next book in the series before anyone else, consider subscribing to me at https://reamstories.com/nicolinodel. You can read the first chapter of the next book for FREE by following me on REAM or subscribe for access to the entire first draft of the book.

Thanks for your support,

Nicolin Odel

SUNSTONE SAGA NOVELS

Book One - The Shepherds of the Sunstone
Book Two – The Children of Skaad
Book Three - The Wayfarers War

PREQUELS

Prequel One – Caste of the Mountain

THE INFLUENCE OF REVIEWS

As an independent or self-published author, marketing and promoting my business is ultimately out of my pocket. One of the most incredible things a reader can do to help with this is to leave a review. This will help other readers who are interested in buying my book and give me more visibility in the marketplace.

If you liked *The Shepherds of the Sunstone,* please leave me a review on the store where you purchased the book.

The Shepherds of the Sunstone

Thank you for your support!

About the Author

Nicolin lives in the Greater Toronto Area with his family, writing books, gardening, or shoveling snow.

For more information:

www.nicolinodel.com

nicolin.odel@gmail.com

You can also connect to Nicolin on social media:

https://www.instagram.com/nicolin.odel/

https://www.facebook.com/NicolinOdel/

Printed in Great Britain
by Amazon

37735685R00142